LP
CAM

D0174363

# MAKE, TAKE, MURDER

**DATE DUE**

| | | | |
|---|---|---|---|
| OCT 1 2 2011 | | | |
| NOV 2 2011 | | | |
| NOV 2 3 2011 | | | |
| AUG 3 1 2012 | | | |
| | | | |
| | | | |
| | | | |
| | | | |
| | | | |

LP CAM
Campbell-Slan, Joanna
    Make, take, murder : a Kiki Lowenstein
scrap-n-craft mystery
A0000004728

W/D

DEMCO

A KIKI LOWENSTEIN SCRAP-N-CRAFT
MYSTERY

# Make, Take, Murder

## Joanna Campbell Slan

**WHEELER**
**CHIVERS**

This Large Print edition is published by Wheeler Publishing, Waterville, Maine, USA and by AudioGO Ltd, Bath, England.

Wheeler Publishing, a part of Gale, Cengage Learning.

Copyright © 2011 by Joanna Campbell Slan.

The moral right of the author has been asserted.

**ALL RIGHTS RESERVED**
This is a work of fiction. Names, characters, places, and incidents are either the product of the author's imagination or are used fictitiously, and any resemblance to actual persons, living or dead, business establishments, events, or locales is entirely coincidental.

The text of this Large Print edition is unabridged.
Other aspects of the book may vary from the original edition.
Set in 16 pt. Plantin.

**LIBRARY OF CONGRESS CATALOGING-IN-PUBLICATION DATA**

Campbell-Slan, Joanna.
    Make, take, murder : a Kiki Lowenstein scrap-n-craft mystery / by Joanna Campbell Slan.
        p. cm. — (Wheeler Publishing large print cozy mystery)
    ISBN-13: 978-1-4104-3967-3 (softcover)
    ISBN-10: 1-4104-3967-4 (softcover)
    1. Lowenstein, Kiki (Fictitious character)—Fiction. 2. Scrapbooks—Fiction. 3. Scrapbooking—Fiction. 4. Large type books. I. Title.
PS3603.A4845M35 2011b
813'.6—dc22                                                        2011017521

BRITISH LIBRARY CATALOGUING-IN-PUBLICATION DATA AVAILABLE

Published in 2011 in the U.S. by arrangement with Midnight Ink, an imprint of Llewellyn Publications, Woodbury, MN 55125-2989 USA. Published in 2012 in the U.K. by arrangement with Llewellyn Worldwide Ltd.

U.K. Hardcover: 978 1 445 83838 0 (Chivers Large Print)
U.K. Softcover: 978 1 445 83839 7 (Camden Large Print)

Printed in the United States of America
1 2 3 4 5 6 7  15 14 13 12 11

To Jane Campbell and Margaret
Campbell-Hutts, the bravest,
coolest women I know. I'm so
proud to be your big sister.
Love always — Jonie

# ONE

I was rummaging around in the trash Dumpster searching for my lost paycheck, when I reached down and grabbed Cindy Gambrowski's severed leg.

Of course, I didn't know it was *her* leg. I didn't know whose leg it was.

In fact, I couldn't even be sure it was a real, live — er, dead — leg at all. I told myself I was nuts. (Which I probably am.) I immediately dropped what I was holding.

"Eeeeek!" I screamed. "It's . . . it's . . . a leg! I found a leg."

"Ha, ha, ha. Very funny, Kiki Lowenstein. When you're finished being a complete dope, how about you find your paycheck so you can get out of there?" said Bama. "We've got our Monday night crop to prep for."

That's my business partner for you. She has all the empathy of a pet rock. Clearly,

7

she was not planning to come to my assistance. She thought I was kidding about the leg. Or wrong.

Well, maybe I was.

I swallowed hard and told myself to calm down.

After all, how could a human shin complete with five toes get inside the big green trash bin? Why would anyone dump body parts in with the paper garbage we generated at Time in a Bottle, the scrapbook store where Bama and I work?

This had to be someone's idea of a sick joke. I must have been mistaken. Who'd put a body part in the Dumpster? Especially in our trash bin? *Don't be ridiculous,* I told myself. *Concentrate on finding that paycheck so you can get out of here.*

If only I could see better!

It's pretty dark inside a Dumpster with the lid propped open only an inch. The day dawned unusually warm for December, but that's St. Louis for you. We tend to swing from one extreme to another. Either we suffer from muggy, ghastly hot days, or we rival polar expeditions for bone-chilling cold. You can walk outside to a clear sky one minute, dodge pelting golf balls of hail the next, and finish the twenty-four-hour period with a pea-soup colored haze announcing an oncoming tornado. It sure isn't boring; I'll give it that!

Neither was my life.

"I need some help here, Bama!" I called. I figured at the very least she'd hold the lid open for me, but no. She had given me a boost so I could climb into the slime pit. But that was all. After I scrambled over the edge and into the trash, Bama stuck a small stick under the metal lid and backed away. Bama didn't care how tough a time I was having. This was her passive-aggressive way of teaching me a lesson.

Unless I also learned Braille, this education was going nowhere — fast. Too darn dark in here to see anything!

"I'm not climbing in after you, Kiki. I won't. Don't ask. Quit whining and find your paycheck. I still have to count out the register and get the store open."

Well, I did, too. I was eager for the activity that would take my mind off how horrible my twelve-year-old daughter was behaving lately.

"This is all your fault," Bama called to me, by way of adding insult to smelly injury.

Duh. That I knew. I should have paid attention. I shouldn't have pushed all those loose papers into the trash can by the desk. I should have put my paycheck in my purse the moment Bama handed it over.

Shoulda. Woulda. Coulda.

And didn't.

When I discovered my mistake, Bama explained she was not about to reissue my paycheck, thank you. "That costs money. Correction: That wastes money. You tossed it, you lost it."

I could tell by the smirk she was proud of her little rhyme. In fact, I bet she was standing outside grinning from ear to ear. All right, I would take my bitter medicine. But I couldn't perform my punishment without more light. "Bama, I'm trying! I want out of here. But I can't see anything! Lift the lid higher!"

"Can't. Don't want to touch it. I'll get dirty." She wore a brand-new, cardinal-red wrap coat that I coveted. I had finally, reluctantly, resigned my old winter coat to the garbage. Moths feasted on the sleeves over the summer. The lining drooped sadly out from under the hem. An unidentified stain crept across the shoulder blades.

I hoped our store was making money. If we were, perhaps I could use a part of the bonus to buy a new coat at the after-Christmas sales. I also wanted to purchase a nice Hanukkah gift for my daughter Anya. She lusted after a pair of Uggs. "All my friends own a pair," she pouted.

But instead of prepping for our upcoming crop or creating displays to entice our customers to spend money, I was stuck here in the trash bin, digging around for my lost paycheck. With no help forthcoming from my "partner," Bama. None at all!

She is so annoying.

"At least go get me some light!" I told myself I must be hallucinating to think I'd touched anything remotely human. But then, I haven't been sleeping well lately. No wonder my imagination shifted to high alert status.

"Hang on," she yelled. "I'll be back. Don't go anywhere."

As if I could! I was too short to climb out of the dumpster without (a) a hand up or (b) a ladder. Instead, I snuggled into the corner far away from the icky, sticky human calf-shaped thing I'd tossed back into the mess. At least in the corner, nothing could come up behind me.

I felt a tickle.

"Something fell down the back of my blouse!" I yelled so loud I thought I ejected my tonsils.

But Bama wasn't around to hear me. I tugged at my top and did the shimmy, hoping whatever small creature was sharing my

11

clothing would vacate the building. Pronto.

"Here," Bama banged her fist against the metal to get my attention. The resulting BONG was as loud as if I were standing inside Big Ben. I could barely make out her next comment, "Got you a flashlight."

The lid opened wide. Sunlight flooded the interior and blinded me. I didn't duck as the big blue plastic flashlight flew by and conked me in the head.

"Bama, that hurt!"

"Sor-reee!" she sang out.

I knew she wasn't.

Ugh. I rotated the plastic cylinder in my hand and clicked it to "on." The stupid beam flickered twice, then died. I knocked it hard against my palm. The light came on. I dug around in the papers and goo of our leftover foodstuffs. When the light wavered, I banged the flashlight against the dumpster wall, and it stayed bright. I shined the beam in the direction of my feet. I moved it left to right in a sweeping motion.

Five pink toes with painted nails winked up at me from between two garbage bags.

"It's a leg! Bama, I'm not kidding! Help! Help! Get me out of here!" I stuffed the flashlight into my waistband and tried to scale the wall of the dumpster. "The lid! Lift the lid!"

Thunk.

Instead of lifting the lid, Bama dropped it. "Phone!" Her voice came from far away. "Be right back!"

"Bama! Wait! Please! Let me out! OUT!" I banged on the wall and yelled some more. I jumped up pogo-stick style and struggled to get a purchase on the rim. I couldn't do it. My fingernails screeched as they slid down the metal.

Carefully avoiding the far end of the heap (or Body Part Village, as I nicknamed it in my head), I heaped bags one on top of each other. When I had a small pile, I climbed them. That didn't work either. They shifted and sank under my weight. I tried again with the same result.

The whole time I yelled and cried and screamed for help.

Finally, I wore myself out. I sank down in the corner of the Dumpster and started to snivel.

Bama took her own sweet time.

I hate that woman.

I really do.

# TWO

"Tell me again why you were in the Dumpster." Detective Stan Hadcho adjusted his weight in the folding chair. My nine-one-one call had brought a Richmond Heights Police Department patrolman who quickly surmised we needed a pair of detectives on the case. We sat across from each other in the back room of Time in a Bottle. His pen poised over an open Steno pad. His dark chocolate eyes never leaving my face. "Go ahead, Mrs. Lowenstein. Take your time. Start at the beginning. You were here yesterday? On a Sunday?"

I swallowed hard and fanned myself. Another swig of Diet Dr Pepper helped me push down the knot in my throat, the bulge threatening to explode along with the contents of my stomach. Staring off into the racks of brightly colored cardstock, forcing myself to focus, I mumbled through the recent events. How a new customer came in right at closing when I worked the sales floor alone. How that new customer was struggling with two howling toddlers. How she needed (a) a break from parenting and (b) more supplies. How I'd bounced said toddlers on my knee while she roamed around the store. Squeezing my eyes shut harder, I visualized the transformation apparent on my customer's face. She had grown more and more relaxed as she thought about the album she was making for a friend's birthday.

The kids were thrilled with the graham crackers I fed them, and later cleaned out of our carpet.

I told Hadcho how the new customer left smiling, dispensing hugs and kisses to her little darlings. A different woman all together from the stressed-out mess who'd stumbled over our threshold.

Crafting was like that. We all grew stronger and wiser when we turned our hands to the act of creating rather than fretting. How many times have I seen stressed-out women, ladies with shoulders hunched around their ears, slowly unwind as they became engrossed in a new project? Too many to count, actually.

Since Bama and I came onboard as part-owners, we'd moved Time in a Bottle a bit more toward papercrafting in general than just focusing on scrapbooking. It wasn't a big change. No way! Just a subtle shift. Dodie Goldfader, the majority stockholder and founder, agreed to give our new, broader emphasis a try.

As a result, our sales numbers were up. Our patron count was rising. A lot of new faces turned into regulars after attending our popular ATC (Artist Trading Card) classes or our latest offering, Décor on a Dime. The young mother of toddlers discovered our store when she saw an ad for our cardmaking class. Despite the downturn in the economy, our business was good.

An inevitable downside of the additional business was more work. Bama and I exhausted ourselves trying to cover all the store hours, plus our prep time and our after-hours work keeping up with stocking, pricing, and market trends. After our new customer walked out the front door last night, toting her happy toddlers and a big bag full of supplies on the back of her stroller, I nearly collapsed against our front counter. Once again, we were closing after our posted hours. Hearing the door minder jingle, Bama stuck her head out of the back stockroom to yell to me, "You still need to clean up after that marathon die-cutting class. You promised to get the holiday decorations up, although those can wait until tomorrow. And, we've got to be here early tomorrow to finish prepping for the crop."

I told Detective Hadcho, "We're open seven days a week. With the holidays coming, our hours are extended. By the time our last customer left, I was slap happy. Totally exhausted. I guess I wasn't thinking straight." I explained how with broad sweeps of my arm, I scooted paper debris into our wastepaper cans. This was unusual. My guilty conscience shrieked, "Recycle! Check for small bits you can reuse!" But, honestly, by that time, I staggered about on my feet. Amendment: My aching feet. In the rush to get home, I grabbed bags from behind the counter, noticed a few official-looking slips of paper that had fallen to the floor, scooped up the whole mess, and wobbled my way through the back door to the Dumpster.

"It wasn't until I got dressed this morning that it hit me."

"You couldn't find your paycheck," he prompted me.

I nodded. I told him how I had dug deep in the pockets of the pants I'd worn the night before and discovered lint. No paycheck. But I knew it should have been there!

Bama had handed it to me shortly before I had eaten lunch around dinnertime, my third day of peanut butter straight from the jar.

Retracing my steps mentally, I formed the only possible conclusion. One of those "official-looking" pieces of paper I'd tossed into the trash must have been my paycheck. It must have fallen out of my pocket and onto the floor.

Ergo, Dumpster-diving.

I must have turned a little green as I recounted my adventure and recalled the squishy feel of cold flesh in my hands.

"You all right, Mrs. Lowenstein?" he leaned slightly forward as if to catch me if I fell.

I shook my head to clear it. "How come . . . how come what I touched felt so soft?" I wondered out loud to Detective Stan Hadcho. His eyes were the color of twin Hershey's kisses. His hair was the sort of jet black you read about, but rarely see. His face was tan and craggy, with high cheekbones that hinted he might have some Native American blood in him. He wore sadness like some guys wear a tired raincoat, loose, threadbare and droopy.

"That's how flesh feels after a while. The body starts to decompose very quickly. Even when it's cold outside. You've probably only ever touched someone newly dead or someone just embalmed, right?"

I nodded. I remembered stroking my husband George's face when he was in his casket. His flesh felt cool and unpleasantly plump, like an unripe peach. I kissed Nana's face as she lay on a bed of white shirred fabric, her small body looking shrunken in a way-too-big metal coffin. By the end of her life, her once lovely skin hung on her bones, but even then there had been a certain resistance to the pressure of my lips. "That's right. I've only touched folks after they've been prepared. If this wasn't the middle of December, if the weather had been hotter, that piece of leg would have been . . . ugh." I shivered and checked to see if the path to the bathroom was clear.

"Mrs. Lowenstein, don't dwell on it," said Detective Hadcho. "It's my job to see and hear things no one should ever experience. I signed on for that. I am willing to do it so you don't have to, if you get my drift." He reached over and squeezed my hand, then released it just as quickly.

I stared at my fingertips. The warmth he'd transferred flowed up my arm. With reluctance, I pulled my hand away from where we were nearly fingertip to fingertip. I didn't want to offend him, but I badly needed human companionship. So much so that I worried I'd throw myself at him and start to sob. His gesture of kindness came scarily close to opening floodgates of pent-up emotion inside me.

Lately, loneliness had been my constant companion.

My romantic life was in the tank. I couldn't even go there. It was too frustrating and humiliating to consider.

I'd never had such a bleak period of parenting, either.

Since Anya turned twelve last summer, she has wanted less and less to do with me. This morning was the capper. She instructed me to drop her off a block away from a friend's house so she wouldn't be seen leaving my car. Shifting in my chair, avoiding Detective Hadcho's eyes, I fought an urge to cry.

Blinking fast and hard, I stared at the spot usually occupied by Gracie, my darling Great Dane. She was at the vet's office. I couldn't think about her. Not right now. It was too worrisome.

I took in a long and even breath. I needed to get control of my emotions. This wasn't the time to succumb to negativity. It was the holiday season, for goodness sake. Ho-

ho-ho, ah, crud.

A little voice inside me announced, "What you really need, Kiki Lowenstein, is a good old-fashioned pity party. A sob-fest. With lots of wine and chocolate."

But I pinched myself hard and refused to let even one little tear leak out. Because I didn't have time for this. I really didn't.

# THREE

Detective Hadcho handed me his business card after scratching another number on the back. "That's my personal cell. You think of anything. You need anything. You give me a call."

His eyes held mine.

A spark flew between us; I swear it.

I swallowed hard.

I needed this like I needed a frontal lobotomy. What was with me and cops? Would I ever learn? Men in law enforcement and I did not play well together. I hastened to shove the card into my back pocket. With any luck, I'd run it through the wash and pick it out of the lint trap in my dryer. I already had one detective on speed dial, and if I'd had any brains, I would have dumped that particular phone number months ago.

A big sigh wooshed out of my mouth.

"I mean that," Hadcho said with a quiet

intensity that told me he knew I was resistant to asking for his help.

"Are we safe?" Bama stepped between me and the detective. Her head tilted, her mouth drawn into a thin, tight line. She waved a pale hand in the general direction of the back door and the unseen Dumpster which was now out of commission. The yellow plastic tape officially designated it as a crime scene. No telling how long it would take for the investigators to go over it. More likely, we'd have to replace that big green box. Visions of dollar signs danced in my head.

"Whoever did that hates women." Bama's voice trembled.

My head jerked up. I hadn't thought of that. She was right and her suggestion sent a chill through me.

"He," and she jerked a thumb at Detective Ortega, the detective who'd been dispatched to interview her in the store's office while Detective Hadcho was chatting with me out on the display floor, "he says you're in charge of this investigation. Lead detective, or whatever. I want to know what you're planning to do to protect us. Someone put that in our trash. They could have chosen another site. They didn't. They chose us."

I gaped in surprise. Bama wasn't much of a talker. I figured she'd answer the other detective in monosyllables and get back to work. In fact, I'd sort of forgotten about her. Separating witnesses was a common procedure. Smart, too. Detective Ortega could compare her responses to mine when he and Detective Hadcho reconvened at the station. Ortega was the stereotypical cop from TV shows. A beefy, blocky body topped off by a face both bulbous and tough at the same time.

Out of the corner of my eye, I saw Detective Ortega flash a message in code to his partner. With only a hint of movement, he spread his hands, below waist level, to suggest, "I tried. What can I do?"

"We'll increase patrols. If you know a reason why someone would dump a body part on your property, you need to tell me. Right now." That last word was a growl. Detective Hadcho's brown eyes turned black as they narrowed.

"A reason? Sure, I can give you a couple! Because women come here. Because if you hate women, you'd want to scare them." Bama's chin was raised defiantly, but the tremor was unmistakable.

"How'd anyone know I'd go Dumpster-diving?" I asked.

24

Three pairs of eyes turned on me.

"Good question," said Hadcho. His face a perfect blank. Dang. He would make a heck of a poker player. "Care to speculate?"

Bama and I exchanged glances.

"How would someone let you know he'd dropped off a startling package for you? Assuming, that is, that his goal was to have you find a severed limb in your own Dumpster? What's your normal routine?" he continued.

Bama marched off, came back fast with three laminated sheets. On them were our Opening Procedures, Hours of Operation Procedures, and our Closing Procedures. She was a great one for lists, rules, and protocol. Without a word, she handed them to Ortega, as he was nearest to her.

He read from the Opening Procedures:

1. Do a quick survey of the grounds. Pick up any trash before entering the store. Bring that sack into the store. (See #6.)
2. Disable the alarm and let yourself in the back door. Bring cash drawer to register.
3. Turn on light banks #1, 2, and 3. Check the phone for overnight messages. WRITE THEM DOWN!

25

Clear the message bank.

4. Turn over sign to read: OPEN. From this point on, customers are your #1 Priority! Listen for the door minder and the phone.

5. Do a quick clockwise surveillance of the sales floor. Return any misplaced merchandise to its correct positioning. Check for loose caps on liquids and inks! Collect any trash from inside the store, including the refrigerator. Bag it, deposit it in the Dumpster by the back door.

6. Check the daily "To Do" list for chores by day and by date.

"Kiki, you were scheduled to open," said Bama. "Did you do all that?"

I gulped and tried to focus. "Uh, no. You said you'd handle the cash drawer this morning."

"But you didn't check the outside? Didn't empty the trash?"

"I emptied it last night, so I knew there wouldn't be any."

"Really?" Hadcho could have filled in for Mario Lopez as one of *People* magazine's most beautiful people. Before you blame me for noticing, let me say in my defense that even an octogenarian with advanced cataracts would gawp at Stan Hadcho. He was too good looking for this line of work. I could only imagine all the catcalls and teasing he took from criminals. I'm not a big fan of men with perfect features, but in Hadcho's case, I could make an exception.

"Since we were running behind, I didn't check the phone messages." I shrugged.

"And you didn't tell me?" Bama's voice climbed to new and irritating heights.

"Um, no. I figured I'd get to them later. Besides, we're both available by cell phone. Everyone in the known world has my cell number. Anyone really desperate could call back."

She muttered under her breath. You know that saying, "If looks could kill"? I'm pretty confident the originator worked closely with Bama. She shot me one of her "roll over, expose your soft belly, and offer up your jugular" glances. I felt myself wince.

Bama is a "by-the-book" type of person. She borders on obsessive-compulsive, actually. I, on the other hand, am the queen of "Wing It." I must admit that her systems caused Time in a Bottle to function more smoothly. Our sales were up, our shrinkage was down, and we rarely had too much or too little of any particular merchandise.

"Let's go listen to your calls." Hadcho led the way to our backroom office.

We squeezed in, huddled around the immaculate desktop. The in-box was empty, the Formica top was spotless, and no detritus of office clutter marred its naked expanse. Bama slid behind the desk with a graceful, practiced movement. Turning to face the shelving unit where the phone base unit sat, she punched the fast blinking "Play Messages" button.

The first message was a call from a customer asking us to place a special order. Bama dutifully and pointedly wrote this down. I sensed a certain restlessness from the two detectives, but neither commented.

The second message chilled me to the core.

"Check your Dumpster out back," intoned a computerized voice flat of inflection and phrasing. Reminding me of a GPS or an automated phone system, the voice droned on without emphasis, "Check it carefully. I left a gift for you. A piece of meat. Shank steak. Take it as a warning — for you scrappers and for all those rich, snotty women who shop at your store."

# FOUR

We never made it to Message #3. The four of us were staring at the phone when the back door flew open. A young man wearing a service uniform labeled Crime Scene Unit came running in.

"Ortega? Hadcho? Found something. You better come take a look."

Both men ran after Mr. Crime Scene, leaving Bama and me to sit like chastised kids in the principal's office. Only, instead of being pale or red in the face, we were a ghastly shade of green. I know this because I caught a reflection of us in the big glass-covered landscape Bama hung on the far wall of the office. The pristine snow in the Colorado scenery bounced back our sickly skin tones. Those evergreens had nothing on us. We were a shade that Crayola might have copied, labeled "bilious," and put in their famous dark green and gold box.

"Crud," I managed. My whole body

sagged. My eyes fluttered, and the pressing insistence of exhaustion pinned me to the chair where I sat.

Bama jumped up to slam her palm onto the desk with such force that the pens and pencils in the top drawer rattled. "I knew it. I knew I shouldn't invest. I should have stayed away! This store is cursed!"

"Huh?" I recoiled. "Cursed? Why on earth would you say that?"

"Nothing good ever happens here. I noticed it the day I walked in. Things have just gotten worse. Dodie has cancer, your husband's killer is chasing you, your stupid dog is sick, Mert has a lawsuit against her, and now this! I should have known better. I should have never tried to set down roots!"

"Wait just a cotton-picking minute," I hissed. "You've made a good living from Time in a Bottle. You've gotten all sorts of praise and attention. What about that cruise ship that invited you to teach? How about the fact your sister makes extra money working here? Or that your niece and nephews hang out here after school and on holidays? How dare you say bad things about the store?"

In the middle of the tirade, I rose to shake my finger at her. She responded by hammering the air with her fist. "I didn't say I blamed the store! It's an inanimate object. This place can't help it if someone worked evil mojo on it. But I'm telling you, there's a curse! A curse! Look at poor Dodie. Look at our first crop and what happened. And now this!"

That capped it for me. Weeks of being bossed around by Miss Perfect, and a solid month of working overtime had worn me down. Last year, arguably the worst in my entire life, Time in a Bottle saved me, my life and my sanity. Dodie's little store offered more than a haven for creativity. This place launched my career. Along with employment came a newfound sense of self-esteem. Never before had I felt successful. Never before had I earned my own way in the world. Thanks to the Goldfaders, I was part owner of a growing retail concern. I carried business cards in my pocket, beautifully printed cards with my own name on them! Folks introduced me with a modicum of respect. Shoot, I was even a member of a Chamber of Commerce! Didn't that beat all?

If Bama didn't like Time in a Bottle and all the relationships this place entailed, she shouldn't have agreed to buy in. When Dodie's husband, Horace, offered us this opportunity, my heart nearly leaped out of my chest for joy. I never expected to actually lay claim to our little shop. I'd have been content to work here as an hourly employee for the rest of my days. This place was that dear to me.

If Bama didn't like TinaB (as we nicknamed the store), she could jump ship any time. In fact, I'd be happy to push her over the starboard railing myself!

Okay, so she was organized. So she ran the place without a glitch. So she knew how to add columns of numbers and fill out complicated business forms.

Big deal.

She was also replaceable. As for the commercial details, I could learn them. I was sure I could. Even if it meant giving up every smidgeon of free time I had left. Even if it meant hiring more help and making less money. I'd do it. I would.

How could she accuse this store of being an albatross around our necks! How dare she! I wasn't about to stand there and let her sling mud at a business I loved with every fiber of my being.

I stepped closer to her, feeling my face flame red as a piece of Bazzill Basics cardstock in Strawberry Orange Peel, and let her have it with both barrels. "You are so selfish. And blind. Totally, blind! Your life is better because of this place! No one forced you to buy in! So why did you, huh? Because it was a fabulous opportunity, you silly goose! You were thrilled then, and you ought to be thankful now. If you aren't, then . . . then . . ."

"Ahem."

I've always seen that word in books, but until Detective Hadcho cleared his throat, I'd never really heard it. Sounds just like it looks, too.

"I hate to break up this love-fest, but ladies, we need another sit-down chat." A sour turn-down tugged the edges of his lips. His wide shoulders filled the doorway in a way that could only be thought of as menacing. The man's entire demeanor had changed in the space of mere minutes. Instinctively, I shrank back in my chair, and I felt, rather than saw, Bama slump down onto the desk chair.

With a scuffle of shoe leather, Ortega flanked Hadcho's right shoulder. "That's right. We need to talk. One of you is holding out on us." From behind his back, he pulled out a see-through plastic baggy with a soggy sheet of paper inside. Detective Ortega waved this artifact like an overenthusiastic cheerleader flounces her pompoms at the crowd. With all that fluttering, I couldn't make out exactly what he had.

Seeing the confusion on our faces, Detective Hadcho reached over and tugged the item from the other cop's ham-sized fist. He cleared his throat. "I'm coming to get you. You'll never get away from me. I'll see you dead first. Remember, I've got a gun."

*Thump!*

Bama hit the floor.

# FIVE

"I never pay any attention to stuff like that." I talked over my shoulder as I waved a bottle of ammonia under Bama's nose. We keep tons of the cleanser on hand. Mixed with one part to ten parts water, the solution offers a thrifty way to clean the ink from rubber stamps. While I waved a plastic container under my partner's nose, Ortega helped his partner prop Bama upright in the office chair.

Her eyes snapped open and she slapped their hands away. Once she calmed down, Detective Hadcho opened his notebook to record my comments.

"You don't pay attention to threats? How come?" His brown eyes registered his bewilderment. "This is pretty strong stuff. Frankly, I wonder why you didn't call us sooner."

I shrugged and ignored the implicit accusation. As quickly as possible, I explained my predicament. My husband had been killed two years ago. His murderer was still at large and had become my own personal pen pal. Wasn't that special?

"You get threats like this all the time?" Bama groaned.

The men cast glances her way. I patted her shoulder awkwardly.

"Usually I just get postcards from exotic locales." Actually the killer picked pretty nice scenes. On bleak winter days, I almost enjoyed them.

"Postcards that say what?"

"The typical message is a variation on 'I'm going to get you.' "

"You're okay with this?"

"What are my options?" I shrugged again and shoved a bottle of Diet Coke into Bama's hand. Saint Bernards might carry whiskey in those cute miniature kegs attached to their collars, but give me a Coke or a Dr Pepper any day, and I'll feel revived. Bama obediently took a swallow. She knew the drill. Shoot, given all the hormones winging their way around our scrapbook store, we must have downed an oil tanker full of carbonated fizz. Point of fact, we offered a Coke or Dr Pepper as our automatic response to most of life's woes.

Worked like a charm, it did. I offered

drinks to the law enforcement officers, but they declined.

Bama peered up at me over the rim of her soda. "Since when did threats bypass your mailbox and come here?"

"Beats me. Like I said, I mainly ignore them. He only wins if he bothers me, right?"

"Hrmph." Ortega snorted. "That's a bit more than your garden variety threat, ma'am. When they get that specific, experts tell us to pay attention."

"Look, I ignore them, okay? I toss them into the trash. I know the murderer has contacts here in St. Louis. It's no secret where I work. I'm not about to forfeit all my freedom to a creep. That's my decision. I didn't share it because it's really none of anyone's beeswax."

Bama inhaled loudly. "You're sure this is all about you. Couldn't possibly be a problem for anyone else. Not even with a severed body part showing up in our trash."

For a person who'd recently taken a nose-dive into the carpet, she managed a lot of sass.

I didn't care for her tone. Not at all.

I shook my head vigorously. "In this case, it's all about me. I know it. This is more of the same-o, same-o nonsense I've been putting up with for nearly a year."

Even as I spoke, an alarm buzzed in my brain. I'd been caught in a lie. This wasn't exactly like the junk mail I usually received. Now that I thought about it, this was different. Actually, George's killer usually stuck to "I haven't forgotten you." That was enough to scare me. This was a longer, more exacting message.

I blew out a sigh and struggled to wipe bad memories from my mental chalkboard. What difference did it make how the message was worded? The point was the same. In a weird way, I was glad my personal monster now sent missives to our store. Until recently, they'd shown up in my home mailbox. Every day I struggled to outmaneuver my teenage daughter so she wouldn't see the threats that showed up regularly.

Lately, I didn't have to juggle bills, junk mail, and threatening postcards with an amazing sleight of hand. Instead, nasty missives had been coming to the store. That was better, much better.

Anya didn't need to see this homicidal nonsense. No twelve-year-old should. But especially not my daughter. She'd been through enough already.

Basically we were talking "sticks and stones can break my bones but words can never hurt me," right? What was an angry note or two?

Three pairs of eyes stared at me.

"I'm not concerned. I'm not in any real danger. So he's changed his modus operandi. Big deal. I'm not about to run and hide from a bully."

I said it with braggadocio, but I fought the urge to shudder. Things had been different when Detective Chad Detweiler was dropping by regularly to see me. Maybe that's why Detective Stan Hadcho appealed so strongly to me. Not only was he super good-looking, but he represented safety. Security. Protection.

The kind of life I wish I had.

The kind of life I once had.

The kind of life that ended when a hotel maid found my husband's dead body.

# SIX

Inside our tiny bathroom, I must have washed my hands twenty, thirty times in scalding hot water.

Bama finished her cola, puttered around her desk with paperwork, and ignored me.

Neither of us asked for details, because really, what was the point? We figured the leg came off a dead body. Where the rest of that poor woman was, well, we didn't know. Neither did the authorities, or at least, so it seemed. The Crime Scene Unit poked around in every nook and cranny of our store. Even if we'd run a customer through a garbage disposal, we couldn't have hidden an entire corpse. Not in our store. Not this month. With the run up to the holiday upon us, every shelf and display unit was stocked to the brim. We were crammed with scrapbooking and craft goodies just waiting to be wrapped and given as gifts.

The cops seemed to understand our situation, but they still had jobs to do. To satisfy their concerns, we offered to open all the boxes in the backroom. Because every day brought more merchandise, we had a good half dozen stacked and ready to check in.

As I wielded the box cutter, I glanced over at Gracie's playpen. The keen pain of missing her added to my already jangled nerves. If she were here, I'd feel a lot more courageous. Gracie wasn't much for barking, but she'd already proved she had no tolerance for anyone who tried to harm me. A hundred and twenty pounds of mad dog is a sizeable deterrent for all but the most foolhardy. One look at Gracie and most miscreants would leave me alone.

Gosh, but I missed her.

Each time the door minder jingled, a frisson of fear raced through me. That's how I roll. I talk a good game, preferring to let my knees knock together in private. As the hours ticked by, I wondered if I had made a mistake. Maybe those notes didn't come from anyone in my life. Maybe we had another problem festering. Maybe I should take back my easy dismissal.

But the words stuck in my craw.

A steady stream of customers milled about. I hoped to use suggestive selling to increase the amount of their total purchases.

A few more goodies in their bags might possibly mean the difference between a bottom line in the red and one in the black.

Fortunately, the gruesome discovery hadn't become common knowledge. Bama and I explained the police were doing a pre-holiday security check. (Which was true in a bizarre way.) I sighed with relief as the hours raced past, and no one greeted me with, "Hi, Kiki, find any spare body parts in your Dumpster lately?" Or even a tamer version like, "What sort of trouble are you in now?"

Our customers waved, stroked paper, examined new tools, and generally "ooohed" and "aahhhed" over the projects displayed in various spots in the store. Instead of asking, "May I help you?" I always say, "Hi, what are you working on these days?" That gleans better information and a chance to show off the latest paper, tool, or product. I greeted each of our guests, a move that Dodie assured us would cut down on theft, and set to work on my latest project, a holiday organizer.

A steady stream of purchases kept Bama busy at the register.

Finally, satisfied there was no more to examine, Detective Ortega had us sign for the Dumpster.

"Sorry, but we need to run lab tests on it."

The two investigators promised to stay in touch, as I let them out the back door and watched them climb into an unmarked car. I locked the door behind them and breathed a bit more easily. Our customers had seemed totally absorbed in their holiday shopping.

Maybe no one had to know we were a crime scene. Or that I'd stuck in my thumb and pulled up a limb instead of a plum (with due respect to the nursery rhyme). Nobody repeated Bama's claim that Time in a Bottle was cursed. Not a single soul had glommed to the fact we were blissfully operating within a crime site.

At least, that's what I told myself. That's what I hoped.

As usual, I was wrong.

43

# SEVEN

"Why didn't you call your boyfriend, the cop?" Bama asked me as we sat side-by-side, kitting page layouts. "Kitting" is the act of dividing up paper and supplies for projects. To be cost effective, we apportioned the paper and supplies accordingly. So, if the project only required a half a sheet of paper and two inches of ribbon, each kit contained exactly that and no more. This type of prep takes a lot of time and planning, but if you do it properly, your final product will be a moneymaker rather than a bust.

Bama sliced large sheets of specialty paper into smaller pieces. I assembled punched bits that would be glued together to create holly leaves and berries. Next we'd cut ribbon, count brads, and print up specialty journaling boxes. As we accomplished each step, I checked off the project elements. Early on, I learned the wisdom of making a supply list just for this purpose so we didn't skip anything and ruin the whole final package.

"I didn't think to call him. Once I got out of the trash bin, I just hit nine-one-one automatically. I figured nine-one-one would get help here faster." Which was technically true but an evasion. To curtail more conversation, I started measuring off ribbon. If I could keep my head low, she wouldn't see the color in my cheeks, wouldn't know how embarrassed I was.

"But why didn't you call him later? He could have at least told Detective Hadcho you're a special friend of the department. That Police Chief Holmes is your mother-in-law's main squeeze. That you couldn't possibly know anything about what you found in the Dumpster."

I bit my tongue to keep from sniping, "Drop it, Bama." A smart retort would only make her more curious. Besides, her questions were only natural. So, I tried a diversionary tactic. "I'm sure Detective Hadcho figured that out for himself. He seemed bright and competent. He didn't need Detective Detweiler's help to see how upset I was."

"But Detective Detweiler would want to know about the severed leg, wouldn't he?

45

He'd want to protect you." Bama shivered. "Shouldn't you at least tell him about that threat on the answering machine? About someone putting a message in our mail? I hope they don't leak this to the media."

"You worried about sales?" My response was blunt, yes, but maybe it would steer us clear of the big rock which our conversational motorboat was bearing down on. I did not want to talk about my love life.

Correction: My nonexistent love life. My big romantic blunder.

Bama took the bait. "Kiki, this is the largest investment I've made in my life. It's not just my investment, either. Speaking of which," and she gave a nod to a customer. "You ready to check out?" Bama rose to help the woman at the cash register.

Bama was right about the importance of protecting our investments. Against all odds, we'd both scraped up $5,000 each to buy a portion of the business. Actually, the Goldfaders had asked for less of a buy-in than I had first expected.

But I also hadn't expected it to be so hard to come up with my share.

My mother-in-law, Sheila, thought I'd come into some compensation for the malfeasance that resulted in my husband's death. After all, George — her son and my late husband — had been a part owner of a successful development firm. But that was wrong, too. The economic downturn of late hit the local real estate market hard. I should count myself lucky that the custodians in charge of shedding Dimont Development's assets were able to write me a small check before they were forced to zero-out all its holdings.

So I muddled along.

Zero can be a wonderful starting spot.

# EIGHT

Even though I was technically broke, I couldn't let an opportunity to buy into Time in a Bottle pass me by. Desperate for money to invest, I'd hocked my engagement ring and emptied my meager savings account. I also cashed in a small life insurance policy I'd bought back when Anya was born. I borrowed $1,500 from my friend and former cleaning lady Mert Chambers. That was a debt I could work off by helping her with her other endeavor, Going to the Dogs, a pet sitting business. After two weeks of going meatless and drinking water instead of soft drinks, I handed my check for $5,000 to Horace Goldfader, feeling a heady combination of sinking heart and soaring hopes.

I was part owner of the store!

I was a single mom with no savings!

Hard to say which emotion prevailed. On any given day, the seesaw of joy versus terror tipped one way and then the other twenty times over. As thrilled as I was at the store's growing success, I spent each waking breath fearful of a personal financial crisis. So far, I avoided putting any emergencies on my credit card, since I was well-aware that its interest rate was sky-high. I suspected if an emergency came up I could do better by finding a loan shark. Or selling plasma. Or a spare organ.

Which brought me back to the body part in the Dumpster.

Ugh.

Idly I wondered if our dismembered corpse had been in debt.

Well, that was for the police to decide. I was staying out of it. I had to protect my reputation and my investment in our store. I couldn't afford to play amateur sleuth. No sirree bobtail.

To recoup the money I invested in Time in a Bottle, I was eating Kraft Mac & Cheese and Campbell's Tomato Soup every night my daughter wasn't home. No way would I let Anya know how broke we were. Not with the holidays coming. She deserved to have a child-like, blissful, and totally ignorant upbringing. Didn't we all? I gritted my teeth and swore I'd do everything in my power to keep our precarious financial position from my child.

That meant working my backside off. Putting in lots and lots of hours. Getting along with Bama. Coming up with new ideas to entice our customers. Creating ever-more interesting classes and projects. Finding outside sales events that would add to — and not detract from — our daily register receipts. Moving scads of merchandise this holiday season. Cutting corners wherever possible.

Bills for our stock were already arriving.

Our utility payments were higher than Bama and I anticipated. This winter had been especially brutal, and the store was always cold. Evidently, there was little to no insulation in our walls. We mainly ignored the temp, but on occasion our customers had complained, and we'd been forced to raise the thermostat.

We were paying COD for the specialty goods we ordered. A lot of those suppliers were struggling small businesses, too. Because our orders were small (at least in comparison to the big chain stores), we rarely qualified for free shipping. We paid extra for quick delivery, mindful that the closer we came to December 25, the less time we had to sell through what we'd ordered.

Bama and I were hoping for a big holiday

season. I could scarcely walk because my fingers and toes were crossed in anticipation. Also because my feet were freezing. I'd worn holes in most of my socks.

The cold weather brought more expenses on the home front as well. Anya had outgrown her winter coat. She pushed up so stealthily that I hadn't realized she'd grown so much until I noticed the sleeves stopped three inches above her wrist bones. Something in my face must have betrayed my dismay, because she pulled the coat right off and announced, "I'll wear that jacket my grandmother bought me instead."

I gave her a grateful look, and felt thankful for my good-hearted kid, the one who co-inhabited a body with the Princess of Petulance.

A glance out of our display window foretold bad weather. The sky was clotted with heavy clouds, threatening to rip open like too-full garbage bags and dump snow all over St. Louis. My breath caught in my throat as I wondered how long Anya could go without new boots. She'd been angling for those Uggs not only because they were fashionable, but also because she needed protective footwear. CALA, which was what the locals called the Charles and Anne Lindbergh Academy, a fancy-shmancy pri-

51

vate school Anya attended, boasted a sprawling campus. Kids trudged from one building to the next as their classes changed. She couldn't go long without boots. She'd surely get sick from having wet feet.

Staring out at the threatening weather, I realized I couldn't put off repairing my old car much longer. My worn-out BMW convertible, the almost worthless vehicle I kept after my husband died, was nearly at the end of its natural lifespan. How long could I ignore the fact that the fabric roof was ripped? Slush and rain dripped on me each time I rounded a corner. The cold and wet had done nothing for my health. My nose had run all week, off and on.

"Achoo!" As if to underscore my mental misery, I gave forth with a hearty and unladylike sneeze. I managed to tuck my face into the crook of my arm so I didn't shower nearby paper with sneeze doodles.

"Bless you!" rang out from customers in all corners of the store.

Bless you. Bless them. They were right.

All in all, I had reasons to count my blessings.

My daughter was happy when she wasn't snarling with the emotional angst brought on by rampant hormones. My mother-in-law was in love and acting pretty nice to me, all things considered. I adored my job. I lived in a snug little converted garage in a nice neighborhood. I had friends. My tummy was full. I was safe. For the moment, at least.

I was healthy, except for a cold I was fighting.

The holidays were coming, and everyone was in a good mood.

Later today or early tomorrow it would snow, and that meteorological magic show would put everyone into the gift-giving spirit. The cash register would ring merrily. The world would look lovely and innocent snuggled in its baby blanket of white. The thick boughs of the evergreens outside my front door would genuflect under their pristine mantles. Noses would turn red as Santa's costume, and cheeks would flush pink as if pinched by elfin fingers.

There was much to recommend this time of year.

After all, if it hadn't been winter, that piece of flesh I found in our Dumpster would have stunk to high heavens. My flesh still crawled as I remembered the feel of the dead skin. I shook my head to erase the sensation and tried to concentrate on the task at hand. It was going to be a long evening. Bama and I had all sorts of inventory to shelve in advance of our pre-Christmas special event.

She came back from ringing up a nice sale and arranged a display of "Suggested Gifts" on an uppermost shelf next to where I was working.

"I'd almost think you were trying to avoid your cop friend."

Would she ever shut up?

Bama assumed I hadn't heard her. She spoke louder. "I said, the way you're acting, anyone would think you were trying to avoid him."

It shocked me that she read my intentions so clearly. I didn't even bother to ask, "Him, who?" I knew she meant Detweiler. Detective Chad Detweiler. She was right. I was trying to avoid the hunky detective. Which was why I turned my back to her so she couldn't see my face. I had to stay strong. I was not going to continue my relationship with Detective Chad Detweiler.

I'd given my word to his wife, Brenda.

# NINE

As I puttered around the store arranging stacks and stacks of lovely paper, my mind replayed the whole ugly scene at the hospital. After being slapped up the side of the head twice with a gun, I had needed ten stitches. Still dopey and pain-stricken, I opened my eyes in the middle of the night to focus on a nurse at the foot of my bed. Her back was to me. She turned toward me, and my breath caught in my throat. There stood a very, very angry Brenda Detweiler. A light from the hospital hallway outlined her thin shape and her lank hair. For a moment, I thought I was mistaken. Then she stepped closer. Her eyes glittering, she moved to my side and hissed, "Look at you. Helpless. All doped up." Her spittle splattered my face as she continued, "Here in my hospital! Lucky me! Because I've had enough of you!"

Grabbing my shoulders with strong hands,

she shook me like a rag doll. "Hear me? Enough! You stay away from my husband. Understand? Stay the heck away! Chad's mine!"

My fingers flayed the air, searched for the call button, and seized upon it.

She shrieked over and over, "Stay away from him! Understand? Stay away!"

My thumb pressed the plastic circle. I saw the light panel brighten with a dot of red, but my shock was so great that I couldn't speak, couldn't argue. Instead, I winced with pain as a jagged knife of agony stabbed deep in my skull. A gurgling sound rose from my throat. My eyes rolled back in my head with the force of her anger.

Suddenly, she dropped me. I fell back onto my pillows. Her hands flew up to her cheeks and she pulled at her skin, distorting her features. "You don't understand," she whimpered. "He can't leave me. Not yet. He loves you. I know he does. I see him staring out into space. He won't speak. He won't eat. It's like he isn't there! I can't lose him . . . not yet. I won't lose him. He's mine!"

With a lunge, she seized my shoulders again. She yanked me toward her, the whites of her eyeballs blazing with fury. "Say it! Tell me you'll stay away! Tell me! Or else!

Or . . . I'll . . . I'll . . ."

I gasped and tried to stay conscious. Her words made little sense. Pain assailed me in waves that caused my stomach to spasm and my throat to constrict.

A thought: She wants to kill me.

And another: I'm going to die.

Either she would do me in, or the aggravation to my injuries would finish me off. My stitches would split. My concussion would worsen. Instinctively I collapsed on myself, trying to back away so I could roll into a protective ball, shielding my soft innards from this mad woman. Beneath all this was another recognition — one that kept me from screaming for help — I deserved this.

I wanted her husband.

I loved Detweiler. I could lie to myself all day, but in my heart of hearts, I hoped he'd walk away from his marriage. Once he had admitted to me his marriage was troubled, I allowed myself to daydream about us, even though there was no "us," and the result had been to weaken my resolve to stay clear. I'd allowed myself the luxury of fantasy. I'd experienced the delicious and unrestrained joy of imagining a future, together. The barricades of my psyche crumbled. All my wildest hopes bloomed and flourished, exploding and expanding, moving from small shapelessness to a larger solid form, like those silly toy capsules that grow into huge sponges when exposed to water.

This was my punishment.

I was no better than my dead husband. George Lowenstein cheated in the flesh, but I'd cheated with my heart, hadn't I?

So I quit fighting Brenda. I went limp as she shook me. I took the abuse, absorbed the pain.

# TEN

But like a decapitated body keeps twitching, my fingers mashed the call button repeatedly. Meanwhile, the ridiculousness of the situation played out in my mind — I was here in the hospital, supposedly to get well, but I wasn't safe. Brenda Detweiler aimed to kill me. A part of me repeated, "You have this coming to you," while another voice responded, "Fight! Fight back!"

My head flopped like a crash site dummy's, snapping back hard as she shook me first this way and then that. The room swam in a fast spinning circle. A sparkling constellation danced across the blackness of my vision. Through all the sensory chaos, came a weak voice, pleading, but distinct.

It was mine.

"Stop, please. Stop hurting me." I managed to add, "I promise."

"What's going on in there?" A voice called from out in the hallway.

The charge nurse must have heard the commotion.

Brenda realized her predicament. She turned loose of me immediately. She jumped back, making it to the end of my bed just as the door flew open. The light revealed Brenda standing there, shoulders hunched as she blinked and shaded her eyes.

The newcomer rounded the corner, her figure haloed in the light. She was nobody's fool. Quickly, she surmised that something — goodness knows what — had happened. "What's going on? Did someone call out?"

Brenda was unable to look the other woman straight in the eye.

I couldn't either. I adjusted my gown so the spots where Brenda had grabbed me wouldn't show.

The newcomer stood in the pie-wedge crescent of light, staring at me, then Brenda, and back again at me. Her voice became more soothing. "Mrs. Lowenstein, are you all right? Is there a problem?"

"Yes," I managed. "Fine. I'm fine."

"You sure?" the woman's voice probed as she picked up my wrist and put her fingertips on my racing pulse. "Your heartbeat is elevated. Your face is flushed."

She turned narrowed eyes on Brenda. "What are you doing here?"

Brenda stared down at her hands. "Um."

"We're old friends," I suggested, tentatively at first. "Brenda came by to say hello."

"Really?" The expression on her face told me the floor manager wasn't buying any of this. "Is that so?"

A long silence followed. I debated what to do. Brenda stood frozen at the foot of my bed.

As Shakespeare would have said, the worm had turned. She was entirely in my power.

I could report Brenda Detweiler. No doubt she'd lose her job. As well she should. She had no right to touch me the way she had. No right to bully me while I was here in her care.

She knew all this. Her face tightened, her mouth turned tremulous, and her hands balled up at her sides. She could tell that I was deciding her fate.

I could get her back. I could make her pay. I could punish her.

But I'm not like that.

I sighed.

Besides, I owed her one. I'd lusted after her husband, hadn't I? So, if she owed me one, and I owed her one, then couldn't we call it even?

If I did rat her out to her supervisor,

things would get very, very messy. Chad Detweiler's name would surely be dragged into the fray. True, he sort of deserved it, but a little voice inside me whispered, "He can't help the way he feels . . . and you can't either."

So I did something rare for me. I kept my mouth shut. In that gap between accusation and evidence, the charge nurse's inquiry fell flat. While we sat there in the empty crater of quiet, I pleated my sheet hem between my fingers. Did a good job of it, too. I'm not sure what Brenda did. I didn't watch her. I put all my energy into pleating.

The charge nurse told Brenda, "Get back to your station."

Her shoes slap-slap-slapped along the floor, moving quickly away from my bed.

After the charge nurse left, I heard her outside my door. I couldn't make out everything she said, but I distinctly heard, "We've got a problem. Brenda's at it again."

# ELEVEN

The morning after my confrontation with Brenda, I wondered if I'd imagined the whole scene. If it was a pain-induced hallucinatory representation of my guilty conscience. If I'd conjured up the whole scenario.

But my doubts ended when my best friend Mert stopped by to bring me a book on tape. (Actually she brought me a bunch of CDs. I can't get used to calling them anything but books on tape. Old habits are hard to break.) I stretched out a hand to examine the CDs more closely.

Mert doesn't miss a trick. She noticed bruises on my upper arms. "Holy Macaroni. What happened to you? These weren't here yesterday."

"Nothing happened to me."

"You call them nothing? You got yourself a perfect set of fingerprints."

"There was a problem. I took care of it."

"Which means what?" Mert scolded and scowled. "I heard that Brenda Detweiler works here. You run into her?"

"No," I lied.

"I just bet," snorted Mert.

"It's none of your business," I snarled. I was tired of my friends being in my business. I was a grown woman. I didn't need Mert educating me on what to do. Last night I'd been "saved" by the appearance of a second nurse. Try as I might, I couldn't erase the image of a furious Brenda Detweiler. Every time I closed my eyes, I conjured up her face and its fearsome expression of anger. A shiver wiggled down my spine.

She could have killed me. She certainly wanted to.

Despite questions from the charge nurse, I held my tongue, nearly biting it off in the process. I'll give her this, she was persistent. After all, she was ultimately responsible for my well being.

"I had a bad dream," I insisted.

When the new nurse handed me a paper cup with a couple of Tylenol in it, I refused the painkillers. No way was I willing to relax. What if Brenda came back? Instead of sliding blissfully into nirvana, I lay in my bed watching the black hands of the clock

64

click off minutes. When the sun brightened my room, I was still watching that stupid timepiece. Tick, tick, tick.

Now I embellished the lie I told the charge nurse the night before. "I had a nightmare," I told Mert. "Flailed my arms about. Hit something."

"That don't give people fresh bruises shaped like fingerprints."

"I bruise easily." That was true.

Mert knew it, but she was too smart for my baloney. "The nurses here are paid to provide a service. Last I checked, that don't include roughing up the patients. I don't care if you ran off with Brenda's hubby on their honeymoon. She's got no call to be mean to you. Hurting you is just wrong."

Of course, I didn't run off with her hubby on their honeymoon. I wish I could have, though. Deep in my heart, I knew that if Detweiler ever came to my door and offered to take me away, I'd step out of this life with only one hesitation — what about Anya? My daughter?

While this fantasy was highly entertaining, I must admit that I often wondered: Would Detweiler and I have this appreciation for each other if we'd met at a different time in our lives? Perhaps we'd have noticed each other and walked on by. Was it the fact we were older, in our thirties, that gave us the ability to truly "see" each other the way we did? A large part of my desire for him was his constancy, his never-ending concern for me and mine. Even after I'd told him to go away, he worried about me and my daughter.

And there was this almost physical, visceral connection between us. I felt this pang, right under my rib cage, whenever he was hurt or upset. He didn't have to tell me something was wrong. I simply knew it.

More than physical desire, he had my respect. I admired the fact he didn't grouse to me about his marriage. He didn't claim to be an injured party or speak poorly of Brenda. Instead, he simply told me they were working on problems, and that he owed it to her and his vows to give it his best shot.

How can you hate someone who's honest like that? Who doesn't deep-six the other person just so he can look good?

While I was reflecting on all this, all these fine qualities that Detweiler had, Mert peered down at my arm, then continued her harangue. "How dare she put a hand on you? Did you tell 'em to write her up? 'Cause you better. They'll fire her so fast her head will spin like Chinese acrobats do them there plates. I can't wait to see it. I want to stand here while they toss her butt right out the front door. See if I don't."

Mert could fuss all she wanted, but I wasn't changing my mind. So Brenda put a couple new bruises on my arms. Big deal. It was over. Done. Fini. I was ready to move on, but Mert wasn't. Boy, was she mad. She was so upset, so off the wall, and so full of vinegar, she was making me queasy.

"Mert, stop it. Please! You know I love you like family, but I'm asking you to back off. Promise me you'll drop it. Promise."

Which she did.

But she wasn't happy about it. Not at all.

# TWELVE

That was a little more than two months ago.

Since then, I had kept my promise to Brenda. I steered clear of her husband. A couple of times Detweiler dropped by the store to see how I was doing. Strictly business, he assured me. After all, my husband's murderer was still at large, and Detweiler considered the case still open.

Fair enough. He was only doing his job.

Life went on. I moved on. If staying away from Detweiler colored my life blue, well, I could manage. Blue wasn't as bad as black. Sure, at night I mulled over what little I knew about his marriage. He and Brenda had split up at least once. They had problems. What couple didn't?

I admit: I did my fair share of fantasizing. And dreaming. A lot of dreaming. In the middle of the night, I would feel the warmth of his mouth on mine and wake up with a face full of covers. Ugh. My behavior, conscious or unconscious, struck me as pitiful.

Why did I always want what I couldn't have?

When things really got to me, I stood in the shower and sobbed. That way Anya couldn't hear me. When I finished, or cried myself out, I dried off, pulled up my big girl panties, and went on my way. As long as Detweiler's path didn't cross mine, I could cope. Growing up in an alcoholic home, I'd had a lot of practice lying to myself. Pretending the real world didn't exist. Living on make believe and magic thinking. All that worked well right now.

Okay . . . it sort of worked. I was giving it that old college try. (Says the woman who dropped out of school. Sheesh.)

Most days, my life worked. Today, not so much. I couldn't stop shivering. Bama, normally a cipher, was clearly upset, too. Shortly after the two detectives left, my co-worker called Dodie and told her about my gruesome discovery.

Good old Dodie must have been rattled. I worked the sales floor as the two of them talked, but at one point, I needed to retrieve a special order from the back. I didn't have time to eavesdrop, but I could hear Bama's voice through the office door. The pitch was unnaturally high, one stop short of shrieking. When she took her place at the register, I thought I saw tear tracks on her face.

That stunned me. Bama never shows any emotion but annoyance.

"How's Dodie?"

There'd been a lull in the surge of shoppers. I asked for the update, hoping to process the news before another wave of customers distracted us. While Dodie's condition was widely known through our crafting community, Bama and I still took steps to guard her privacy. Our "boss" needed all her energy to fight for her life, and while our customers were well-meaning, sometimes their interest could be more tiring than helpful.

"She's nearly done with her chemo and radiation. The cumulative treatments are tiring her out. The doctors are going to do more tests, and then decide what's next. If they haven't gotten all the cancer, they'll schedule a laryngectomy."

The thought of Dodie silenced hit me hard. This was a day for being knocked low. A world without her terse wit and wisdom would be a sadder, stupider place. I felt sad just thinking of her loss, but I reminded myself this wasn't a forgone conclusion. Not yet.

Work was my ticket to forgetting what ailed me, so I concentrated on the tasks at hand. If Bama would just keep her mouth shut and not bring up Detweiler again, I might be able to salvage the day. We had wasted a lot of time with the detectives. Tonight was a crop night. I needed to put the final touches on our projects and toss together some nibbles. I also planned to decorate the store before our croppers arrived. This was iffy. Lights and I did not get along together. Heck, screwing bulbs into fixtures challenged me. Those itsy-bitsy fairy lights could be a real hassle. They rarely cooperated. Dodie bought these strands years ago, and they were flirting with early retirement.

I sighed, made a pit stop, blew my runny nose, scrunched my curls, wiped on heavy-duty undereye concealer, and decided to tackle the hardest job next.

First, I used the ladder to get down the box of lights from the shelves in the backroom. Then, I tested my first couple of strands. So far, so good. Next, I dragged the ladder to the front display window and climbed up. Even then, I stood on tippy toes to reach the upper edge of the window frame. I strung the lights across the top, secured it with thumbtacks, climbed down, and plugged it in. It refused to light. I pulled it down by carefully unhooking it from the tacks, retested it in the back, re-draped it, and swore under my breath while those dud lights hung there sadly like spent sparklers. On my fourth try, a ding-ding-ding in my brain reminded me my problem could be the socket. Which it was.

I flipped the strand around to the opposite end so I could run it to a socket on the other side of the window. I draped the strands again. Climbed down. Pushed the plug into the wall and zap!

All the lights went out.

To the groans of upset customers, I made my way to the backroom and reset the breakers. Then I returned to the front of the store. This time I brought an extension cord. I plugged it into a "good" socket and watched the formerly dark fairy lights brighten into miniature sparkling Tinker-bells.

A splattering of applause came from our customers.

Time to tackle lights over the door. I dragged the ladder over to one side of the door. Once up on it and stretched to my limits, I managed to rest the light cord awkwardly along the doorsill. However, it hung low in the middle. That had to be fixed, *tout suite.* With a mouthful of thumb-tacks, I climbed the ladder again and started to secure the strand. But I didn't get far. The door minder dinged. The front door flew open. The wires jerked out of my hand. The whole string came crashing down, and I nearly did a back flip off the ladder.

# THIRTEEN

My mother-in-law Sheila sputtered up at me. "I could have tripped!"

Crunch. Her boot heel came down on two of the lights.

"Drat. I just got those up and working."

"So what? I need to talk to you."

"Anya okay?"

Sheila snorted. "Of course my grand-daughter is okay. If she wasn't, I sure wouldn't come running to you."

Grrrr. That Sheila. What a pip. Count on her to brighten my day. And she wasn't done yet. Not nearly. "Grab your coat and come with me."

"I have a ton of work. There's a crop tonight —"

"Whatever. I said I need to talk to you. You must not be listening carefully." By golly, she actually stomped her foot.

I continued with my to-do list. "Food to prepare, and I haven't eaten lunch."

"I'll buy lunch."

That was a pretty good deal. The best I could possibly get. I told her I'd be right back and raced into the stockroom. "Bama, I'm off to buy food for the crop. You'll need to wait on customers." With that, I grabbed my jacket, an old navy-blue pea coat I found at Goodwill last week for five dollars. I wasn't sure why they'd discounted it so heavily, but it fit, and so I snatched it up. Inside the neckline I tucked a scarf I had crocheted all by myself. Sort of. My friend Clancy was teaching me, and I was pretty awful. Instead of being shaped like a long, thin rectangle, my scarf was a wonky triangle. One end had fourteen stitches fewer than the other. But Clancy assured me that improvement was my only option. (She discounted that I should maybe quit and let sheep all over the world graze contentedly without fear.)

Still, I liked the spot of color that my new turquoise and blue scarf added. I needed all the extra insulation I could muster because it's hard to heat a convertible, especially an old one like mine.

By contrast, you could fry eggs on the vents in Sheila's Mercedes. Slipping into the passenger's side, I flipped the heated seat switch and wiggled with anticipatory joy. Sheila slammed the car into reverse, then into drive, and capped that off by pulling out in front of a semi-tractor trailer. I saw the red Kenworth logo on the radiator grill as we squeaked by. "What the . . . ?" I gulped. "Are you trying to kill both of us? Because if you are, my sister in Arizona will raise Anya. Believe me, that's not what you want."

Sheila stomped the brake at the next light. The motion rocked me violently back and forth.

"Sheila? Sheila? Are you all right? Do I need to drive?"

"All right? Do I look all right to you? Do I seem all right?" her voice ended on a screech.

"Um, not exactly."

"Huh. Sometimes you are such a fool, Kiki Lowenstein."

I blinked hard and thought about this. If Anya was okay, what could be bothering her? That's all Sheila cared about. Anya and . . .

"Robbie? How's Police Chief Holmes?" I squeaked out as she right turned in front of a line of oncoming cars. "He okay?"

*Thump. Bump. Thump.* She ran over the curb in front of St. Louis Bread Co. (Everyone in town pronounces "Bread Co."

to rhyme with "bread dough." Sort of cute, isn't it?)

Her front bumper scraped a concrete parking block. She slammed the car into park and turned the key to off. For a long moment, neither of us spoke. Instead, Sheila worked her jaw this way and that, her eyes staring off in the distance.

"Sheila? Is Robbie all right? I mean, he's not . . . he's okay, isn't he?" The police chief suffered a heart attack several years ago. Since then, he'd had angioplasty, adhered to a better diet, and seemed the picture of health. There was one other explanation, one other reason Robbie Holmes might be unwell.

"He didn't get shot or anything, did he?" I sputtered. Robbie did more desk work than street work, but even so, several years ago, a gunman opened fire at a city council meeting in Webster Groves, a St. Louis suburb. The violent deaths brought a new realization that elected officials and city workers were at risk in ways previously un-imagined. Five people died at the scene, not including the shooter. Later, the mayor suc-cumbed to complications from his injuries, bringing the total to six, again excluding the shooter. That was a day we all cried, a day none of us in the community would ever forget.

Surely if there'd been another tragedy we would have heard. Someone would have phoned the store. Bama would have caught it on the radio that Dodie left in the back office.

Then I remembered that Bama had purposefully turned off the radio after our visit with the detectives. "I've had enough bad news for one day," she'd said and I concurred.

But this day had started out so horribly, of course it would continue downhill.

What if Robbie Holmes had been shot or even stabbed? Maybe a disgruntled citizen or a criminal seeking revenge made it past the metal detectors outside his office and . . .

"Sheila, tell me Robbie's all right!" I grabbed her arm.

She jerked away from me. "Of course, he's all right!"

I shivered in my seat. With the engine off, the car cooled quickly. "Then what on earth is bugging you?"

A tear spilled over her cheek.

"Whoa," I whispered. That droplet slowly rolled down her face and kept me mesmerized. I was in shock. Sheila never cried. Well, sure, she did when George died. He was her son, after all. But other than that, she never showed signs of emotion. She brought on tears, boy, did she ever! But she herself never cried.

Sheila shook her head, flicked away the moisture with a gloved finger. With a shudder, her lips parted. I heard her exhale. Heard her sigh. I held my own breath. What could have possibly happened?

"That stupid fool asked me to marry him."

# FOURTEEN

Sheila was right. If Robbie Holmes wanted to marry her, he was indeed a silver-plated, addle-pated fool. I mean, why? They practically lived together. His neat little bungalow on Pernod Street afforded him a place to escape when Sheila went on a tear. Her gorgeous mansion on Litzsinger gave them both a formal place for entertaining. Why ruin a perfectly good relationship by cohabiting? Heck, I found staying overnight at Sheila's stressful. Sure, Linnea, her maid, must be a direct descendent of an angel handmaiden. True, the place on Litzsinger was spacious. You could go for days and not have to interact with anyone, thanks to the well-thought-out floor plan and generous square footage. Yes, the Litzsinger house was a graceful haven where Queen Sheila personally stood guard. The comfy beds were made with Frette sheets, cashmere blankets, and hand-quilted comforters. Each bathroom featured a heated towel rack loaded with lavender-scented fluffy towels. The huge Sub-Zero refrigerator burgeoned with yummy cheeses, cut veggies, chopped up fruit, and sliced meats.

My mother-in-law missed her calling. If she hadn't signed up for the pain-in-the-butt master class, she could have been a very successful hotelier.

But why would Robbie Holmes feel the need to make a change? To combine their residences? To legalize their union?

As I pondered all this, Sheila rummaged in her Coach purse for a tissue. Pulling one from the nifty leather case designed to hold an entire pack of Kleenex, she sniffed gently and dabbed at her eyes.

"You are right. If he wants to marry you, Chief Holmes is nuts. You don't suppose his mind is going, do you?"

She shot me a blistering look. "For goodness sake, Kiki. That's the most ridiculous, malicious pap I've ever heard."

I shivered. "Let's discuss this inside. I want a sourdough bread bowl of their black bean soup."

Once I sat down with the fragrant brown bowl in front of me, I tried another approach. "Did Robbie tell you why he wants to, um, tie the knot?"

"Because he loves me, of course. He's absolutely besotted with me. Always has been."

I tore off a piece of the bowl, savored the tang of the sourdough, and let the warm richness of the black bean soup languish on my tongue. "Always?" I sipped my green tea. Delightful and healthy, too. For dessert, I'd chosen a fresh fruit cup. I love Bread Co.

"He tried to date me in high school, but my father put his foot down." A stain of crimson began at her neckline and slowly rose toward her face. "Although we did manage to see each other on occasion. School dances and so on. But never alone. For the most part." She set down the sandwich she was nibbling. Her cheeks glowed a bright, very un-Sheila-like red.

"But you met Harry and fell in love."

"I met Harry and recognized we would have a wonderful life together. That's not exactly the same thing." She frowned.

I admit; I was surprised by this revelation. George always portrayed his parents as the love match of the century. Unfortunately, Harry died shortly after his son and I married. But up until he drew his last gasp, I often observed my father-in-law staring at Sheila with eyes full of adoration. Now I was stunned by the realization that perhaps that worshipful affection hadn't been returned in equal measure.

Sheila sighed. "I married Harry because we were a better fit."

"But Robbie is a great guy! He's thoughtful, kind, considerate, ambitious —"

"Don't be ridiculous, Kiki. I know exactly what sort of man Robbie Holmes is. I also know what sort of young man he was. As the twig was bent, so grew the tree."

"Then, what did Harry have that Robbie didn't? Family money?"

She gave a tiny mew of exasperation, which along with a flick of her fingers, indicated I was the loose nut at the top of the old oak tree. "For pity's sake, Kiki. It's obvious, isn't it? Robbie wasn't a Jew."

"Oh, yeah." I suppose I can be forgiven for overlooking this teensy little detail since having a mixed marriage didn't stop me — or her son, George — from plighting our troth. "He's Roman Catholic, right?"

Sheila nodded. A tight, thin grimace pulled her face into an unhappy mask. "Exactly. My father called him a papist."

Her casual use of the term surprised me. Her attitude rankled. Why'd she have to repeat what her dad said? The pejorative repulsed me. She knew better. I wiped my face with a brown paper napkin, but the anger didn't go away. Instead, it surged within me. "Good news, Sheila. Your father's dead. Your Jewish husband is dead. Your reproductive organs are Missing in Action. If Robbie Holmes is dumb enough to want to be with you 24/7, I say, 'Have at, buddy.' Good luck to the poor sap."

"Trust you, Kiki, to make sport of a serious situation. Here I picked you up hoping to have a rational discussion, a deep theological conversation, and you . . ." she trailed off.

"I what? Threw a big, cold bucket of honesty into your face? Robbie's a nice man, Sheila. Scratch that. He's a wonderful man. A good, caring, decent fellow. You couldn't find better if you ran a classified ad in the *Jewish News*. As for the difference in religions, what difference does it make? It can't possibly matter now, can it?"

With that, she tossed her sandwich onto her plate. The top slice of bread bounced off and into the middle of the table. "How can you say that? Especially to me? You know how I feel about having a Jewish home."

I leaned closer to her so the rest of the diners couldn't hear me. "I say it because it's true. You aren't going to convert him, and he's not going to convert you. How long do you figure you have, Sheila? Another fifteen healthy years? Twenty? That would make you, what? Seventy-seven? Nearly eighty years old? How do you want to spend those last years? Alone in that big honking house or in the arms of someone you love? I know what my choice would be."

A vision of Detweiler's face popped into my head. What would I give to spend my life with him? Here Sheila was, passing up a man who loved her. Kids weren't part of the picture. No lack of respect was involved. Each attended services at the other's house of worship. Both donated money to their chosen faiths. Both had raised children according to the dictates of their religion.

So now, in the twilight of their years, what kind of God would keep them apart? What sort of supreme being would rather these two people — a couple who were much better together than apart — live without love?

I rubbed my face with my hands. What was it about religion that brought out the worst in us? That caused us to turn away from love, friendship, and kindness in the name of narrow dogma? How could God want this for us? I couldn't believe he did!

Sheila was so lucky. Her soul mate was

asking for her hand in marriage.
Mine was already taken.

# FIFTEEN

With that angry, bitter thought, I pushed my chair away from the table, got up, marched to the counter, and ordered muffies and cookies for the evening crop. By the time the food was bagged and paid for, Sheila had cleared our table or corralled someone into doing it for her. Struggling with my purchases, I held the door open for my mother-in-law and watched her stomp to her car. I was smacking the pavement pretty hard myself. Each of us was irritated and feeling sorely used.

"I need to run an errand on our way back to your store," she announced. With that, she cranked the heat onto high.

Errand? Did she say "errand" in the singular? Indeed, she did.

And she lied. She stopped first at the dry cleaners (where she fought with them over a spot they couldn't remove), next to Barnes & Noble Booksellers (where she fussed about a book cover she thought lurid), on to a drugstore (where she complained about problems with the federally mandated "childproof cap"), and finally to a cobbler's shop (where the nasty man who ran it got the better of my mother-in-law, but then he was famous all over town for being a first-class jerk). At the last stop, knowing what a turkey that shoe guy is, I stayed in the car and cranked the heat down. A honking-mad Sheila climbed back into the car. "He says my shoes are old. I pointed out people don't generally repair new shoes. Why would they? What a fool! Doesn't he know what business he's in?" She continued to grumble under her breath as she cranked the heat higher.

As the temperature rose in the car, an unpleasant fragrance filled the air.

In response to the growing stench, I closed the vents on my side.

Sheila responded to my move by cranking the heat to its max.

With all her errands, we'd strayed a long way from my store. The drive back took a while. We'd been riding a good ten minutes when Sheila's nose wrinkled in disgust. "What *is* that smell?"

I sampled the air, too. She was right. There was definitely something stinky aloft.

Something pungent. Something gross. I turned my head and sniffed at the bag from Bread Co.

Not coming from there. So where was it?

I leaned toward the back seat and took a deep breath.

Not there either.

At a stoplight, Sheila sniffed delicately around the steering wheel, following the long expanse of dashboard from her side to mine. "It's coming from your side of the car!"

I closed my eyes and sucked in air, sharp and ugly. Sheila was right. It *was* on my side. The pungent smell wafted from where I sat. I let my nose lead me, down, down, down, and slowly bent my face to my jacket. Sniffing and concentrating, I followed the stench to my sleeve.

The car's interior was now toasty warm. Almost hot, in fact.

The heat activated the smell. Energized it. Caused it to bloom. In response, I dialed down the thermostat. "This isn't helping."

At another long light, Sheila leaned toward my side of the car. We were now sniffing in tandem, two hound dogs on a fox's trail. She scooched as close to me as our seats would allow. I followed the scent, my head bending nearer and nearer to my body. I raised my arm, pulling it up to my nose.

"Pee-yew!" said Sheila.

"Ugh. It's coming from my coat." I took a long discerning snort. "Yuck."

"Is that jacket new?"

"Um," I hedged. I didn't want her to know I was shopping at thrift stores. I especially didn't want her to know I was shopping at thrift stores and buying from the markdown racks. "Not exactly. I just started wearing it."

Sheila sniffed in my direction and broke out with a cackle. "Better stop wearing it. You stink of cat pee."

# SIXTEEN

Sheila was still laughing as she turned the corner to my store. Her laughter died when she spotted the TV trucks. "Are they there to interview you? Are you in some sort of jam again?"

I closed my eyes. This was bad. Really bad. How had word leaked out so quickly?

"I found a severed leg in our Dumpster this morning."

"You what?" Sheila shrieked.

I filled her in quickly. We had time because the line of media cars blocked our parking lot entrance.

"And you didn't think to tell me?"

"You didn't exactly give me the chance. Besides, it's just garbage. Unusual garbage to be sure, but it's only trash. Bama and I are thinking it might be from a local hospital. Maybe even a prank pulled by a med student." Over the past two years, I learned to lie with casual finesse. This wasn't exactly a skill I planned to perfect. However, its usefulness could not be denied.

"Why in the world did they decide to use your Dumpster?"

She stumped me. (Pardon the pun.) We weren't close to any of the college campuses with a med school. The nearest funeral home was blocks away. No local bar or pub was situated within walking distance. The only response I could muster was a shrug.

"Thanks again for taking care of Anya tonight," I said, "and for taking her to Hebrew lessons today. Thanks in advance for picking her up from school and feeding her dinner tomorrow. I think I better hop out here and see if Bama needs help. She's a very private person." With that, I unbuckled my seatbelt, grabbed the bag of food, and leaped out in one smooth move. Right before I slammed the car door, I said to Sheila, "About marrying Robbie Holmes. Why not go see Rabbi Sarah? She can give you guidance."

Sheila's thoughtful gaze offered me a new-found respect. "Good idea. I might just do that."

As predicted, the teaming mass of media hounds turned on me like a fire ant colony on an invader. Questions flew. Microphones were shoved into my face. Hands tugged at my jacket. The swell of bodies pressed closer and closer. Media totally surrounded me.

Just as quickly, noses wrinkling in distaste, folks started to back away.

Maybe stinking like cat pee was a brilliant idea.

Or then again, maybe not.

My good pal Clancy Whitehead was the first of the Monday night croppers to arrive. "What a mob scene outside! I heard about your problem on the news. Totally gross, but also exciting. Really fascinating. How totally weird." Her face pinkened up. "You know what I mean," she added.

I nodded. I knew she was lonely and bored, so I didn't take her comments the wrong way. Clancy came across as cool, calm, and collected, but that polished exterior hid a sensitive soul. Rather like an armadillo with all those interlocking plates perfectly aligned for the purpose of protecting the defenseless creature at the core. I nodded to show I didn't think she was being callous. "You're right. Who would have ever guessed that among those paper scraps would be something so gruesome?"

Then I shuddered, "Being in the Dumpster with a severed body part was awful."

She had the good grace to look chagrined. "I imagine so. What do you think happened?"

I groaned. "I hate to think. The way the leg was chopped off, how cold the skin felt, that'll stay with me forever. Ugh. I'm hoping that a med student dumped it off as a prank. Or maybe some weirdo went through the trash at a hospital and found it, took it, and then thought better of the whole scheme."

"I doubt it. Usually they put body parts in an incinerator. Three questions come to mind. One, where did the severed limb come from? Two, who had custody or access? Three, why drag that thing to your store to dump it?"

"Beats me. I expect we'll know soon enough. The police were all over this."

Clancy's eyes sparkled. "Will Detweiler get involved?"

"I hope not. I've cut off all communication with him."

She raised an eyebrow at me.

"What are my choices? He's married. Until that changes, I'm begging for more heartbreak."

"Well, then, this should get your mind off him. It sure sounds like a mystery to me. I know you are busy around here, but this might be a welcome diversion." She laughed. "Ouch. I'm sounding like a really sick puppy, but you know how I love mysteries and how boring my life is. In fact, I was thinking. Do you need any help over the holidays? I'd be happy to help out."

"I'm not sure we can afford you."

"Come on, Kiki. You know I'm offering gratis."

"I can't ask that of you. That's taking unfair advantage of a friend."

She turned sad eyes on me.

Clancy could be Jackie Kennedy Onassis's twin sister. From the arched eyebrows and brightly piercing eyes to her tasteful clothing choices. Today she wore a simple powder-puff pink cashmere v-neck sweater, a statement necklace, brown gabardine slacks, and crocodile loafers. Despite all that stunning wardrobe and personal charm, she threw off misery like a dog shakes off water. "My ex and his new bride invited both my kids on a ten-day Caribbean cruise over the holidays. Try to compete with sun, sand, and endless free-flowing liquid when your kids are young adults struggling to get by."

I said nothing. The thought of being entirely alone this time of year totally choked me up. I coughed to recover my powers of speech. She patted my back.

"You know," Clancy said, "loneliness is the most powerful emotion known to man.

Or woman. I like my own company, I do. But to have children and miss them, to have loved and go to sleep each night by myself in a California King bed, well, it drains the soul of all energy, doesn't it? I feel like an empty tin can being kicked down the highway of life."

With that, I hugged her. Clancy's a bit stiff, but after a second, she melted. "Don't feel sorry for me. I'm not asking for that."

"Come help us. We sure could use the extra pair of hands. Bring your crochet, and if you get bored, you can high tail it to the backroom. Think you can stand Bama? I might have to check with her first, before I give you an official okay."

"When I taught middle school, I put up with hormonal teens, overly involved parents, and other teachers who were totally bonkers, as well as school administrators with only one clear goal in life: making other people miserable. I think I can handle Miss Cold Shoulder."

# SEVENTEEN

I laughed. We sneaked back to the stock-room where she could examine my crocheting. "You're coming along. Remember to trust the yarn and the hook. Your work is a bit too tight, and that comes from worrying your piece will slide off."

I nodded. Clancy hit the proverbial nail on the head. My hands ached from clenching the yarn tightly. I worried my projects would slip from the hook and unravel at any juncture. "At this rate I'll never finish the scarves I plan to give as gifts."

She grinned. "I can help with that, too. Now show me where you found that piece of shin. I'm curious."

Our other Monday night croppers showed up one by one, moving past the last of the media. Once inside they dispensed hugs and holiday greetings. Of course they wanted to know what happened to draw the attention of the news trucks, but Bama quickly brushed the questions aside with, "It's no big deal. Just something Kiki found in our garbage. We're confident it's a prank."

Most of the women were our regulars; we'd been through a lot together. While my gross discovery caused a few nervous glances, they were more interested in their crafting projects than someone's failed anatomy lesson.

Miriam Glickstein brought a Hanukkah page she started and hoped to finish, Maggie Earhardt (her daughter Tilly attended school with Anya) carried a box of Christmas cards she was working on, Rita Romano baked a fabulous batch of cornbread with chiles to share with us, and Jennifer Moore (her daughter Nicci was Anya's best friend) brought a small album chronicling the history of her family business. Lanetta Holloway showed up in her signature purple, including the coolest low boots I've ever seen. She was putting together an album of her favorite new sci-fi/fantasy books. Bonnie Gossage showed up looking the same color I did after I pulled up that severed limb. As the women settled into their spots, Rita placed the cornbread on the side table we reserved for food. (Keeping it separate from the crafts was a priority. Nothing like a spill to ruin weeks of work.

Even dry items like breads and cookies can leave oil stains on paper.)

Five other newcomers rounded out the group, including the young mother of twins I had stayed to help the night before. "My name's Daisy Touchette," she said shyly. "You were so nice to me that I had to come back. Told my husband that having a hobby was way cheaper than divorce court." With that she gave a nervous giggle.

The minute the foil wrapper came off the cornbread and its lovely aroma filled the air, Bonnie hopped up and ran to the back room. She returned with a slight sheen on her skin, and one hand pressed to her lips. It didn't take med school to figure out she'd been sick.

"Hope you don't mind. My tummy's upset so I helped myself to a Sprite from the refrigerator," she said.

"Of course not." Bonnie once helped spring me from the county jail. As far as I was concerned, she could drink Lake Superior dry of colas, and I'd gladly foot the bill.

Bama frowned at the attorney from behind our customer's back. Boy, oh, boy. Miss Pinch-a-Penny was the life of the party. I hissed to my partner, "I'll pay for it," and Bama recovered enough to welcome our croppers. She passed out goody bags with a sheet detailing our holiday store hours, a cute little die cut of stacked presents, and a coupon for special discounts. I hadn't seen the final schedule until Bonnie withdrew hers from the bag. When I did, I bit my lip to keep from moaning. I love the store, but staying open until 9 p.m. and occasionally 11 was going to make holiday shopping impossible for me. As for celebrating Hanukkah, forget-about-it. Eight days of festivities were always hard to pull off, but more so when I only had one or two waking hours at home.

Bama ended her portion of the event by reading a note from Dodie, Time in a Bottle's founder and majority owner. Dodie explained her chemo and radiation treatments would end soon and she missed everyone terribly. A coda from her husband thanked all of us for our support and good wishes.

"Tonight's project is a holiday organizer. I think you'll find it incredibly useful for staying on top of all your activities. Jane Dean, that fabulous United Kingdom scrapbook artist, showed a similar project a few years back." I handed out the materials kit and a color copy of the *ScrapBook inspirations* article with Jane's project in it. The resulting oooohs and ahhhs went a long way toward making me feel better. But then, crafting always makes me feel better. I know I'm not alone.

# KIKI LOWENSTEIN'S HOLIDAY ORGANIZER

*Inspired by a similar project by Jane Dean, published by* ScrapBook inspirations *magazine.*

1. Buy a cheap 3-ring binder of light cardstock.
2. Cover the front and back with holiday appropriate paper. If desired, cover the inside covers as well. You might wish to lightly sand the outside if it is glossy. (Tip: I like UHU Glue Stick for gluing paper to cardstock. You do need to get the glue all the way to the edges or the paper might peel up, but the glue stick won't bubble like liquid glue does.)
3. Create inside pages out of cardstock. Label these: Calendar, Gifts, Recipes, Events, Decorating. (Tip: Use a punch in the shape of a label tab and stagger the tabs so they are all readable.) Remember to leave a margin on one side so you can punch holes and not ruin your design.
4. Decorate these inside pages. You can find calendars online for your calendar page. You might also want

to create some inside pages with pockets. On other pages, add room for lists that you will make as you go through the holidays.

5. Between the decorated pages, add empty plastic page protectors for notes.

6. Assemble your organizer.

# EIGHTEEN

The crafters decided to create a "get well" card for Dodie. As a result, we closed a half an hour later than predicted. How could I stop them? Especially when the extra time went for such a good cause? I knew the card would perk up her spirits. Horace phoned during the crop and told Bama privately his wife might be back at the store next week. I hoped so, but I also hoped she would take time to recover from her treatments. The aftermath of chemo and radiation could be as brutal as the treatments themselves.

My house was dark and deserted when I arrived home. It wasn't that I'd forgotten to turn on the porch light. I was hoping to save a little money by leaving it off during the day. Instead, I carried a flashlight in my purse. The sweep of the beam picked up a figure walking toward me, and I nearly wet my pants.

"Kiki?"

I recognized the voice of my landlord, Leighton Haversham.

"Didn't mean to scare you. Hoped I'd catch you. May I come in? Is your porch light not working?"

"Um, I forgot to turn it on when I left."

Mr. Haversham smiled and held my door open for me, which was very helpful because I was loaded down. "I'll have an automatic light sensitive timer put in. That way you won't have to remember. Where's Gracie?" he said as he took my bundles from my arms. I brought old magazines from the store with the hopes they'd inspire me for future projects. I also carried a sample project, the leftover Bread Co. food, paper to cut for upcoming projects, and small scraps of paper that needed sorting. This I fished out of the trash with the hopes I could use them on my own holiday cards that I hadn't yet started.

"Gracie's staying overnight at the vet's office. She's got a bad case of 'happy tail.' "

"Happy tail?" He pulled out a kitchen chair and settled in. Leighton has that old world gentleman thing going. His salt-and-pepper hair was slicked back in a *très* European manner, and his slacks always draped as though made from very expensive material. I'm not sure if his loafers were Italian, but I imagined they were. There was this overall elegance about him that always caught me slightly off-guard. Especially when he also managed to look entirely comfortable in my kitchen.

"Repetitive injuries after her tail got caught in a car door," I explained with a wince. My best friend Mert's son Roger had been fooling around. At twenty, Roger's a big man-kid. He didn't mean to slam the door on Gracie's tail, and fortunately, he caught it mid-slam so the full impact wasn't realized. But Mert just about killed her son over it. "Fiddle-farting around and he knows better!" she hollered. The wound should have healed quickly. Gracie, like most dogs, is a totally forgiving creature; her response was to give a loud yelp and then to quickly love up Roger. He knelt at her side, tears forming in his big hazel eyes, his whole body trembling, as he repeated, "I'm sorry! Gracie, I'm so sorry!" When he offered to pay for the vet's visit, I said, "No way!" but Mert insisted. "Serves him right. He gotta learn that actions have consequences."

When her tail didn't heal after the first trip, I took her back to see Dr. Tailor. His demeanor told me more than his words. He rubbed his jaw and sighed. "We call it 'happy tail.' Happens a lot with your big breeds. Poor girl keeps re-injuring herself as she wags it."

He suggested that they keep Gracie overnight, which stretched to two nights. At the clinic they put my baby in a special crate lined with pads to minimize the impact of her wagging and gave her a shot of antibiotics.

Leighton drummed his fingers on the table. "That's too bad. I hope she recovers quickly. I heard about your Dumpster-diving episode. Imagine bringing up part of a corpse. That's an assumption, of course. The other option is too terrible to consider."

He was right about that.

He continued, "I stopped by because I need help. I'm leaving town on a mini-book tour. Do you have a few minutes? I could show you how to care for Monroe."

Petunia was his scaredy-cat pug and Monroe his pet donkey. In return for reduced rent, I bartered my services as pet sitter. "Of course."

A few snowflakes danced in my porch light as we stepped out my front door. The air actually felt warmer than it had at noon. Leighton called out to Monroe as we approached. A clatter of hooves on cold hard ground greeted us, his breath clouding the frigid air. In the center of Monroe's pen was a sturdy shed over a concrete floor covered with sawdust and straw for bedding. The fencing attached to each side of the enclosure. A simple gate with a lift and drop latch completed the enclosure.

"Monroe hates the color white," Leighton explained while he scratched his pet under the neck. "He's a rescue donkey. Spent his formative years at a petting zoo. Little kids loved to pull on his ears, and Monny has sensitive ears, don't you, buddy? But donkeys are smart. Monroe figured out that if he head-butted kids in diapers, they'd stay away from him. As a consequence, my sure-footed friend thinks anything white is worthy of target practice."

I laughed. Monroe wore a bright blue blanket. Leighton explained that he had been "rugged up" as protection from the cold, and his garment was changed and laundered frequently. To my surprise, Monroe appeared every bit as affectionate and personable as a dog or a cat. He followed his owner around like a lovesick puppy. His big velvety lips tugged at Leighton's barn jacket, as he leaned his forehead against Leighton's arm.

With a quick toss, Leighton lobbed an apple at me. "He can only have one of these a day. I saved this treat so you could give it to him." Suddenly I was the center of Monroe's world. I flattened my hand and offered up the fruit, which Monroe delicately removed. His soft lips tickled my palm, and I couldn't help but crow with delight. "He's so sweet!"

"Unless you are wearing white," said Leighton. "Then he's a fur-covered bulldozer calculating how to mow you down. But I can't blame him, can you? He was only trying to defend himself. A very noble response. Anthropologists say humans have two overwhelming drives: procreation, or adding to our species, and self-preservation, or maintaining our species. Surely Monroe has the right to self-defense. Why should we wish to deny him that?"

I also learned that most donkeys don't like dogs. "But Monny is very tolerant of them. Lucky for us dog lovers, eh?"

Leighton showed me Monroe's food and gave me instructions on how much to feed him. "Don't let those brown eyes sucker you into extra food. It's not good for him. Oh, and there's a heater in his water supply, so it won't freeze up."

The cares of the day evaporated as I learned how to care for my new friend. Leighton opened the back door to his home and called Petunia, his pug. The shy little boy-dog ran to me with his tail tucked between his legs, wriggling with joy. Tunie and I had been pals for ages, so I scooped up the cute smashed-nose pup and gave him a cuddle.

"By the way, Kiki, you do know you can turn me down for pet sitting, right? I don't expect you to be available every time I ask."

He's such a nice man.

I assured him that caring for Petunia and Monroe wouldn't be a problem. In fact, with Gracie gone, I was eager to take Petunia home with me that very evening.

I was sincere in my intent, but after I locked my front door and got the dog settled, I wondered how on earth I could manage to care for Leighton's pets, help Mert with her dogsitting, meet my store obligations, and take care of holiday celebrations with my daughter. I opened the organizer I'd created as an example for our croppers. There just weren't enough pages or open spaces in it to accommodate my overflowing schedule.

So I closed it and went to bed. This had been one of the longest days of my life. I kicked off my shoes but didn't bother to undress. I tossed and turned all night,

imagining the feel of cold, yucky flesh
against my skin.

# NINETEEN

*Tuesday, December 15*

I woke up with a head full of junk. My dressing routine was interrupted by several fits of coughing and sneezing. A couple of squirts of nasal spray helped me start breathing through my nose instead of my mouth.

I hate colds. Hate 'em.

My spirits brightened as I approached the pen. Monroe was thrilled to see me, and I quickly dispatched my responsibilities in the shed. Petunia wiggled around on the passenger's seat. I cracked the windows for him while I raced into the vet's office to pick up Gracie. Dr. Tailor instructed me to keep Gracie from any excitement. The less wagging, the better. I wondered how I could do that. By nature, Gracie wasn't a barker. My big, beautiful Harlequin Great Dane didn't make a peep for months after I acquired her at a pet adoption fair. But she was always a lover and a happy pup. Almost anything could set Gracie's backside a moving like a metronome. I studied the bandage on her appendage and crossed my fingers mentally. Maybe if I positioned her in the backroom where she couldn't see the comings and goings, she'd stay calm.

*Fat chance,* said a voice in my head.

I situated both dogs in the playpen. Heated water in the microwave for a cup of Earl Grey, brewed it, squished out the moisture and kept the bag tucked away in a ramekin for another cup or two. I started the opening procedures and heard the buzzer sound at the back door. With any luck, I'd open it to a delivery of more stock.

I was all out of luck.

Detective Chad Detweiler stood there.

I gulped.

I hadn't seen him for nearly a month. My mouth went dry. My hot tea sloshed over onto my hand.

"Ow!" I cried and dropped my mug. Behind me, my silent wonder-dog, Gracie, yodeled with joy. Detweiler is her favorite person in her world and mine. Heck, in my own way my tail was wagging, too.

Without speaking, he took me by the arm over to our bathroom sink. There he pressed against me and held my hand in cold water.

113

"It keeps burning after the liquid is gone. You need the cold to stop the progress."

The heat in my hand was quickly replaced by a warm tingling south of my belt buckle. I considered splashing a little water all down the front of me. I sure needed it.

"That's better," Detweiler said as he stepped away. My wobbling legs nearly collapsed.

But sanity and sheer grit rescued me. I straightened, caught a glimpse of myself in the mirror, and flinched. My nose rivaled Rudolf's for redness.

"I assume you're here for a reason," I managed, but that's all I said before the buzzing of the back door minder interrupted us. Detective Hadcho wore a grim expression as he stood on the threshold. "I see Chad's already here. Your business partner is just pulling in. We need to talk."

Bama came in and we all took seats in the office. Hadcho and Detweiler explained that the police received a strange message the night before on their Tips Hotline. Detweiler withdrew a small recording device from his pocket and hit the "play" button.

"My name is Cindy Gambrowski," said a quivering voice. "I'm afraid for my life. If anything happens to me, talk to Kiki Lowenstein over at Time in a Bottle. She'll

114

have the answers."

"I have no idea what that person is talking about. When did you say you found this?" I cradled a new mug of tea. The old one with its broken handle had been relegated to the trash.

"One of our technicians brought it to us this morning. They followed up last night with a call to the Gambrowski residence, but no one answered. Without anything to follow up on —" Hadcho opened his palms in a gesture of defeat.

"Is Mrs. Gambrowski one of your customers?" Detweiler tapped his pen against his Steno pad, a habit of his I knew well. The pen moved at the rapid pace of his thoughts.

"She is."

"What else can you tell us about her?"

I floundered about, not so much because I was being coy as how do you describe someone without being cruel or petty? Cindy had a bit of the floozy about her. Too much makeup. Too-low tops. Too-tight pants. Always wore high heels. No doubt her wardrobe was all very expensive stuff, but it was also too tight and too showy. Her taste veered toward cheap, or at least to the obvious, and there it remained. Her husband Ross was the driving force behind several subdivisions including Rossman

Acres, a trendy but tacky subdivision on the south side of St. Louis. I once went to a Tupperware party there with another customer. (I usually avoid home parties because you feel obligated to make a purchase. But in this case, I needed their cupcake server for the store, and Tupperware is the best.) The walls of that little two-storey house shook whenever big cars drove by. The carpet obviously had been glued directly to the floor. When a toilet flushed on the second floor, I thought we'd all been instantly transported to Niagara Falls.

But why tell this to Detweiler and Hadcho? These were only opinions, not facts. It wasn't like I'd ever had a heart-to-heart with Cindy.

Except . . . except . . .

"Did she take that journaling class you offered? The six-week one?" Bama mused out loud. "Journaling Your Life Story, right? Wasn't that the name of it?"

I nodded.

"You keep any of her writings?" Bama drilled me.

"No. I expressly do not keep them. My goal is to encourage women to be honest on paper. You can't do that if you worry other people will read what you wrote. They did most of their writing at home. I suggested they decide what was for public consumption and put that small portion of their work in their scrapbook albums."

Everyone sat there without talking for a few minutes.

"You sure you don't have anything of hers?" asked Detweiler. "Stan and I are here because we've been assigned to the Major Case Squad."

Suddenly the import of all this hit me hard.

"You think she's dead?"

## TWENTY

Bama gasped, "Then you think that leg was . . ."

"Oh, my, gosh!" I sat my mug down so hard the tea splashed across the desktop.

Detweiler and Hadcho exchanged smoke signals with their eyes. Detweiler's face softened as he directed his comments to me. "We don't know whose leg you found. Ross Gambrowski didn't report his wife as missing. However, he can't account for her whereabouts. We have a BOLO — that's Be On the Look Out — for her car. The last time he saw her was Friday night. He claims he came home late, found the bedroom door locked, and fell asleep on the sofa. Says the next morning, Saturday, there was a note on the kitchen table from Cindy. Said she was off bright and early for a Bible study group. That night he got a text message from her phone." Here Detweiler flipped to a page in his notepad and read, "Be home late. Went to a scrapbook crop."

"Did you have a crop here Saturday night?" Hadcho asked.

"No, we didn't."

"Who did?" Detweiler's voice turned staccato. For the first time, I examined him more carefully. His eyes wore a tired, careworn expression. A few gray hairs mingled in with the brown hair at his temples. Most telling, his shirt sported wrinkles across the chest. This, a seemingly insignificant personal tidbit, surprised me. He was a total nut about ironed shirts. Did them himself. Used spray starch. He liked to press the yoke on the back from one side and then the other so the fabric would lie down neatly. We had a good laugh about how anal that was.

"I like what I like," he grinned. "Since I'm willing to do them myself, why not? I find ironing therapeutic. Too bad you can't iron all the wrinkles out of life."

That preference must have fallen by the wayside.

"Are you serious?" Bama dropped all pretense of nice. "Any one of a dozen groups could have held a crop on Saturday. There are Creative Memory crops here all the time. We have a lot of active representatives in the St. Louis area."

"As well as other private crops," I chimed in. "But the Creative Memories folks are very well-organized. You could check with them. They all know each other." I wrote a phone number on a card. Our store had a wonderful relationship with the local CM reps. More than once I suggested folks check out their classes, crops, and products.

Another idea occurred to me. "Just a sec." I popped up and hurried to the front of the store. With any luck, we could send the two detectives on their way and get cracking on the day ahead.

Positioning the small ladder against one of the side walls of the store, I steadied it against the wall and started to climb.

Detweiler braced it from below. "This doesn't look safe. Get down and let me up there."

I ignored him. Focusing on one of the pages pinned to the wall, I dug a thumbnail under the tacks. Moving carefully, I backed down the ladder. Detweiler didn't step away. An inch, maybe less was all that stood between us.

His lips touched my ear, and the sweet scent of soap tickled my nose. "I heard about what Brenda did. You should have reported her."

"Excuse me?"

He set his hand over mine, as it lingered on the ladder. "Kiki, don't do me any favors. Not like that."

A blaze of anger started, hot and slow. "Favors? What makes you think I did you a favor? I don't know what you're talking about."

"The heck you don't. She shook you. And you let her get away with it. Out of some misguided allegiance —"

"Excuse me?" Detective Hadcho's voice called over from a fixture. "What did you find?"

Detweiler and I broke apart like two guilty teenagers. I suspect my face pulsed with fury because Bama rounded the corner immediately after, and she stopped in her tracks at the sight of me. "Wha . . . ?"

I waved the page at the two of them. "This is Cindy's entry for our All about Me Contest. I thought it worth looking at more carefully."

But before we could take the layout to the cropping table where the light was better, Detweiler and Hadcho's cell phones rang in tandem. Both men clapped their mobiles to their ears. *Sotto voce,* they grunted in unison. It would have been funny, but a frisson warned me the news wasn't good. Hadcho clapped his cell closed and abruptly stood up.

Detweiler put out a staying hand. "No need to hurry. Let's look this over first."

"I'll make you each a color copy," I said. I walked to the copier and loaded the page face down on the scanning bed. Detweiler appeared at my elbow.

"Listen," he whispered. "I'm not upset with you. I'm furious with her. I know you let it slide to be nice. But don't ever do that again."

"I don't intend to," I said. On one level I understood my emotions. Embarrassment, desire, and anger all roiled within me. On another, I simply didn't care how mixed up my feelings were. So what if I let anger rule? Wasn't that better than seeming like a victim?

"Good." He reached over and gave my hand a small but tender squeeze. The gesture was fast, intimate, and nearly brought me to tears. "It makes me sick that anything happened to you while you were helpless. She had no right. I wish . . ."

That half-sentence didn't add up to much. It certainly didn't shed any light on what happened. In my mind, it was simple: Brenda had been angry and I had been helpless. What was he going on about? The copier finished its scan and spit out the warm duplicate images. "I hope these help," I managed.

"I do, too," he said. "But right now, I can't imagine how. I have a bad feeling it's too late for Mrs. Gambrowski."

# TWENTY-ONE

Detweiler and Hadcho were nearly at their cars when Mert's truck jumped the curb and headed straight toward them. Hadcho shot her a dirty look, hopped in his Impala, and burned rubber in his way past her. Not that Mert noticed. She almost sideswiped him on her way into a space. Her driving had taken a decided turn for the worse over the past thirty days. She had a lot on her mind, I'll grant you. A client accused Mert of breaking expensive décor items while housecleaning. Rather than argue, Mert let her insurance pay the first claim. But the second time, she stood her ground. "I ain't taking it no more. I didn't break that there vase. Or that serving bowl. Iff'n I had, I'd a said so. But I didn't. This'll jack up my rates, and I won't stand for that."

So Mert was prepping to appear in Small Claims Court. "You would just know it had to happen during the holiday season when ever'one and her sister needs housecleaning right here, right now." She thumped around in my kitchen as she explained her situation.

I wished her luck.

She didn't need it.

Mert's a lot smarter than people credit her. There's that book about the many types of intelligence. I figure "people smart" must be on the list. Mert has that covered twenty ways to Sunday.

Now she muscled the truck into a space, slammed the Chevy S10 into the parking curb and tossed open her door. The sound of dogs barking followed her out onto the pavement. She waved down Detweiler. The two put their heads together.

A sick feeling started in my gut. I had a hunch Mert was the person who told him about Brenda shaking me. Now the two people I loved most in the world next to my daughter were in cahoots, plotting against me. Drat, drat, double drat. Like I needed that! What was Mert on about? She knew I'd decided to keep my distance. So why was she chatting him up? Did she hope to snare Detweiler for herself?

I shifted my weight from one foot to the other and back again.

I chastised myself for the unworthy

thoughts.

Detweiler nodded a goodbye to my friend. She waited for him to back out before unloading three dogs.

Detweiler pulled into the traffic on Brentwood.

"This here Chihuahau's name is Izzy, ain't he cute?" Mert reached into her cab and handed me a tiny black and brown fellow with bat-shaped ears. Izzy and I gave each other the once-over. He must have decided I passed muster because he yawned. "I got you this springer spaniel named Fluffy. I expect someone ought to shoot his owners for violation of the Stupid Pet Name Code. Then there's Jasper, and he's part poodle, part Bichon." She dragged Jasper and Fluffy toward me as they pulled on their leashes in two different directions.

Fluffy was a buff-colored, spring-loaded, bouncy toy of a dog. White-and-peach-spotted Jasper cocked an eyebrow at me, promptly sat down, and scratched behind his right ear. That's when I noticed that Jasper was short a leg.

"He's only got three legs!"

"Dang it. He had four when we left the house!" Mert hurried over to look at him. I stepped up next to her and stared hard, too.

My jaw dropped. I only counted three legs.

"I was just fooling. Got you good, too."
Mert started laughing. "Jasper's a rescue
pup. Poor thang. His old owners left him
outside till the fur wrapped around his left
leg and cut the circulation off. Had to be
amputated. You'd never know he's missing
it, would you?"

No, I wouldn't. Better yet, Jasper didn't
seem to care. "He's pretty perky."

Mert squatted down and loved him up. "I
love this here dog. He's a walking reminder
to take life in stride. He don't fret none
about the past, about what he don't got, or
what people done to him. Ever' day he just
wakes up eager to see what good news the
Lord hath wrought. A person could learn a
lot from good old Jasper."

I was not as willing to leave the past
behind. I waited until we were near the
doggy playpen to pounce on Mert. "You
told Detweiler, didn't you? About what happened in the hospital? With his wife?"

Mert didn't miss a step as she stooped
down to give Petunia and Gracie a little loving. "You betcha. After I tole him what happened, I called up that wife of his and
explained a few facts of life to her. Said if
she ever, ever, ever touched a friend of mine
again — or your child — she better hightail
it for the North Pole 'cause I planned to

run her feet first through a blender and turn her into chowder. Then I'd feed her to the crocodiles or alligators or whatever it is that lives down there in the Everglades."

I didn't know whether to laugh or cry. Mert's startling ability to turn violent always caught me by surprise. Coupled with her hardscrabble style of talking, I envisioned us in some creepy Cohen Brothers movie. A St. Louis version of *Fargo,* maybe. "Mert, give me space. You can't go charging in after people on my behalf. What if she reports you to the authorities? You're already on the court docket."

"Yep, I am. Guess what? Mr. Hunky Detective said he'd check the pawn shop records for me."

"For what? A gun?"

"No, ma'am. I'm thinking that my former employer Mrs. Springer done broke those things to get some spending money."

"So?"

"Maybe she also pawned stuff and just says it's broke. She could be lying."

"But isn't her husband that super-rich attorney? Handles all those big corporations over in Clayton. Why would she need money? They're supposed to be loaded."

"There's loaded his style and loaded her style," my friend carefully delineated this with two unequal portions of air divided by her palms.

"You lost me."

"See," Mert made a big distance between her hands. "He's got all this money, right? But he don't share none with her." Next she made a tiny sliver of airspace with her hands. "So iff'n she wants something or needs something he don't want her to have, she's stuck."

"Why not charge it or write a check?"

Mert snorted. " 'Cause she don't got no credit or checking account. He gives her cash for everything. I seen this list in their kitchen. She had to write down everything she bought. Turn in the receipt, too."

"You are kidding me."

"No, sirree, doggies. Some of these men think they gotta keep a wife on a real short leash. I suspect old Mr. Springer's one of them. I mean, look at him. Ever seen his photo? He's just a tiny little squirt of a man. Wears his pants up around his boobies. Got this yellow hair sticks out every which way. Ugly, too. Don't you think he worries about what she sees in him? Can't be his charming physique. Or his noble chin. Cause he ain't got one."

"Isn't that a form of abuse?" I wondered.

"Being chinless?"

129

"Withholding spending money. I mean, especially if you have it. I think of marriage as sharing. For one person to dole out pennies seems pretty mean to me."

"It sure qualifies as abuse in my book. I wouldn't put up with it. In fact, my first husband was abusive and I didn't put up with it."

# TWENTY-TWO

"You never told me that."

"Invite me over for a glass of wine this weekend, and I'll tell you the whole sad story."

"I'd love to but I'm working here every day until Christmas."

"No breaks at all?"

"No."

With that, Bama stuck her head out of the office. "Five minutes 'til store opening. Have you paid attention to the schedule, Kiki?"

"What do you mean?"

Bama came over to where Mert and I stood petting the dogs. She gave Mert a nod. That passed for a gracious greeting from Miss Frosty. "I don't see how we're going to cover all our open hours. My sister can't help us. The catering business is her first priority since they pay her health insurance. Even if you and I both work every

131

open hour, we'll need help. We can't have adequate coverage with just one person, or even two."

I decided not to tell her that Clancy had volunteered. As long as I held out, I was holding a handful of aces. If I played my cards right, I could offer Clancy's help to Miss Smarty Pants, and I'd look like a hero for coming up with a solution to our problems. So instead of explaining that help was standing by, I studied the schedule Bama handed me.

Good. Clancy's help was definitely needed. The hours of covering our sales floor totaled more than I expected. "I don't see any way we can do this. How were we going to manage? It's not just a stretch; it's an impossibility."

"It's worse than it looks."

"You mean because we have prep duty? Paperwork? Ordering supplies?"

"No," said Bama. "I mean we have another problem."

"You mean Dodie won't be able to pitch in next week."

Bama nodded. "There's that, too. Horace called. He thinks she's too worn out to help. Besides, he says the chemo has muddied her thinking."

"That's hard to imagine, but if he says it's

true, it must be." My heart felt heavy as I passed the schedule to Mert. She was a wizard with management problems like this. Even so, she took one glance at it and shook her head. "What's your other problem?"

"We need better floor coverage, and we need it now. Someone's shoplifting merchandise. We've lost four Cricut cartridges in the past five days. Two of our most expensive albums are missing as well."

She could have punched me in the stomach. Her words knocked all the wind from my lungs. I didn't want to believe this. All the women who shopped here were our friends! Who would do this to us?

"Clancy volunteered to help. I'll call her and ask when she might work," I said. "Even so, we'll still need help."

"I got myself a young friend named Laurel Wilkins, and she needs a job," said Mert. "I can vouch for her honesty personally. How about if I send her over? She'll work cheap, and I know she's been laid off from the Ford car plant. She's real bright. Likes crafts. Got a great personality. Lots of pep."

Bama and I nodded our approval. "Sounds good," said my partner. "With Clancy and her, we can probably make do. Besides, we'll need help when I leave to teach on that cruise to Cozumel in January."

"But won't that cut into our earnings? I was hoping we'd make a little extra during the season. For holiday shopping," I added without needing to go on.

"If someone's stealing from us, they are taking our profit. The way I see it, it's six of one, half a dozen of another. I'd rather pay someone a fair wage than have stuff stolen from under our noses. Plus when it's stolen, we lose those sales twice over."

"How do you figure that?" I picked up Izzy and gave him a cuddle. This was why having dogs in the backroom was such a great idea. They offered their own brand of doggy Prozac without the hassle of a prescription.

"Unless I'm mistaken, this person is probably selling what she steals. She might even be taking orders online. That's why she took multiples of the same item. So, we're losing our investment in the product, our opportunity to sell and make a profit from that product, and we've lost the element of timing with the holiday season." Bama held up three fingers as she ticked off her reasons.

Mert shook her head. "You're losing out another way, too. See, the consumer who buys the stolen merchandise online ain't buying it from you. She might even quit coming here and walking out with something extra 'cause she saw it in the store. So you've lost that revenue, too."

Someone I trusted and liked was stealing from us. It couldn't get much worse, could it?

Of course it could.

## TWENTY-THREE

I turned the front door sign to OPEN and readied the cash register.

Mert brought in the dog food, an instruction sheet, leashes, beds, and bowls. She dialed Laurel and passed her cell phone to Bama so the two could work out a time for an informal interview. I started waiting on customers. By the time I had the chance to come up for air, Mert had already left. I hadn't gotten to say goodbye. I plunged right into restocking our hanging displays, moving back and forth among the racks quickly. Over the soothing sounds of "Snowfall" from *The Christmas Album* by The Manhattan Transfer, the store phone started ringing. Almost instantly, Bama and my cell phones rang in unison.

"What the . . . ?" Bama and I could only stare at each other.

My phone displayed a text message from Sheila. "News about your leg," it said.

"Huh?" I wondered more to myself than to anyone but Izzy. I was carrying him tucked inside my zip-front hoodie. I don't know who was enjoying this cartage more, Iz or me.

"There's a news bulletin on the TV," said Bama as she closed her cell and sprinted toward the office.

A reporter stood in front of a late model Lexus convertible. Yellow crime scene tape encircled the car, and a phalanx of folks wearing Crime Scene jumpers were swarming the vehicle. The newscaster said, "Police tell us that this was most certainly the scene of a crime, and probably a fatal one at that."

"How can they tell?" asked the unseen anchor. A news ticker bar ran across the bottom of the screen announcing, "Blood-soaked vehicle found at Lambert Airport in long-term parking."

"Given the amount of blood in the car, no one could have lived through the assault," said the reporter.

"The police are sure it belongs to the missing woman?" the anchor prodded as the screen flashed the car's interior. The leather seats had been blackened with what was obviously blood.

"Yes. This 2009 Lexus is registered to

Cindy Gambrowski of #20 Ladue Forest Drive."

I'm not sure what Bama was thinking, but I fought the urge to upchuck. I'm real squeamish about blood. I'd love to donate mine to the Red Cross, but I've heard fainters need not apply.

"The missing woman's husband is Ross Gambrowski, the builder," the reporter continued.

Bama moaned.

"He says he hasn't seen his wife for four days." A screen shot showed a publicity photo with the name "Ross Gambrowski" underneath. "Mr. Gambrowski told the police that he thought he and his wife had simply missed each other in passing. Seems they both have busy schedules. A spokesman says Mr. Gambrowski had no reason to suspect foul play. But that's not the only reason the police have their suspicions."

The anchor's voice interjected, "There was a body part found at a local scrapbook store, right?"

Bama covered her eyes.

"Right. The store's name is Time in a Bottle. That's over on Brentwood, south of the Galleria. The body part turned up in their trash Dumpster. The police have impounded the bin, and all they'll say is that their investigation is ongoing."

"But you think that body part might belong to our missing woman?" prodded the off-screen anchor.

"That's right. An anonymous tip to our newsroom suggested the severed leg found in the Dumpster behind this scrapbook store" — and a shot of Time in the Bottle appeared — "belonged to Cindy Gambrowski."

Cindy's smiling face filled the screen.

The anchor's face concluded, "If anyone has any knowledge of Mrs. Cindy Gambrowski's whereabouts, they are encouraged to call this phone number."

That was all I could take. I reached over and turned off the set.

Funny how fast the grapevine transfers "knowledge." Our phones rang non-stop, our cell phones jingled, and car doors slammed in the parking lot.

This time the media burst through our front door.

"Out! Out! This is a place of business! It's private property!" I shooed them past the merchandise and toward the door. Using my forearms as shields, I backed reporters and cameramen out of the store. "Bama?" I yelled. I flipped the sign to CLOSED and turned around.

Bama had disappeared.

# TWENTY-FOUR

The reporters started pounding on our front door.

Robbie Holmes pulled up, the bubble light and siren both going full-blast on his official car. He hopped out and waved his arms. "People?"

The media turned as if it were a Hydra, whose many heads just caught sight of a ship full of sailors. "Police Chief Holmes!" they screamed.

"People, this is private property, and you are hindering an investigation." His voice rose over the din. "I will answer two questions if you promise to vamoose."

"Is Cindy Gambrowski officially dead?" yelled a woman in the back.

"Folks, you know how this works. We still need to search for the woman or her remains. At this point, Mrs. Gambrowski is a missing person." His tone conciliatory and his big hands open, Robbie Holmes spoke with the ease of a man who has nothing to hide. His years on the force and his personal demeanor underscored every word with an easy authority. From my spot by the front door, I watched the crowd's collective shoulders relax in response to his words.

"But you might have found a portion of her leg!" shouted a man in the back. "And all that blood was in the car!"

That animal, the crowd, raised hackles again. A slight surge of body weight brought them a skosh closer to Robbie. But his stance didn't change. In fact, he busied both his hands in his pants pockets like a kid on a playground fishing around for a lost stick of gum. Then he rocked back on his heels and smiled. His face appeared totally guileless.

"Now you know as well as I do, we can't say if that was her leg. Or her blood. Not yet at least. As for her disappearance, if after a sufficient length of time Mrs. Gambrowski is officially missing, her husband Mr. Ross Gambrowski can petition the court to have her declared dead," Robbie stood head and shoulders over most of the crowd. His commanding posture quickly dampened their herd instinct. Instead of jostling about, they stood quietly, photographed him and listened.

"But doesn't the amount of blood tell you something? No one could lose that much blood and still live!" This came from another man at the back of the crowd as he waved a big black microphone in the air.

"Ah, come on, people. We haven't run any lab tests on what we found. Folks, we aren't a fancy TV show like CSI. You all know that! We're real professionals working with a limited number of labs and technicians. Besides, you all are jumping the gun, aren't you? For all we know, that's cow blood or pig blood some prankster splashed in that car," he chuckled. His ease of manner was infectious. You could tell he faced down the press on numerous occasions. "Makes for mighty fine speculation, doesn't it? But you don't want to get yourself caught up reporting the wrong thing, do you? You all are having a field day pouncing on wrong conclusions. Heck, you're professionals. You know things are usually more complicated than they seem." Robbie Holmes flashed an "Aw, Shucks!" grin. That and the stunning dollop of common sense shut everyone up. But only for a hot New York minute.

"What about the messages? We heard there were messages from Mrs. Gambrowski suggesting someone named Kiki Lowenstein is involved!" I shivered in my Keds. Terrific.

I was about to be dragged into this kicking and screaming.

Or skulking. I stepped away from my spot behind our locked front door. I decided I'd go hide in the backroom. But when I looked around the store, Bama was already gone. My plan — sketchy and hastily conceived — was to ask her to take my place up in the front of the store. Since her name hadn't been mentioned in that dastardly message, she could easily defer all these pesky questions.

But Bama was MIA.

I found her huddled in a corner back in Dodie's office. Her skin wore the sheen of perspiration and her teeth chattered. "Put your head between your knees," I ordered her. Those years of Girl Scout training came in handy. "Do it, now!"

I grabbed a cola for her and shoved it under her face. "Drink."

My cell phone rang. I recognized Robbie Holmes' number and read his text message: "Let me in the front door."

I left Bama long enough to go unlock the front door and allow Robbie entrance. As I did, I noticed that the media circus was folding its tents and heading home.

"Thanks," said Robbie.

"No problem. Thank you. You did a masterful job of bearding the lion."

"I promised them a press conference later." He chuckled. "That's the media for you. I once went on a fox hunt out in Virginia. You know they don't kill foxes here in the States, don't you? That wily animal always stayed two steps ahead of those hounds, running down gopher holes, hiding in trees, climbing over fences. Hounds can scent the fox, but their eyesight stinks. I saw that old red fox pitter-patter in front of those dogs easy as you please. There's a lesson in that. Don't run from them." He jerked a thumb over his shoulder. "You just heard the baying hounds, Kiki. Problem is: They've caught the scent of a big story. I don't need to tell you, this isn't going away."

From the back of the store came a scream and the sound of barking.

# Twenty-Five

"Get out! Get out! If you don't leave, I'm going to sic these dogs on you! They're trained killers!" Bama yelled.

Fluffy cocked his head at her as if to say, "Who, me?"

As Bama shoved her shoulder against our back door, she hollered, "Out! I've got a gun! I'll blast your heads off! I tell you I will!"

Robbie Holmes pushed me behind a shelf unit. "Is she armed?"

"No way," I whispered, and I trotted up alongside her. "Bama? You okay?"

"He . . . they . . . he . . ." She shivered and shook. "A photographer knocked on the back door. I thought, I thought it might be that Fed Ex delivery we're expecting. They called while you were up front. I opened the door. A flash went off. He took . . . he took . . . my picture!" and she broke down sobbing.

"Slow down. I can barely make out what you're saying. It's okay. Police Chief Holmes is here. Shhhh." I grabbed her and pulled her toward me like I would my own daughter. Her shoulders trembled as her tears soaked my blouse. I didn't know what was most shocking: (1) her reaction (2) her letting me comfort her or (3) her allowing us to see that under that Ice Queen exterior was a very frightened and emotional woman. Sobs shook her body. Bama grabbed my sleeve as if she never planned to let me go.

You never really know another person. Oh, you think you do, but all you see is the cold exterior serving as the ice-cutter, the reinforced nose of the ship designed to bully its way through the frigid water. Beneath the waterline, beyond the bulkheads, another world carries on, loving, living, surviving on a more intimate level. A swirling mass of emotions exists beneath our public exterior, a heaving jumble both unseen and unshared. But once the ship hits the ice floe, the battle for survival demands all hands on deck. With so much at stake, pretence is tossed aside. This shipwreck of a woman was the real Bama. We exchanged glances, fractional, lasting seconds only, but an unspoken truce passed between us.

*So,* I thought, *that tough, cold exterior is just an act.*

"Shhh," I tried again, keeping my eyes locked on hers. "Calm down and talk to me. I need to know what happened." I couldn't imagine why she was so upset. After all, weren't we in the business of taking and saving photos ourselves?

"He took my picture!" she wailed and pointed at the door, gesticulating over the yelps of the dogs. I could imagine what was on the other side. Photographers. Videographers. Reporters. But that wasn't such a big deal. Not really.

"Well, see? You're okay. That's nothing."

"They . . . they're going to print my picture!" she cried out, pulling away from me. So much for comforting my business partner. My words only encouraged her to toss her head back and howl. She clenched her fists and shook them at the big police chief. "You tell them they can't. Tell them it's illegal. Stop them! You have to!"

"I'm not sure I can. You lose a lot of your rights to privacy when you own a business open to the public. And, sad to say, when a crime occurred on your property. Or at least when Kiki found the evidence. Your rights collided with the public's right to know," he touched a gruff paw to her shoulder lightly.

148

"Now, it's not such a big deal, is it? Having your picture taken? Maybe they won't even use it."

"What if they do?" she asked him.

"That's great publicity for us," I answered. "You represent the store well; you're so stylish."

"No! I can't. I don't want my picture in the news!"

"Why don't you get her a cold drink, Kiki?" Robbie suggested. "I'll take a cup of coffee if you have any."

The refrigerator and coffee pot were on the other side of the stockroom. It took me a while to mix Robbie's coffee the way he likes it with creamer and sweetener.

On my way back with the drinks, I paused long enough to check on the dogs. From my spot by their playpen, I could see into the office where Bama sat hunched over with a pinched, pained expression. Robbie squatted next to the desk and spoke in low tones. I caught a few words: "Careful . . . my number . . . check on you." I thought I heard something on the order of "let Kiki know," but to that Bama shook her head violently.

Whatever. I guess we hadn't really connected. That moment of comfort I'd offered her must not have been the start of a beautiful friendship.

Robbie took his coffee with him as he headed back to the station. By the time Bama finished her cola, Her Frosty Majesty was back on the throne.

# Twenty-Six

The rest of the evening moved along slowly. Most of our customers bought supplies that they intended to use while finishing up holiday cards or special gifts. This worried me. We hoped they would buy gifts for themselves. Or send in family members and friends with instructions to make purchases for them. All along the walls, we draped yards of gold-colored silken cord that Dodie had snapped up from a resale shop for pennies. (Normally we couldn't have afforded such luxury. That stuff was more per yard than many fine fabrics!) From these "ropes," we attached festive red and green striped paper cut-outs of stockings. In between these, we tied cinnamon sticks. The air was fragrant with the spicy aroma. Around the "fur-trimmed" top of the socks, customers printed their names. On the various stripes they printed product names on their "wish lists."

Our idea was to make it easy for customers to shop for each other. Their significant others could also come in and see what they wanted.

But so far, we'd only seen a few of the desired products rung up at the checkout counter. This worried me. We put a lot of money into that inventory.

I concentrated on finishing a holiday e-mail blast while Bama sat in the back and balanced the credit card slips. My computer terminal sat to one side of the front counter. Perched on a stool, I could survey the store as I worked. When Bama came up to do a quick count of Cricut cartridges, I asked, "Did we lose any more?"

"Nope." Bama's eye makeup had smeared during her upset, so the woman in my sights looked a tiny bit wonky, like a speckled reflection in an old mirror.

I wasn't in much better shape. My schnozzle was running like a garden hose. I tried to wipe my nose gently, but the skin was sore and tender. Plus, I was losing focus. After so much dripping and mopping, I gave up and took a cold medicine designed to dry me up. My throat ached and my head pounded. I probably needed to take a sick day but that was out of the question. At least maybe I could sleep in one morning. I asked Bama, "What did you work out with Laurel?"

"She's coming in to sign paperwork. Maybe even tonight. She's supposedly been scrapbooking for four years. Knows how to work a cash register. Really, we only need another set of eyes. And hands."

Bama hesitated. "I need to take off early. We have that special Last Minute Gift crop tomorrow night, and I need to finish my holiday shopping."

I knew she was lying. She bragged to me earlier in the month about how organized she was, how all she needed to finish was getting gifts wrapped. I thought about calling her on it, but really, I figured she needed a graceful way to end a bad day. I must have waited too long to respond because she rushed in with, "Hanukkah's only two days away, right?"

I nodded. "Go ahead and leave if you need to. Did you give Clancy a call?"

I could tell Bama was considering refusing my friend's offer. We'd talked before about the problems associated with hiring good customers. Frankly, I didn't think we had a choice. I added, "Clancy's willing to work for free."

"How come? Nobody does anything for free."

"She likes to keep busy." I didn't divulge my friend's family problems. They were none of Bama's business.

Bama chewed her bottom lip. "Clancy would do a good job here in the store. She's smart, professional, and she catches on quickly. Between her and Laurel, I think we could put an end to our shoplifting problems. But I don't think we can let her work for free. That's not right. It's taking advantage of your friendship. I'm surprised you'd suggest it."

"I'm not suggesting it. I just wanted you to know how willing she was. I'm thinking we should offer her store credit. She's new to scrapbooking. That would give her a chance to buy more supplies."

I guess my tone of voice betrayed my irritation. Bama agreed with the store credit idea on the spot. In fact, she seemed downright conciliatory. I decided to push my luck. "Any idea if we're ahead of projections? Will there be a Christmas bonus?"

"I'm still working on the accounting. A few of the manufacturers offered discounts if we paid quickly, so that's my priority."

She watched the store while I took my small, mobile canine herd around the block for peeing, pooping, sniffing at, and general overhauling of the neighborhood landscape.

That airhead Fluffy must have tangled her lead five times in the first five minutes alone. At one point, I could have doubled as Gulliver after being tied down by the Lilliputians, I was wrapped so thoroughly in leashes. With a lot of hopping and tripping and ducking under and over the cords, I managed to get back to the store so Bama could leave. She was on her cell by the time I put my charges in lock-down mode. Okay, call me a bad person, but I eavesdropped. I overheard her say, "I don't know . . . don't panic . . . think of something . . ."

Not very interesting stuff.

The next few hours dragged on and on. My eyes drooped and I actually almost fell off the stool once.

At 6:20 I closed out the register. Laurel hadn't stopped by. I worried a little that she changed her mind about helping us. Maybe after hearing about our garbage fiasco, she decided ix-nay on the impromptu anatomy lesson we might offer. I couldn't blame her.

When I checked the numbers on our cash register reconciliation form, the paltry sales figures concerned me. Where were all our customers? Had they all been scared away?

I started to awfulize, to think of the worst possible scenarios. Maybe the rest of Cindy's body had been found. Maybe she'd left another missive pointing to me. Maybe we were the lead story on the evening news. Ho, ho, ho. That sure would put a kibosh on the old holiday spirit.

Discouraged and exhausted, I loaded up the dogs, popping Izzy into my purse and carrying him to the car over my shoulder. His apple-shaped head bobbed along as I walked.

It wasn't until 6:35 that I pulled out of the store parking lot. It took me a few minutes to wipe all the dog slobber off the inside of the car windows.

I managed to catch the end of the half-hour newscast on the local radio station. The broadcaster repeated the story about Cindy's disappearance, the body part, and the bloody car. Fortunately, the reporter left out our store's name and substituted "a local merchant." Fine by me. I got the dogs settled at the house. It was nearly seven by the time I drove over to Sheila's house to pick up Anya.

I guess it was too much to expect that my mother-in-law might go easy on me because I'd had a tough day.

As usual, Sheila had her own agenda.

# TWENTY-SEVEN

"She's not studying her Hebrew. At this rate, Anya won't be ready for her bat mitzvah. By the way, where's her coat? She told me she was fine in that jacket, but she couldn't possibly be. What about her footwear? She's going to need boots. She can't be wandering around CALA without something besides those silly Birkenstocks all the children wear. The very idea of slapping around in clogs. Without any back to them. And thin socks! How could you let her leave the house like that? You know she's just courting a bad cold." Sheila's eyes narrowed. "Speaking of colds, you have one? Stay away from me. Go wash your hands. Did you take any of that Airborne stuff? It works. I take it all the time. Here, I bought a couple canisters and I don't like the grapefruit flavor." She shoved a tube into my handbag.

Over my shoulder, on my way to her

bathroom, I called out, "Anya's bat mitzvah isn't until next May. That's a year and a half away. She'll buckle down. I'll talk to her."

I locked myself in and slumped onto the closed toilet seat. I leaned my head onto a stack of guest towels. Maybe I could close my eyes for a bit, and Sheila would go away.

*Bam, bam, bam.*

"Kiki? You in there? Anya asked me if you two were going to buy a Christmas tree tonight. You know I don't approve. Not in a Jewish household. That's just not . . . not . . ."

"Kosher?" I asked as I flushed the toilet twice. That forced her to yell over the noise. What she was saying, I couldn't make out. Nor did I care. Instead I slowly mopped my nose and pressed a damp cloth to my eyes.

Giving her grief seemed fair enough. Sheila always seemed to know exactly when to turn the thumbscrews on me. In fact, I bet she installed an internal alarm system in her brain that buzzed loudly when my mood hovered near rock-bottom. Without fail, she'd choose the worse possible times to climb on my back, ride me around the block, and use her words to beat me senseless.

"Christmas trees aren't . . . You shouldn't . . . The very idea . . ."

158

I kept hitting the toilet handle and turning on the tap.

Wow. This was certainly the day for Morse code conversations. I only caught every third word, but I didn't need to hear more. I opened the bath door and Sheila nearly toppled over.

"I can't stay. Got things to do. Thanks for picking up Anya. I'll come get her tomorrow night after seven. You have a date with Robbie this week, don't you?" Oddly enough, her tirade had energized me. If Sheila didn't like an idea, I was all over it. No way was she going to tell me what I could or could not do with my own daughter. Or with my life. Or my holiday plans.

I beamed what I hoped passed for an embarrassed smile. "I think I clogged your toilet," I lied.

I took great satisfaction in watching her turn pale.

Once I stepped out into the foyer, I hollered up the stairs. This sent Sheila right over to the dark side. She hated and feared plumbing problems, and she absolutely loathed with a passion having people yell to each other in her house. Unless, of course, the yell-ee was her.) "Anya? Yo, Anya? We need to go!"

My kid galloped down the stairs. She'd

borrowed a knitted scarf from Sheila and wrapped it tightly around her throat. She also had on one of Sheila's old coats. It nearly fit her. That stunned me. My, how my baby was growing up.

"See you, Nana," said Anya as she scooted past Sheila, who was giving Linnea detailed instructions about unclogging toilets.

Linnea raised her hands in surrender. "I don't do plumbing, Miss Sheila. You know that."

Sheila stamped her foot. "Get me that plunger, right now!"

*Ha, ha, ha. Ho, ho, ho. Merry Christmas,* I snickered.

Anya must have read my mind. "To the Lions Club Christmas tree trailer?"

"How'd you guess?"

But I didn't move quickly enough.

"What about that leg you found?" Sheila stomped over to me, waving the plunger. It was dripping all over her floor. Two paces behind my mother-in-law, I saw Linnea rolling her eyes and shaking her head with dismay.

"Hey, you're going to splash that on your clothes," I told my mother-in-law. "Shouldn't you be wearing rubber gloves? It's more sanitary."

Sheila tossed down the plunger and

160

erupted with a string of curses. Very unlady-like. We both watched it bounce along the hallway.

"Now you've got, um, whatever all over your nice floor," I pointed out helpfully.

I could see Linnea standing behind Sheila, and her shoulders were shaking with mirth. While Sheila jumped back to inspect the wet spot, Linnea and I exchanged winks. I just loved Linnea. She was such a hoot.

Sheila raced around to block my egress. One foot slipped, and I instinctively grabbed her before she hit the ground. She brushed me off and struggled to regain her dignity.

"Kiki, I demand to know about that part of a person you found. What on earth were you doing in the trash? Did you take total leave of your senses?"

"Anya, go get in the car."

"Geez, Mom. You aren't seriously trying to keep this a secret, are you? Everyone is talking about it. Three of my friends phoned to get details."

Sheila blanched. "Your friends? People are talking about this? Anya, go get in the car now!"

"Not my fault," I said when my daughter was out of range of hearing.

"Of course not," said Sheila. "But you did happen to be at the epicenter, didn't you?

My granddaughter is at risk! Robbie told me they suspect murder. That poor Cindy Gambrowski. Murdered and dismembered. You need to be careful, Kiki. I know all about Ross Gambrowski."

"You do? What do you know? Fill me in."

"Everyone in town knows about Ross."

Well, la-di-dah. I hated this. The "Old St. Louis" grapevine regularly sent messages to its members. What was my mother-in-law going on about?

From the driveway, Anya honked the horn on my Beemer.

Sheila leaned out her front door to shake an angry finger at my child. I was fast on her heels. What a sight she made in her gabardine suit, her pearls and a plunger for a scepter. Queen of All She Surveyed.

Sort of.

"Everyone knows what about Ross Gambrowski?" I prompted.

"He put Cindy on a pedestal. One she couldn't get off. Set her apart. Kept her under a long protective arm. At least that's what he called it. Had high expectations. His love for her is —"

The horn honked again. This time more impatiently.

I'd had enough. "I'll catch you later," I

told Sheila.

What the heck did she know about love?

# TWENTY-EIGHT

Anya chattered on about the upcoming holiday sock hop at CALA, Charles and Anne Lindbergh Academy. "What I really want for my big gift is a pair of Uggs. All the girls have them. I could wear them to the party, and to school and when I go out."

I nodded. Go out? I never let the kid out of my sight. Personally, I thought the Ugg boots a wizard combination of ugly-cute. On spindly teenage legs, I had to admit, they were darling. But they were also out of my price range. Hanukkah is eight days long. That means a week and a day of gift-giving. George adored shopping for us. Every evening we lit the candles on the menorah, sang the song about the dreidel, played the game, and ate brisket and latkes. I actually mastered the art of a mean latke. The secret is instant potato flakes. George said mine were even better than Sheila's. (Um, Linnea's, actually. Sheila doesn't cook. She occupies the command post.)

After we celebrated, George would proudly hand both of us a package in a signature robin's egg blue box. Every Hanukkah, he gave me a gift from Tiffany's on the first day. On successive days, he alternated books (hard-cover bestsellers), Godiva chocolates, scarves (He loved shopping for scarves; ironic wasn't it?), and finally, on the last day Anya and I would each receive a totally outrageous big gift.

I always bought George the same gift for Day Eight: nail clippers. This was a standing joke between us. He lost nail clippers like some people pop off buttons. So every year, I bought him a new pair, and he'd say, "Kiki, sweetie, you shouldn't have."

Ours was not an ideal marriage, but there are all sorts of love, and we certainly loved each other. He was my best friend. Sort of. I could depend on him. He knew he could depend on me.

That's why I had been so willing to put myself in jeopardy and solve his murder.

But that didn't matter now. I was officially out of the murder inquiry business. I shook my head and yanked myself back into the moment.

We pulled up into the darkened lot a few store fronts down from a big Dierbergs

165

grocery store. There sat a tired white trailer, festooned with old fashioned large bulb Christmas lights. Under an awning, a wood-stoked fire blazed in an old oil barrel. A group of men wearing hunting jackets, thermal overalls, and those hats with ear flaps stood warming their hands over the fire. Their work gloves stayed tucked under their armpits until we approached closely.

"Hey ya, Mrs. Lowenstein! Miss Anya! How you've grown, young lady," said Elmer Peters.

I gave Elmer a big hug. He was a fixture at this particular Lions Club temporary location. George, Anya, and I started buying our trees here when she was only a toddler. I stepped away from Elmer and watched my daughter give the big man a happy embrace. As time went by and George's memory faded, I hoped that times like this would remind Anya of outings with her dad.

"What'll it be this year? A Scotch pine? A Douglas fir? A Colorado blue spruce? Let me show you some beauties."

I squirmed a bit. Live trees aren't cheap. Elmer pulled on work gloves and dutifully walked us up and down the aisles. Rows of fresh cut trees rested against wooden A-frames. Anya was drawn, of course, to the

166

biggest and most expensive trees. I had to remind her we were on a budget. My nose ran profusely as the night grew colder. Under the artificial lighting, the trees took on a magical quality, but with each trudge of my feet, a deeper sadness weighed on me. Why wasn't I earning enough to satisfy my child's needs? I knew that millions of parents the world over shared the sentiment.

Anya fixated on one particular tree, returning to it after exploring other options. I knew the money went to charity, but I still was having trouble justifying the expense. How could I let my daughter down? She didn't ask much, but this was more than a stupid tree. It was a memory. It was our tradition. It was something her father would have done for her.

My vision clouded with tears that I managed to mop up before they spilled. While I held the tissue to my face, a voice boomed, "Elmer? Load that tree up for them. Add it to my bill."

I turned to face a tall man in a black cashmere coat, his face framed by an expensive Burberry scarf. "Ross Gambrowski. You're Kiki Lowenstein, right?" and he squeezed my hand in a painful grasp. "I hope you don't mind. I followed you here."

"Anya? How about you go with Elmer to

167

make sure the tree's tied down." I had no intentions of letting a stranger pay for our purchase, but I didn't want my daughter to overhear this conversation.

"What can I do for you?"

"Cindy was my whole world."

I stared at his red-rimmed eyes. The man's nose had been broken and never set properly, and he towered over me. His shoulders proclaimed him a linebacker, and I could easily imagine him with black greasepaint on his cheekbones. Even in the near dark, his skin glowed with a healthy tan. I seemed to recall Cindy talking about the tanning bed they had in their home.

"I don't know what I can do."

"You found her leg."

"Are they sure? I mean, it could have been —"

"It was hers. I recognized a scar on the inside of her right ankle. She tripped a lot. For a woman so beautiful, Cindy could be very clumsy. She was always falling over her own feet." He raised a beefy hand to his eyes to shield them. His lower lip trembled. "I told her not to go places without letting me know. I worried about her. Didn't like her friends. They were undependable. But Cindy could be very willful. She didn't always listen to me like she should. The minute I saw that leg, I knew it was hers."

We stood in silence. He added, "I just have to trust God that she's all right."

"You don't know where she went? Where did she say she was going?"

"I thought she was at the house. Or at Bible studies. I even got a text message from her. I figured she went to church services. That's where she was supposed to be on Sunday. She knew better than to take off without telling me. I just got home late Friday night because of a business meeting. I figured she was in the other room. Sometimes she liked to take a sleeping pill and get a good night's rest. I thought we'd just missed each other. Have you seen our house?"

I shook my head. I caught a whiff of his breath. Alcohol.

"I built that palace just for her. Over by the Ladue Country Club. Fifteen thousand square feet. More with the finished basement. No other builder in this town could top it. Heated floors. Indoor pool. Sauna. Jacuzzi tub. You name it. Even built a craft room for her so she wouldn't have to run to those what-you-ma-call-its? Crops. I wanted Cindy home with me." He grabbed my shoulders. "The cops think I did something to her. My Cindy. After all I've done to protect her, to keep her safe. You don't know where she is, do you? Please?"

His grip tightened on my jacket and he squeezed enough for me to murmur, "Ouch."

## TWENTY-NINE

Then his nostrils flared and he let me loose. "What's that smell?"

*Saved by the cat pee,* I thought as I took a step away. "Um, I don't know Cindy well enough to help you."

"But she told me all about that class she took at your store. I gave her permission to go. I saw her writing about all the happy parts of our life. How you encouraged her to get down her happy memories. She even showed me that contest entry."

I nodded. We'd put one of her pages on display so our customers could vote on a favorite in the All about Me Contest. In fact, that reminded me I needed to clear space on our crop tables. Which meant, I'd have to clear the tables and reset them for the evening event. By myself. I sure hoped Bama would get on the stick and hire Laurel or Clancy to help.

But that sidecar quickly derailed. Ross

Gambrowski grabbed my hand out of my pocket. One of my good gloves had gone missing, so all I was wearing was a thin pair of mittens. "Tell me where she is. I only want to help her. She can't be dead. I'd know it. I'd feel it here," and he tapped his heart. "We're connected. Soul mates. Have been since the day we met. I told her we'd never be apart, and I meant it. I have to find her!"

I glanced away. Anya stood beside our car, blowing on her fingers.

"I'm sorry but I can't get involved."

"How can you say that? Don't you see what it's doing to me? How am I going to manage? Can't you see how hard this is on me?"

I'd been in his situation. I knew exactly how hard it was. I gulped and tried to push my own sad memories out of my mind. I couldn't afford to drag myself, my child, or my store into a potentially dangerous spot. Still, there was something I could do. Something small and safe. "I'll ask the other scrapbookers if they've seen her."

"Tell me you'll look for her. That you'll call me." He pressed a business card into my fingers. "Anytime, day or night."

I fished one of my cards from my pocket and handed it over.

"You lost your husband didn't you?"

I nodded.

"George Lowenstein, right? We played golf together. So you get it. You know what I mean. I can't live without her. At the holidays? What will I do?" He dragged the back of his hand over a set of fleshy lips. Ross Gambrowski would never be called a handsome man, but from him came a raw masculinity which I'll admit was very attractive. He was a guy's guy.

"How do you get by? How do you manage without the person you love? Tell me! Because I don't think I can. But you've done it and raised a daughter. I can't imagine what I'll say to our Michelle. How I'll tell her what happened to her mother. You have to help me. You know how this feels!"

I certainly did. On this night of nights more than ever. But not because of George's death. All his ranting and raving brought back the night my sister Catherine disappeared. That was a time I worked hard to forget. I'd locked my memories away and promised myself I'd never revisit them. But Ross Gambrowski's pleading caused a sick twisting in my stomach. I blinked hard to hold back my own tears.

"How can I raise my child without my

wife?" asked Ross.

I nodded. I wondered the same thing almost every day since George died. Until his death, I never, ever spent the holidays alone. Now, what was I doing? Worrying about gifts? Scraping around for proper coats? Unable to buy my child what she needed? And who would buy gifts for me? This was all too much. I couldn't stand here and think about it. I had to get away from this man, or I'd lose it.

"Mom?" Anya called out to me. "I'm going to get in the car and start it. I'm cold."

My baby. My poor, poor baby. I cleared my throat and started to inch away from Ross. "Sorry, but I need to go."

"But you'll help me, won't you?"

"Um, what do the police say?"

He roared like a lion. Ironic, really, considering where we were. "They're trying to blame me. Me! The person who loved her most in the world. The guy who worshipped her. Those jerks. While Cindy's out there, lost, needing me — or worse yet, hurt — they're messing around, wasting time, asking me all sorts of stupid questions."

I sighed. In the hours immediately following George's death, suspicion briefly centered on me. Ross Gambrowski was right. The police would blame him. After all, he was the surviving spouse, and therefore, the logical suspect.

"It's the not knowing that's killing me," Ross added. His voice dropped to a whisper. "What if she needs me?"

"Got to go," I said. I couldn't let him see how upset I was. I understood exactly what he meant. I wondered the same thing all the time. Not about Cindy Gambrowski, of course.

I wondered about my sister Catherine.

# THIRTY

*Wednesday, December 16*

The next morning I woke up early, mixed a cup of instant coffee, and sat in the winter morning dark to admire our tree. Anya had loved trimming it, and I did, too. I took a slow tour of the evergreen, delighting in the fragrance, the lights, and the years-old ornaments so full of memories. Despite the fact he'd scared me, I wrote Ross Gambrowski a thank you note for buying the tree. I guess my mother's years of drilling in good manners outweighed my personal discomfort. I set the finished note aside with a heavy heart. Now I owed him the return favor of asking around about his wife.

Last night before bed, I examined Gracie's tail carefully. She mouthed me, her eyes suggesting that she wasn't happy to have it disturbed. I could quickly see why. The skin puffed up around the stitches. I rewrapped it and said a prayer. This morning, it was even worse. I decided to try talk therapy. "Gracie, darlin', show a little restraint when you're wagging that thing. Please?"

Monroe nickered softly as I entered his shed. He rested his forehead against me, hoping for a long scratch behind his ears. I was filling a bucket with fresh food for him when the weight in my hands suddenly lifted.

Detective Chad Detweiler was holding the bucket. "Let me do it."

My emotions were on red alert from worrying about Gracie, thinking about Cindy, and trimming our tree. I didn't have the energy to argue with him. "Okay."

"That leg belonged to —"

"Cindy Gambrowski. Her husband told me. But he still doesn't think she's dead."

Detweiler straightened. Those beautiful Heineken beer-bottle green eyes darkened. He lifted the bucket as easily as I might a glass of water. He expertly dumped the pail into Monroe's feeder. The donkey twitched his ears happily and began munching on his food.

"Stay away from Gambrowski, Kiki."

"Don't tell me what to do."

"You have no idea —"

"You're not the boss of me."

He set the pail down. "Please," he reached for me.

I was too spent to fight him. I rested my face against his jacket, then pushed off. "Don't . . . we can't . . ."

He pulled me tight as he whispered. "I can't let anything happen to you. And I can't protect you."

"From what?" Before he could answer, I added, "From you? You need to leave."

Holding me at arms' length, his troubled green eyes searched mine. "You can't possibly imagine how much blood there is in the human body. Eight to ten pints. Every ounce of that woman's blood was spattered all over her car. Someone out there wants you involved. The messages were designed to draw you into this mess. I'm begging you —"

"She better help me!" Ross Gambrowski bellowed at us. "She better!"

Detweiler and I turned to see him standing a few feet away. For a big man, he moved quietly, opening the gate and slipping into the small paddock. Neither of us had heard his approach. Monroe brayed at the man and moved nervously.

"It's okay, Monny. It's okay," I stroked his neck.

"I think you know what happened to

178

Cindy. Where she went and why," said Ross, pointing at me. "Tell me! Did she go to Cozumel? She loved it there. She wouldn't have left without her photos. Did you help her make duplicates? Help her get ready to leave? Is that where she is?"

"But her leg," I shook my head. "How could that have happened?"

Detweiler moved in front of me. "Mr. Gambrowski, no one could have lived through that mess in her car."

"But she did live through it! I got a phone call last night! Someone saw her!" Gambrowski kept advancing on us. Now he and the detective were almost eyeball to eyeball. Detweiler shoved me behind him. His hand moved to his service revolver.

This was not going well.

"Mr. Gambrowski, I told you I'd ask around," I said. "But you have to quit yelling. You're upsetting the donkey."

Ross Gambrowski suggested the donkey have sex with himself.

"If someone called you last night, then you need to come with me down to the station and tell us about it," said Detweiler in an entirely reasonable voice.

"I'm talking to you here!" Ross Gambrowski pulled a white cotton handkerchief from his back pocket and mopped his

179

forehead. Even though the day had dawned cold, he had worked up a sweat in his cashmere coat and Burberry scarf.

"Your call. You come in, maybe we can trace that phone message. Right now, you've done a heck of a job stopping us from using our resources."

"Your resources? What a penny-ante, pitiful excuse for real cops you are! My wife's gone and you can't find her!"

His hollering brought another round of braying from Monroe. His eyes were wide with fear. He started pacing, moving back and forth in his enclosure in a violent way.

"Shhhh, Monny, it's okay, it's okay." I walked over and took the donkey by the bridle, rubbing his ears and soothing him.

"I've had about enough of you. You're on private property and you're an unwanted guest." Detweiler grabbed Ross Gambrowski by the arm. "Whoever made that call is playing games with you. Let's drive on over to the station. We'll track the caller down. You don't need to bother Mrs. Lowenstein." With that, Detweiler began to lead Ross Gambrowski out of the pen.

With an abrupt jerk, Ross Gambrowski wrenched free of Detweiler and ran back toward me. "Come on lady, tell me where my wife is!" He lunged at me, but I stepped aside to dodge him. His right fist, the one with his handkerchief in it, slammed Monroe in the jowl.

"Eee-aw," the donkey brayed as he jumped back.

"How dare you! Get out. Get out now!" I yelled at Gambrowski. "Monroe, buddy, are you okay?" Monroe rolled bovine eyes at me, but he seemed to be unscathed.

"That's it. One more word, and you're under arrest," said Detweiler, grabbing Gambrowski's coat and hauling him toward his car.

"I'm calling my lawyer," Gambrowski said.

"And he'll tell you that this is private property, and you are trespassing," said Detweiler. "I'll walk you to your car."

They moved past me, but Detweiler's voice floated back to where I stood. "Just a piece of friendly advice: I better never catch you anywhere near Mrs. Lowenstein again. You got me? This is one line you really don't want to cross."

# THIRTY-ONE

I was all kerfuffled when I dragged the dogs through the back door at the store. Part of me puffed up with joy because Detweiler had arrived in stereotypical knight-in-shining-armor fashion, but a generous portion of my mind and heart ached for Cindy Gambrowski. What had befallen her? Was it really her leg and her blood? Was she hurt and alone somewhere? Who had called her husband?

I reached for my cell and started to dial Detweiler. I wanted to hear what he was thinking about Ross Gambrowski's assertion that someone had seen Cindy alive.

Then a tiny voice reminded me that I'd sworn to steer clear of Brenda Detweiler's husband. But this wasn't my fault was it? I hadn't dumped a body part in our trash. I hadn't splashed blood all over an abandoned car.

My fingers hesitated over my phone number pad. Finally, I snapped my cell phone shut.

I didn't need to go chasing Brenda Detweiler's husband just because he had a job to do.

Eager for a distraction, I poked my head in to say, "Hi" to Bama, but she was on the phone turned away me. All I could see was the back of the big, black desk chair. The urgency in her voice warned me not to interrupt her conversation.

"I'm asking you to keep a special eye on my kids. All three of them. My photo was in the paper," I heard her say.

That was odd, because R J, Virginia, and Harley were her sister Katie's kids, not hers. Still, family was family, so it didn't really matter. I parked Jasper and Fluffy in the playpen and headed back out to get Gracie and Petunia. Izzy rode shotgun in my backpack. After everyone was situated, I walked to the front of the store, flipped over the OPEN sign, and noticed a copy of the St. Louis Post-Dispatch on the counter. Bama was right. On the front page was a color photo of her waving away the media. The cutline read: "Gruesome finding in store Dumpster leads police to suspect woman's dismemberment."

Fortunately, the name of our store wasn't

mentioned in the story.

Unfortunately, you could read our store name from the photo. Dodie had it painted on the side of the wall in big block letters two feet high.

Well, we hadn't budgeted for advertising, and what was that old saw? Any publicity was good publicity? I hoped so.

Footsteps told me Bama was approaching. I looked up and nearly fell over in shock.

Yesterday she wore her hair in a chin-length black bob. Today, it was carrot-red, cut short and spiky. A pair of small glasses rested on her nose, and whereas before her eye makeup had been subdued, today she laid it on with a trowel.

"What are you staring at?" she snapped at me.

"New look?"

"None of your business!"

The front door minder saved us from more scintillating conversation. In strolled a tall, thin blonde with an unnaturally large chest. A mental image flashed in my brain of her toppling over face first and not being able to get back up. The newcomer's dark navy jeans fit like they were spray-painted on. A hint of black turtleneck showed at her collar under a quilted, hip-length black jacket. "Hi, I'm Laurel Wilkins," she said in a voice full of sunshine and lollipops. She offered a slim cool hand to first me and then Bama. "Mert Chambers suggested I drop by. I tried to stop in yesterday, but there were a lot of media trucks blocking your driveway."

I groaned. Of course. I thought our sales were slow, but I hadn't realized people simply couldn't get to us.

"You didn't fill the spot, did you? I'd really like to pick up some Christmas hours." Her pretty blue eyes widened. "I'm a quick learner. I like all sorts of crafts. I know how to use a cash register, and I'm good with customers. Especially with the grumpy ones. You could say that's my specialty — um, hard-to-please customers."

I just bet she was good with the grouches. A big dimple at the side of her mouth made you want to smile along with her. Even if she was simply too pretty to be real, she was instantly likeable. Well-prepared, too. She pulled two big envelopes from her handbag and handed them over. "My resume is inside. References and phone numbers."

"When can you start? Mert's say-so is good enough for me," I said.

"Right now?" asked Laurel. "If that's okay

185

with you?" and she turned to Bama.

"Fine." Bama clomped off toward the backroom.

I showed Laurel where to put her things and got her started counting merchandise. Meanwhile, I took down and set up pages for the All about Me Contest. After each was propped up in a special holder, I added a tiny sticky dot with an entry number. Laurel suggested that she type up a voting list. That took her no time at all. The girl was fast, smart, and efficient.

In between, both of us waited on customers. Laurel proved a quick study. If she didn't know, she'd ask me, but she managed to do so in a way that made customers feel fine with standing around. She also knew how to up-sell. Twice I heard her reminding people that mysteries featuring a scrapbooker were a great holiday gift. She was even familiar with the series! "You can read them gently and send them off to a friend. Easy to mail, too. Don't you love giving a gift that isn't hard to wrap?"

Merchandise fairly flew out of the store. At quarter of one, Laurel offered to run out and buy us all something to eat. Bama grumped, "I brought my own."

My morning planning had been thrown a curve ball by the encounter with Ross Gambrowski, so I sent her out with an order.

Laurel reappeared in no time, waving a fragrant teriyaki chicken sub at me, and handing back more change than I expected. "The guys at Subway gave me a discount." She shrugged. "People are so nice. That happens a lot to me."

"Let me guess," I laughed. "You were waited on by men, right?"

She looked up at the ceiling and fingered her bottom lip. "I guess. I didn't pay much attention."

Oh, boy.

We had a mid-afternoon lull. I took a fifteen-minute break to do a little crocheting. "Hmmm, chain two instead of three along the side," Laurel suggested as she looked over my shoulder. "Then tighten your first inside stitch. Your edges will be smoother."

She was right.

"I'll never get this done in time. Hanukkah is tomorrow night."

"But you have eight days, right?" Laurel kept straightening shelves. Really, what a find she was! She managed to work and carry on a conversation at the same time.

"Yes, but I also planned to make a shawl for Dodie Goldfader." I pushed the pattern across the table.

"The other owner, right?" Laurel picked up the photocopied sheet and studied it.

I nodded.

"If you have the yarn here, I can start the chain for you."

I wasn't about to turn her down, because the chain is the hardest part.

While she took her break and started my project, I finished the prep for our "Last Minute Holiday Gifts" class. Our customers had signed up for three different projects over the course of the past six weeks. Tonight they would finish their "Holiday Recipe Collection" project by bringing in twenty copies of one of their own family favorites. Dodie, Bama, Mert, Sheila and I also contributed a copy of one of our family hits. Since we had fifteen people in the class (plus the five of us), each participant would take home a set of twenty different recipes. The pages were assembled inside decorative covers and bound with three metal rings. Since we used empty cereal boxes for the album covers, the project cost us next to nothing but looked absolutely fabulous. Best of all, the class registrations brought in a tidy sum.

Unlike most of our evening crops, this one started promptly at five and ended up at seven. That meant we needed to hustle. Our patrons knew they were expected to finish the project at home, so the trick was getting them started and then packed up and out the door without making them feel rushed. Which was exactly what I felt, rushed.

Assembling all the supplies, counting the paper, checking my list twice got me into a lather. People don't realize how heavy scrapbooking tools are. Die cut machines particularly. And paper? Shoot, it weighs a lot, plus the edges of it are sharp. I wound up with a nasty paper cut that forced me to grab the tube of Super Glue and ask Laurel's help.

"You really glue your skin back together?" Her blue eyes widened big as dollar pancakes.

"Yep. Otherwise, the cut splits open again. I'll cover it with a bandage so I don't ruin the paper, but this happens a lot. Especially in cold weather."

"Your hands are so chapped!"

"I'm missing a glove. I don't like to wear my knit mittens because they keep snagging on my hangnails." I was also still wearing my eau d'kitty jacket. And my nose? Let's not go there. Suffice it to say, I was a mess. Standing there in front of Miss Victoria's Secret catalog model, all my inadequacies loomed bigger than Santa's big belly. With all the treats pouring into the store, Santa and I would soon be wearing the same pant size.

But that was stinking thinking, and I didn't have the time or energy to waste.

Laurel finished wrapping my index finger with a Band-Aid about the time the door flew open, and in walked Mr. G. Q., my sometimes boyfriend and almost fiancé, Ben Novak. The sight of Laurel's loveliness stopped him in his tracks. The man was only human. But Ben was a sharp cookie, so he recovered admirably and managed a weak, "Kiki? Thought I'd check about our date."

"Oh, gosh. I totally forgot." My cheeks grew hot. I forgot because I didn't much care. For that I should be ashamed, and I knew it.

Laurel started to back away. I caught her arm. "Ben Novak, this is Laurel Wilkins. Our newest staff member."

Laurel flashed that dimpled, darling grin. The two sized each other up. I secretly wished they'd lock eyes and vow to run away together — that'd save me lots of trouble — instead, they shook hands with perfect civility.

After she went to find the hole punches for our class, Ben segued back to our plans. "That's fine because we're busy at the paper."

His parents owned *The Muddy Waters Review*. Ben was an only child. His parents, Leah and Alvin, made no secret of the fact they hoped we would marry. Sheila had one foot on my back pushing me toward the same conclusion.

Ben was a wonderful man. In fact, everything I told Sheila about Robbie Holmes was equally true of Ben.

The problem was me.

# THIRTY-TWO

I wasn't in love with him. I did, however, find him lovable. If that sounds confusing, well, it was.

"Could I send a reporter to talk to you about that body part you found?"

That request surprised me. Ben rarely asked anything of me. I nodded quickly. Maybe he would forget about our date. "Sure. Best to have him or her call me. It's our busy time of year."

"Got you. Let's reschedule seeing the *presepios* on The Hill. I thought maybe Anya would want to come along. Sheila says your daughter loves Italian food."

My eyes narrowed. Sheila knew that Anya adored Detweiler. If my daughter also adored Ben, that would move our relationship along. It wasn't that Anya didn't like Ben. She did. But Detweiler had won over her heart as easily as he had mine.

"How about next Tuesday at five. We

could have dinner, the three of us."

I had to give him that. Ben was incredibly considerate. How could I turn him down? I hadn't suggested we get together for one of the nights of Hanukkah, I kept that to myself because I didn't want to encourage the man.

Which was stupid of me.

Ben Novak, all six-foot-two-inches of him, would make a fabulous catch. After recently returning from a publishing conference in Cabo San Lucas, his dark blond hair gleamed with natural gold highlights, and those smoky topaz eyes caused my heart to flutter. Truth to tell, I wasn't letting myself fall for Ben. Call me perverse, because I certainly am.

Ben was everything I needed in a man.

Then he proved it. "I heard Anya is struggling with her Hebrew. After the holidays, I could work with her. If that's all right with you."

My heart tumbled and a lump formed in my throat. Usually Ben steered clear of Anya. He was solicitous, but he kept his distance. As an only child himself, maybe he didn't seem to know what to make of her, didn't know how to engage her in conversation. Whereas Detweiler always exuded ease around Anya — and Gracie —

Ben proceeded like a man picking his way through a minefield. Sheila once told me Ben worried about making the wrong moves. "He's such a good-looking man, and you have a young daughter. Remember, *The Muddy Waters Review* broke the story about that St. Louis attorney who allegedly molested his pre-teen stepdaughter. Ben had a front row seat for that circus. Later, the girl admitted she was angry because her new daddy wouldn't buy her a Mini-Cooper. Ben's no dummy. He's a cautious man. An upright man. He's smart to take it slowly."

I gave a lot of thought to what Sheila said. Mert and I discussed the situation at length. "Any woman with a young daughter oughta think twice about who she brings into her home," Mert said. "I seen it time after time." She was, of course, referring to her own stint in foster care. While Mert never talked directly about her past, I knew it must have been a nightmare.

Bama appeared at my shoulder. She fisted her hands on her hips as she faced me down. "You going to stand here all day or you planning to get ready for that crop? Get busy!"

"She is busy," said Ben. To my surprise, he pulled me into his arms and kissed me soundly in front of my co-worker. Chills ran up and down my spine and my body melted into his. I caught a good whiff of his expensive cologne and thought I'd dissolved into a puddle on the spot. I have to admit, my whole body tingled. Even my sore little nose. Maybe I underestimated this man.

I kissed him back, too. My lips were nearly numb before we were through. At some point in the clinch, he lifted me off my feet.

As he set me down gently, he said over his shoulder, "You must be Bama. Are you always this rude?"

# KIKI LOWENSTEIN'S HOLIDAY RECIPE COLLECTION PROJECT

*Tackle this super idea with a group of friends. You'll all enjoy the results. Why not make a few extra to give as gifts?*

1. You'll need one empty cereal box per album. (Yes, cereal boxes make great crafting supplies!) Cut the box apart. Trim the front and back of the box to a desired album size such as 7 by 7 inches. Using sandpaper, buff off the shiny outside of the box. (Tip: This is pretty dusty work, so wear an apron and use a microfiber dust cloth to get up all the fine dust.) If you don't buff off the shiny surface, it's hard to get the cover paper to adhere.

2. Cut paper with a high cotton content to one inch larger all around than the box pieces. (For example, if your final album will be 7 by 7 inches, cut the high cotton content paper to 9 by 9 inches.) Center the cereal box pieces on the high cotton content paper, wrap and glue the edges down around the cereal box pieces. (Tip: I use wooden clothes pins to hold the edges

down.) Once dry, line these covers with contrasting pieces of paper one inch smaller all around. (So, as per our example, the contrasting liners pieces would be 6 by 6 inches.) (Tip: I like to use a corner rounder on the inside liners. It looks very nice.)

3. Let the covers and liners dry thoroughly. Once dry, carefully measure and punch three equi-distant holes along one side of the covers. For a 7 by 7 inch cover, the holes might be 1/2 inch in from the outside edge, and then punched at these intervals: 1 1/2 inches, 3 1/2 inches, and 5 1/2 inches.

4. Cut double-sided scrapbook cardstock to the same size as above (7 by 7 inches) for inside pages. Punch holes using the cover as a template.

5. Print out your favorite recipes and add them to the interior pages. Add photos of the prepared foods as desired. Be sure to include the history or some interesting facts about the recipes, such as who usually cooks them and when you eat them.

6. Decorate the interior pages.

7. Use one of the interior pages as a

table of contents.

8. Bind the recipes inside their cover with round metal ring binders available from office stores. Tie a ribbon around the whole album before you give it as a gift!

# THIRTY-THREE

I staggered out of Ben's embrace. I mean, he has always been such a gentleman, and that's good and bad. In our heart of hearts, every woman longs to be swept off her feet. We want to think we're irresistible. So his politeness hadn't served him well. See, when I met Detweiler there were all these emotions rampant: loss, fear, danger, and of course, attraction. Admittedly, Chad Detweiler intrigued me from the start. But Ben seemed too perfect. Too cool. Too calm. Too collected.

But not any more. Whew. He'd blown that image to smithereens.

My head was still spinning as he set me back on my feet. I grabbed at the lapels of his cashmere jacket.

"Oh." (That's all I could muster. But believe me, my senses were working overtime.)

Bama grumbled at us under her breath,

but for once she was put in her place. And I learned something else through this encounter. I learned that bullies can't stand to be challenged. They fold like cheap tents.

I walked Ben to the door. In many ways, this felt like a first date, the kind of first date when you hope he'll call you . . . soon. After he left, I had a hard time concentrating on my prep work.

Around 4:30 the croppers filed in, one by one — a merry bunch loaded with loaves of homemade nut bread, plates of cookies, jars of candied nuts, scented candles, bags of gifts, and their own supplies. Laurel proved a charming hostess, taking coats, helping folks get settled.

This particular class attracted our regulars: Bonnie Gossage, Clancy Whitehead, Ella Latreau Walden, Maggie Earhardt, Jennifer Moore, Dana Churovich, Nancy Weaver, Olivia Kormeier, as well as several women who were new to our shop, including our newest shopper Daisy Touchette.

Bonnie must have been over her tummy bug, because her blouse buttoned awkwardly as though she'd gained weight. Dark circles ringed her eyes. She brought along a selection of water crackers, Ritz crackers, and a store-bought cheese ball tightly wrapped in plastic. The latter surprised me because Bonnie makes this fabulous dip with shrimp in it, and everyone always raves over her treats. Usually she brings her dip as a kindness to all of us fans.

"Your lights are out," noted Clancy.

I cranked my head to stare at the strand along the window frame. She was right. Dang it. And I still hadn't gotten around to putting up outside strands at home. I was definitely a dim bulb in this season of lights. Maybe instead of hanging around so many cops, I needed to find an electrician and settle down.

Bama shoved a paper into Clancy's hand. "Heard you want to work. Can you cover these hours? If so, you can start tomorrow."

As we watched her stalk off, Clancy said, "My, that was pleasant. Did someone do an unsuccessful makeover on her? Was she the victim of a personal stylist with a Carrot Top fetish?"

I rolled my eyes. "Beats me."

"Explain to me how she gets to go teach scrapbooking on a cruise ship while you sit home twiddling your thumbs."

"Oddly enough, there was a call for teachers on the Internet, and Bama sent in a response to their RFP, Request for Proposal. I didn't see it, or I would have submitted an idea, too. Imagine hot sand and gorgeous beaches when we're suffering through our annual ice storm. She pinned up their itinerary in the office. I guess they're traveling along the Yucatan Peninsula."

"I heard about the idea she proposed. Sounds like a rip-off of that journaling class you do." Clancy shook her head. "That should have been you."

I kept my mouth shut, but I couldn't agree more. What could I do? Bama had filled out a lengthy proposal form. I hadn't. Yes, we'd worked together on the journaling class, and yes, it would have been nice for her to at least give me some credit, but she hadn't. There was nothing for me to do but be gracious and move on.

Jennifer Moore came over and asked me about my holiday plans. She wondered if I planned to buy Anya a pair of Uggs. "That's all Nicci talks about. That and bugging me to go to the mall. I think our daughters are learning the joy of shopping early."

I tried to laugh light-heartedly, but instead I worried about how I'd pay for those silly Austra boots. I knew Anya and Nicci talked Jennifer into dropping them off at Galleria now and then. I also knew Sheila and Anya made frequent stops there, although Sheila was strictly a Frontenac shopper, because that was where all the "old money" in St.

Louis made their purchases. There and downtown Ladue.

Mert strolled in. "Heard there's a shindig here tonight. I can sure use myself a little girlfriend time. Just don't ask me about what happened with my court case, okey-dokey?"

Right about then, someone unwrapped the cheese ball. The pungent smell filled the air. Bonnie turned green as a sprig of holly and raced to the backroom. When she returned, Mert eyeballed her. "When're you due?"

"In June," said Bonnie.

A general hurrah went up from the crowd. Bama paused while ringing up purchases to sigh. "I remember that first trimest—"

With that she shut up and concentrated on the cash register.

I stood there with my mouth open. Here I thought she'd never had children!

After the slip about her own pregnancy, Bama stayed in the backroom. She finally showed her face ten minutes before the crop ended. "I need you to finish up," she said. "Don't goof anything up. You miscounted the change last night."

The croppers looked at her in shock.

"Bama, may I speak to you in private?" I

asked with a pleasant smile plastered on my face.

Once we stepped into the backroom, I let go. "Your behavior is totally out of line. I'm sick of it. Don't you ever, ever treat me like that. Did you see the expression on our customers' faces? They were shocked and horrified. You made a fool of yourself."

She staggered backward.

"Message heard?" I persisted. "You are more than free to go. In fact, you don't even need to come back if you're going to be a horse's rear end."

"It's your fault. You got everything stirred up. Got the media to come here. Just when things were going right for me, you ruined it!"

"Oh, yeah. My fault. I purposely decided to find Cindy Gambrowski's leg in our trash. I planned to go Dumpster diving. Which reminds me, you neglected to cut me another check. Please do it first thing tomorrow. I don't think the police will be returning anything from our trash anytime soon. By the way, have you listened to yourself? You are just downright nasty." I shook my head. "It's pathetic."

Her face changed from defiant to thoughtful. "Maybe I do need a day off. The schedule I handed Clancy gives me tomorrow off.

Between her, you, and Laurel, the floor will be covered."

"We'll handle it." I felt myself softening. "Go do something fun. You need a break. I'm truly sorry about the hassle. It's not my fault, but I still wish it hadn't happened. Ross Gambrowski stopped by my house this morning, and —"

"What did he say?"

"He was pretty upset. He thinks Cindy's still alive. For some odd reason. Says he got a phone call from someone who saw her."

"Seriously?"

I nodded. "I hope she is all right. Maybe the police have it wrong. Maybe she's okay. Look, I'm just trying to compartmentalize. You need to, too. Whatever we think about each other, we have to get through this holiday season. I feel bad about Cindy, but what can I do? Except pray. And I do plenty of that."

"Did you know her well?" Bama shivered again, and so did I.

"That's the weirdest part. I swear, I barely knew the woman. Why would anyone bother to involve me? I mean, if I knew something, don't you think I'd tell the police?"

"Maybe you want to string this along so you can get attention from that detective friend of yours."

"You can't be serious. I can't believe you said that!"

She shrugged. "I've seen how he looks at you. Better yet, I've seen how you look at him. It'll take more than his wedding ring to keep you two apart. That poor guy who kissed you in the store today hasn't got a chance."

# THIRTY-FOUR

A few minutes later, Bama bid us all good-night and left through the front door.

Most of our croppers finished what they were working on quickly and headed for home. Daisy, the young mother of twins, acted like she was in a special hurry to get home. Laurel cleared away the mess so quickly I didn't need to hang on as long as usual. She climbed into an old Mustang convertible and roared off into the night. Mert and Clancy helped me walk the dogs to my car and load them up.

"Excuse me?" A man stepped out of the shadows.

The mutts went wild.

Mert's hand dipped into her purse. Missouri is a concealed carry state, and I knew exactly what she was fishing for, a small handgun. I stiffened and stepped to the front of our crowd. My goal was to protect the man from Mert. The last straw would be a shooting in our parking lot.

"I hoped to catch up with Bama Vess," he said as he showed us a dozen roses in a big glass vase. "I have instructions to deliver these to her personally. They're a surprise from a secret admirer."

"You missed her." I studied the intruder in the half-light of the streetlamp. He was a big guy, broad shouldered and muscular, wearing a baseball cap with "Floral Delivery" embroidered above the bill.

"Will she be in tomorrow? Could I have her home address?"

I studied the flowers. They would certainly do her a world of good. She needed cheering up. "I'm not at liberty to share that with you. She'll be in late on the next day, Friday. She's working the crop."

He tipped his cap to me politely. "Have a good evening," and he climbed back into a big black van.

"She could use a bouquet," muttered Clancy. "Of poppies. To put that little witch to sleep."

I laughed.

Mert kept her hand in her purse as she watched the van pull out of the lot. "Maybe. Or maybe not. This don't feel right to me."

"That's because you're in a take-no-prisoners type of mood," I joked with her.

"How is the court case coming?"

Mert grumbled. "She's had her say. Done accused me of stealing money, breaking stuff, and what-not. Her hubby's managed to bump into me twice in the halls, accidental-like, but hard enough to send me flying. I get my say tomorrow. We'll see what happens then."

"Are you defending yourself? They say the man who defends himself has a fool for a lawyer." Clancy's eyes twinkled in the half-light.

"That's talking about men. Not women. I ain't no fool, but this woman sure is. By the way, your boyfriend Detweiler really came through for me."

"He's not my boyfriend," I retorted angrily.

"Maybe, maybe not. Any whosis, he got a hold of some pawn shop records that prove I ain't no thief."

Good for him, I thought to myself. And good for Mert. At least the two of them had something to be happy about.

I sure didn't.

I picked up Anya from Sheila's house. Linnea was there, but my mother-in-law wasn't. Once again, all my daughter could talk about was the upcoming dance at school, and what she intended to wear with her new

Uggs. That optimism that everything will come out exactly as you wish is one of the joys of youth. It didn't seem to dawn on Anya that I might not be able to afford the boots.

I guess she was right. She knew me well enough to know that I didn't want to disappoint her. While we watched *Miracle on 34th Street* for the umpteenth zillion time, I put down my crochet hook long enough to put a pencil to paper. With the dogsitting money coming in, I could cover the cost of the boots if we kept our grocery costs to a minimum over the next month. My calculations didn't include any possibility of extra income from the store. As Anya did her homework in her room, I went online to Zappos and ordered her a pair of the classic short boots.

My daughter accompanied me to check on Monroe. She giggled with delight as he ate pieces of apple from her palm.

After adding water to the tree, I unwrapped Gracie's tail and gently cleaned the area. The skin around the stitches seemed even more puffy and angry to me. After Anya put on her jammies, we snuggled on her bed with the dogs. Izzy yawned from his perch on my daughter's shoulder, looking more like an exotic bird than a canine companion. Fluffy and Jasper curled up on the floor, while Petunia spooned against Gracie. Anya had borrowed a Madeleine L'Engle book from her school library, and I had a book Clancy had suggested I read on charting your own destiny. Suddenly my child set down her book and gave me a hug. "I miss Daddy, don't you?"

I nodded. "Especially when I think about Hanukkah starting tomorrow. Gives me a lump in my throat."

"Me, too. Not only do I miss him, but I liked it better when you didn't worry so much about money."

"Who says I worry about money?"

"Mom! I'm not a baby. I can see it in your face. You tense up."

"I'm not going to lie to you. Things are tight, but we'll get by. The store is doing well."

Anya smiled. "You're a survivor, Mom. I'm down with that."

"Huh?"

"I mean I appreciate that you're a survivor. I love you for it. I just wish you didn't always have to work so hard."

Moving Izzy aside, I hugged my daughter close. "I wish I didn't either, honey. How about if we plan something special for the weekend?"

"Our schedule's already pretty busy. Tomorrow's the auction at my old grade school. Friday night's the school dance. Don't forget, you said I could spend the night at Nicci's house."

"Okay, how about Sunday? Do you want to visit Santa's Magic Kingdom? Oh, and Ben wants to take us for dinner on The Hill on Tuesday."

"He wants me to come, too?"

"Yes, and he's planning to feed us both Italian."

"Yum, yum. Doesn't he have any idea how much spaghetti I can eat?"

"I hope not."

The two of us fell asleep on her bed with visions of pasta dancing in our heads.

# THIRTY-FIVE

*Thursday, December 17*
*1st Day of Hanukkah*

My daughter's boots arrived at the store early the next afternoon. I quickly wrapped them and locked them in the trunk of my car. Clancy helped me with my crocheting in between waiting on customers. A steady stream walked in and out with large bags of merchandise. Our page kits quickly disappeared, and I settled in to make more. Double-page spread kits are one of our best startsellers, so we normally stock two albums worth of designs. While I gathered more supplies, I decided to do a quick check on the Cricut cartridges.

"Crud!" I rocked back on my heels. "Another three are missing."

"You checked them against the POS?" Clancy asked.

POS was a Point Of Sale inventory system that could give us a running total of almost any item in the store. I showed her how to pull up the POS. Sure enough, we lost three cartridges and a set of Cricut tools.

I stomped my foot and snarled. "How can someone do that to us? That's like stealing money right out of my purse."

Clancy turned about face, marched into the backroom, and handed me a Diet Dr Pepper. "You need this."

She was right.

I did.

Laurel tottered in on mile-high boots. She wore a fake leopard jacket and a pair of sleek black pants. I bet she came directly from auditioning for America's Top Model. Whatever. I could still be thrilled to see her, and she was such a sweetheart I couldn't hate her for being gorgeous.

"All we can do is keep a closer eye on customers," I said.

"That and concentrate on activities that make a lot of profit for you."

"Page kits," I said. "Especially those that use up some of our less popular paper."

Two husbands showed up to buy gifts for their wives. I think they rode over together as a "buck up" buddy precaution before entering an all-female zone. They made a lot of guffawing and sports references, but when the two got a gander at Laurel, the testosterone really started to ooze along the floorboards. I saw a way to work this to our advantage. I excused myself and went over to where Laurel was cutting paper. "Wait on them, will you? I'll take over the page kits."

She did.

Boy, oh boy, did she ever.

She sold $525 to one guy and nearly $700 to the other, and they loved every second of her attention. Both men staggered out under their purchases. Clancy whistled through her teeth. "Gotta love the weaker sex. They had no idea how to resist Miss December, did they? By the way, did you check her for staples across her midriff?"

"Meow." I shook a finger at Clancy.

She laughed. "Just call me Catwoman."

With Laurel knocking them out of the park and Clancy restocking, ringing stuff up, and doing displays, I knuckled under and finished the auction items for St. Louis Day School, Anya's old preschool. I prepped a "Scrapbooker's Dream Supply" donation, filling a canvas tote with punches, stickers, chipboard letters, and slabs of paper. Next, I completed the last pages in a customized 8″ by 8″ album with the school's logo on the front. Finally, I framed a one-of-a-kind layout that could be modified to feature any

St. Louis Day School child.

I was typing up the descriptions when Clancy called me over to the computer terminal at the front of the store. "You need to see this."

My jaw dropped. Mommy's Memories to Go was the name of an online store with a mailing address less than five miles away. Under the heading "New — Just In!" were photos of all the Cricut cartridges that had turned up missing during the past two weeks. No other cartridges were displayed but the specific ones we'd lost. The photos were blurry, the merchandise casually arranged, and the feel of the site was amateurish. We clicked on the site and discovered it had only been up a couple of weeks.

"I googled 'New Merchandise Online' and 'Cricut' and pulled this up," Clancy said.

"Please call a couple of the other nearby stores and ask if they've lost cartridges, too," I suggested.

Needless to say, I was badly shaken by this discovery. If the clock didn't say that the auction started in forty-five minutes, I would have moped around the store. Instead, I fished around in my wallet and handed a card to Clancy. "Here's the number of the Richmond Heights Police Department," I said. "Detective Stan Hadcho has been here a couple of times for that Cindy Gambrowski investigation. Call him, please."

Clancy nodded.

"You need a night off." Laurel put a hand on my shoulder. "Try not to let it bug you. You'll get to the bottom of this, and we're here now to help. We'll make a special point of greeting every customer. Once they know you've noticed them, it's harder for them to steal."

"Let's start asking customers to put any large carry-alls behind the counter," suggested Clancy. "That might help. Our thief must have carted these out in a purse or a bag."

I nodded.

"I'll also check into getting a closed-circuit TV installed. Don't tell me you don't have the money. Let's see what they cost first. Hey, how about I take care of the dogs for you tonight? Show me what needs to be done to Gracie's tail."

After I explained the procedure of checking her wraps, Clancy also offered to drop the dogs off at the house for me. "Isn't tonight the first night of Hanukkah?"

"I'm going to Sheila's to light the candles. Then there's the auction at Anya's old preschool. Anya and I will exchange gifts when we get home. We have our big celebration on the last night."

I didn't add that since George died, Sheila, Anya, and I worked hard to avoid the first night. His loss brought such pain that it was difficult to properly celebrate a day that involved such special traditions. I suppose we were all running away from reality. We couldn't bring George back. We couldn't imagine the first night without him. So we indulged in a sort of fantasy by omission. If the first night didn't happen, we didn't have to come to grips with our loss, did we?

"You can't go to an auction at St. Louis Day School dressed so casually," said Clancy. There wasn't a smidgeon of meanness in her voice. Protectiveness, yes; snarkiness, no.

Laurel loaned me a recently dry-cleaned white blouse from her car so I wouldn't have to run home and change. (Wonder of wonders, it fit. Could I possibly be that chesty? I guess so.) Clancy handed over her black cashmere cardigan, which went well with my black slacks and turned the simple shirt and pants into an outfit. After a long survey of my appearance, Clancy retrieved a red and black print silk scarf from her coat pocket and tied it around my neck. The effect surprised me. I looked polished and professional.

A few minutes later, I was looking fine as I pulled out of the parking lot with the auction items on the passenger seat.

What would I do without my friends?

## THIRTY-SIX

I hit Sheila's at a run. The sun was sinking quickly, and since her house was west of the store, the colorful sky reminded me I needed to hurry.

We gathered around the menorah. Anya took the shamas candle and recited the time-honored prayer: *"Barukh ata Adonai Eloheinu melekh ha-olam, asher kid'shanu b'mitzvotav v'tzivanu l'hadlik ner shel hanuka."*

In translation, my daughter said, "Blessed are You, Lord, our God, King of the universe, Who has sanctified us with His commandments and commanded us to kindle the Hanukkah light."

Sheila handed over a big package to my kid. "Open it fast, we have to go."

Count on Sheila to make every moment a Kodak moment.

Anya ripped into the paper and found an Uggs box.

I gnashed my teeth. Why hadn't Sheila

talked to me first? Hadn't we agreed long ago to consult each other on major gifts?

"Mom, isn't this great? Just in time for the dance!"

I wouldn't ruin this for her. It wasn't her fault her grandmother regularly overstepped her bounds. "Thank your grandmother, honey. What a thoughtful gift."

That was a stretch.

"My gift for you is at home," I told Anya. "We need to get going." Back at the house, I would give her another gift from my Hanukkah shopping list. Fortunately, I bought her a nifty purse at a crafts fair two months ago. I knew she'd love it. I dreaded sending her boots back to Zappos, but I comforted myself that they had a great return policy. And Sheila's gift had eased my holiday budget woes.

I struggled not to give in to sadness as I drove to the hotel. Anya was coming with Sheila, who still needed to change. That was fine. Sheila's Mercedes had heated seats so my kid would enjoy a warm tushie on the way over. Meanwhile, I was freezing because I didn't dare put my cat pee coat on over my friends' borrowed finery.

How I missed George! Especially on this, the first night of the Festival of Lights! I sat in the cold car and shivered, trying to get on my game face. I even applied lipstick. I was willing to do about anything to man up for the event, even if manning up meant going girly. When I couldn't take the cold in my car any longer, I wiped my nose and gave myself a good mental slap. I stepped out with my items in tow and joined the stream of the happy couples chatting their way into the Marriott ballroom.

I walked quickly past the area where people handed over their credit cards to get a bidding number. George had loved events like this nearly as much as I hated them. He was as social as I was introverted. How he enjoyed perusing the auction offerings! Especially if the item was a special opportunity, a once-in-a-lifetime event. He would win the bidding, then surprise Anya and me with something fabulous. One time he bought seats in the dugout of old Busch Stadium for batting practice. It was so much fun. Anya and a group of friends still talked about that outing. Another time, we had box seats for *Phantom of the Opera,* plus a special after-the-play meeting with the cast members.

I blinked and wiped a tear from my eye. At least I had happy memories to console me.

Sheila walked in with Anya about the time

I finished displaying the Time in a Bottle items. My mother-in-law wore a beautiful periwinkle blue dress with a pair of silver strappy shoes. A cashmere shawl was thrown carelessly over her shoulders and fastened with a large broach of opals. Everyone overdressed for this occasion. One woman even sported a sequin-covered cocktail dress and dangling diamond earrings! These were definitely people with too much money, too much time on their hands, and not enough places to go. I was doubly glad that my friends bailed me out on the wardrobe department. In fact, Sheila sidled up to me and said, "You are underdressed, but you look better than usual."

I think she meant her remark as a compliment.

Anya and I took seats at a table while Sheila wandered around placing bids.

"Don't you want to look, Mom?"

I shook my head. "I have everything a person could want."

"Except a signed Mary Engelbreit print."

I gawped. "A signed print? By Mary Engelbreit? Oh, my gosh. She's a goddess!"

My kid pulled me to my feet, and we searched the bountiful tables crammed with all sorts of trinkets, until my eyes spied a framed poster in the signature bright color

223

of St. Louis's own favorite and most famous artist. I stood and stared at her whimsical work. The title block said, "Queen of Everything." It had been a long, long time since I felt like a queen of anything. A quick glance at the sheet told me the silent bids already reached stratospheric heights. I shook my head. No way could I participate.

"Wouldn't that look great over your bed?"

"It sure would, Anya, but I think I'd put it over our kitchen table. If I am Queen of Everything, you are second in line for the throne."

We laughed and returned to our seats. Sheila bounced up and down the whole night, checking on this and that.

By the time dinner arrived, the seats next to us were filled. I introduced myself to our tablemates. Every fifteen minutes, a bid station closed. My work fetched a pretty penny, and maybe more importantly, I was asked to stand and have my efforts acknowledged. I hoped that would translate into more business for Time in a Bottle.

"You work at that store where Cindy Gambrowski's leg —" began the woman on my left.

"Yes," I interrupted her. "We're all very worried about her. She's in our prayers."

She introduced herself as Gwen Bordeau.

"I know, sounds like a bad joke, doesn't it? This is my husband, Mitch."

He shook my hand and said, "It's a little late for worrying about Cindy. Everyone knows what happened."

# THIRTY-SEVEN

"Excuse me?" I set down my fork.

Gwen leaned over and cupped her hand over my ear. "Ross beat that poor woman like a boxer uses a punching bag. He got by with it, too, because of all his doctor and lawyer friends. They belonged to the same country club, see? He built them mansions at special prices, and in return, they kept their mouths shut about poor Cindy. The docs treated her. The lawyers shut her out so she couldn't seek legal help. Everyone protected Ross and turned their back on the woman. Over the years, he got smarter and smarter about how to beat her so the damage wouldn't show."

I thought I was going to lose my meal. Saliva flooded my mouth. I'd heard about wife-beating spouses, but I never thought this included the privileged upper class. It never occurred to me that women sporting expensive jewelry and furs lived in fear.

"Cindy always seemed so . . ."

"Normal?" Mitch laughed. "For an abused wife? What choices did she have?"

"Hon, keep it down," warned Gwen. "Mitch used to golf with Ross. After Ross bragged about pummeling Cindy, Mitch walked off the course. Refused to take his calls."

"I always knew he had a bad temper." He shook his head. "If Ross picks a fight with me, at least he's squaring up with someone his own size. Look, there was nothing normal or healthy about their relationship. She got regular plastic surgery to keep up with Ross's whims. She was his personal improvement project. He beat her if she gained weight. Then it was her bust. And her nose, because he'd rearranged it. After their daughter, he wanted her to have a tummy tuck. God knows what else he had done to that poor woman. Makes me sick to think about it."

Gwen shielded her mouth with a hand so she could talk to me. "Everyone knew what was happening because Ross is such a braggart. He couldn't keep his mouth shut. You can look at photos of Cindy over the years and see the changes. Most of them were pretty obvious. She didn't have any friends. Ross wouldn't let her make them. To him, she was an object, a prize, a thing."

"He let her serve on charity boards, though. That was good for his image." Her husband tore off a piece of his roll and buttered it.

"But she had to tell him when and where and with whom, and she checked in frequently."

I recalled Ciindy watching the clock during our scrapbooking class. Last in, first out, she grew increasingly nervous if we ran a little behind.

*Detweiler,* I said to myself. *I have to get word to Detweiler.*

"How could I have missed this?" I wondered out loud. "She took a class at our store."

"You missed it because Cindy was too darn scared to let on," said Mitch, "and because Ross paid people to keep it under wraps. When you have that kind of money, you can make a lot of problems disappear. Ross sure did. Once I stood next to him at the country club, and he reached over and grabbed his wife's —"

"Mitch," his wife warned him.

Mitch lowered his voice. "Ross grabbed Cindy's private parts and announced to everyone, 'This is mine. Bought and paid for.' "

I pushed away my dinner, which was a crying shame because I hadn't had a nice meal like that in ages. The raw prime rib didn't seem very appetizing all of a sudden.

"She mentioned she loved your class," Gwen said. "I'd like to come take one myself."

I reached into my purse and offered Gwen a "One Free Crop" coupon that I devised just for situations like this.

"A few of us are planning a memorial service for her on Sunday," Gwen tucked my coupon into her purse. "You might want to come. She has — had — a lovely daughter, Michelle. She'll drive over from the University of Illinois in Champaign."

"So you're pretty sure Cindy is dead?"

Gwen's shoulders drooped. "I'm friends with the dental hygienist at Cindy's dentist's office. The police called and asked them to pull her records. The blood in the car was definitely a match. The cut on the leg was done with a buzz saw, the kind builders use."

Mitch added, "Somebody found Cindy's cell phone in that grass that runs along the Lambert Airport's long-term parking lot. A pal in the police department told me they have an incoming nine-one-one call that corresponds with her disappearance."

"Mitch! You didn't tell me that! What did it say?"

"A woman said, 'My husband is going to kill me. He says he's going to cut me into a thousand little pieces.' "

# THIRTY-EIGHT

I excused myself and slipped out of the ballroom. I phoned Detweiler first, and then Hadcho. I left messages for both of them outlining what I learned. When I got back to my seat, the live auction was over.

"Anya, go on to the car, please. Here are the keys. I'll be there in a minute. Go ahead and start it up, honey." I pushed my daughter forward as I pulled Sheila back into an alcove between the restrooms. "Why didn't you tell me Ross Gambrowski abused his wife?"

"I tried to. You didn't listen."

*Friday, December 18*
*2nd Day of Hanukkah*
After tossing and turning all night, I finally gave up on sleep. After I drank my instant coffee, I took care of Monroe. The cold weather suited him just fine. Certainly his "rug" looked warmer than the nasty jacket I

231

was wearing. He frolicked around in his pen, kicking up his heels and braying. Picking up on the mood of general frivolity, the dogs ran around and around in circles inside my fenced-in yard.

I cleaned the kitchen and then brought them inside and unwrapped Gracie's tail. It was definitely worse. Yellow pus crusted around the stitches. After soaking a soft cloth with warm water, wringing it out, and dabbing carefully, I managed to clean the area. All the while, my poor dog cast me doleful glances. The tail was hurting her, I could tell. I called the vet's office and left a message on their machine.

Anya rode to school with Izzy in her lap and Jasper at her feet. She used her arm as a gate to keep Fluffy from piling into the front with us. Petunia sat on the back seat, casting amorous glances at poor Gracie. Short and dark with bulbous eyes, he definitely wasn't her type. Nope, my dog loved long, lean, and human. She had only one name on her dance card: Detweiler.

All the fairy lights were out at the store. I settled the dogs and messed around with the breakers. Once everything came on, I blinked in astonishment. Clancy and Laurel had outdone themselves by stocking shelves, dusting, emptying the trash cans, and even making new displays and signs. By the front register was a handwritten note. I recognized Clancy's careful script.

"(1) Called the detective. (2) Ordered the Cricut cartridges from that online place. (Paid extra for overnight shipping. They should arrive here tomorrow. I also ordered a few using a different online address, and those will come to my house.) (3) I will bring you lunch at noon! Try not to fret! Hope you had a good evening.

C —"

Laurel left a note, too. Her script was rounded with smiley faces for dots. "Tallied the votes for the pages in the contest. They're in this envelope. That way we won't have so many to count next Monday when it ends. Laurel."

The back door slammed so loudly I heard it from the front counter. Bama stomped in.

"Have a good day off?" I asked.

She grunted.

Ducky. Just ducky.

Before she could hide in the office, I stopped her with, "They've planned a memorial service for Cindy Gambrowski. It's Sunday, before we open."

"They're that sure she's dead?"

"I guess."

The rest of the morning moved at a fast clip. At noon, Clancy appeared with a Wendy's bag for me. "Eat. Keep up your strength. By the way, Laurel and I worked on that shawl for Dodie. If the three of us keep at it, it'll be done by tomorrow. Nice pattern. Easy, but pretty. She'll love it."

I munched on the burger and shared the sad insight I gleaned from the auction.

"What sort of man hits a woman?" Clancy asked.

"A sick one," said Bama. "A man who can't control his anger, who learned his behavior at his mother's knee, who has poor impulse control, who might be under stress, and who manages to convince a woman she has to submit. It's a national epidemic with more than 10 percent of the population suffering at the hands of an abuser."

"Many believe it's a form of psychopathy," said Clancy.

"Which means what?"

"That spells 'sick' in all caps," said Bama.

"In other words, spousal abuse is a form of mental illness," said Clancy. "But other theories suggest that it happens when a man is so fearful of abandonment that he's threatened by any sign his partner might leave him. That beating is actually a sign of a man's deep-seated and fearful needs."

"Right. Like the deep-seated need to pound on someone," Bama said. "Someone weaker."

"No, it's more complicated than that. These men fear being rejected. Many of them can't conceive of life without their relationships, so they want to be sure the women can't leave them."

"By breaking their legs," said Bama. "Or arms. Or noses. Or fingers."

"By starting a cycle. He hits her, he apologizes, they experience a form of closeness and bonding that's unusual and highly emotionally charged. She fantasizes it won't happen again, he tells her it happened because of his love —"

"And then round two and round three and so on," I supplied. I wanted to change the subject. This was intensely uncomfortable for me. The conversation stirred up old memories, times of my childhood and adolescence that I didn't want to revisit.

But I didn't need to change the subject because a new topic walked in the door. A willowy young woman with nervous eyes carried a beautifully wrapped package under her arm. After balancing it precariously on the edge of our counter, she said, "Is Kiki

235

Lowenstein here?"

I rose from the stool behind the cash register. "That's me."

"I'm Michelle Gambrowski. Cindy is my mom."

I noticed she used the present tense. I'd done that a lot in the months after George's death. I didn't see the family resemblance between this girl and Cindy, but then, if Cindy had all that surgery, perhaps I didn't see a resemblance because it was no longer there. Although Michelle wore almost no makeup, she did have the same coloring. Like Cindy, the girl also seemed skittish and of course, her face had the blotchy spots you get from crying. She pushed back too-long bangs as her eyes darted around the store like finches flit about in a cage.

"Mom wanted you to have this." Pushing the package toward me, she jammed her hands deep in the pockets of her down jacket. Underneath I caught a peep of a bulky sweater, a pair of loose fitting jeans, and hiking boots. Odd. Cindy always dressed in figure baring, skin-tight clothes.

I corrected myself. Actually Michelle's mode of dress wasn't odd. Cindy had dressed the way her husband, Ross, wanted her to. He wanted her body displayed for all the world to see. Michelle was clothed for comfort.

And to hide her body. That, too, seemed interesting to me. The girl's posture caved in on itself, as though Michelle was trying to disappear entirely. Or at the very least, not be noticed.

"Nice to meet you," I said extending my hand. "We all liked Cindy. We're so sorry for your loss."

She ignored my gesture and just stared at the wrapped gift. Later, Clancy would say Michelle had a curiously flat affect. In other words, you could have sworn nobody was home.

Depression could do that. However, a voice inside told me, *She's purposely not reacting. This is more than holding back.*

"Um, I guess you want me to open this now?" I glanced over at her hands. Their outline showed through the pockets of her coat because she jammed them in so hard. Her lips pressed together as though she was afraid she might speak.

Instead, she nodded.

Carefully and slowly, I peeled off the tape, untied the curling ribbons, and unfolded the paper. (That I intended to save. The pattern was an artful rendition of a book shelf filled with colorful, leather-bound tomes. My mind raced with ideas for copying and reusing the design.) Inside the package were three books. What a contrast these were to the heavy classics on the wrapping paper. I found an *I Spy* children's book, a copy of *Where's Waldo Now?* with a bookmark stuck in the page showing him and the Aztecs, and *The Magic of M. C. Escher,* a book about the famous artist's optical illusions.

What on earth did these presents mean?

# THIRTY-NINE

Michelle's eyes didn't move from my face. She was waiting, waiting, waiting, but for what?

"Gee, this is really kind of your mother. I love all of these. But I'm curious. Did she mention why she chose these for me?"

"I guess she thought you'd like them."

A more important question buzzed around my brain. "When did she buy them?"

If my questions lacked a bit of finesse, no one seemed to care. After all, things really couldn't get much more awkward, could they?

"A couple weeks ago. She always does her holiday shopping in advance. I, um, just remembered she wanted you to have them."

"It's very, very kind of her. Again, please accept our condolences. Of course, a group of us from the store will attend the memorial service."

Michelle nodded.

Still, I felt exactly like you do when someone hands you a piece of the jigsaw puzzle and expects you to place it where it belongs. But I couldn't. The books were a missing piece, probably a corner or a part of the border. But exactly where they fit, I couldn't say.

Clancy strolled over and looked at the pile. "I assume there's a message here? Or some reference to a conversation you once had?"

I flipped each book open to where there might be a signature or a personalization. In the front of the *I Spy* book, a tight handwriting said:

To Kiki,
    Who knows where to look for secrets.
                              Cindy.

"I'm not sure I understand this."

Michelle shrugged.

My shoulders fell, and a weight dampened my spirits. The joy of these presents deflated like a burst balloon because in my heart, I knew something was afoot. But what?

*Come on, Kiki,* I told myself. *A woman's life might be at stake.*

"What's that noise? Back in the back?" Michelle tilted her head toward the sound of the dogs barking. "Animals?"

"I dog sit."

"I love animals." Her face lit up. "Would you like to come back and meet my friends? Can I get you a cola or hot tea?"

"I've got the floor covered," said Clancy.

A surge of happiness filled me. Clancy and Laurel both displayed intuitive understanding of their roles in our business. Without asking, they moved to help me before I asked.

I seemed to be on their wavelength, too. When Dodie was here, she commanded from on-high. That was cool. She founded the store and still owned the majority of stock. When Bama was here, I constantly needed to watch my back and worry about what picayune (which we always pronounced "picky-you-nee") problem she'd have with whatever I was doing.

But I meshed better with Clancy and Laurel. So far, all three of us worked together harmoniously. There was no attitude. No drama. I liked that. Liked it a lot.

Michelle shuffled after me toward the back. I squeezed my new books to my chest and wondered why and how they came to be mine. Did Cindy really know me so well? Anya and I spent hours pouring over the *I Spy* and *Where's Waldo* books. After she fell asleep, I would carry the books into another room and continue our search. I found the process totally absorbing. Small victories can mean so much when you're a stay-at-home mom.

Michelle crouched next to the doggy playpen, cooing and stroking my furry friends. "Wow."

That was it for a while. Just, "Wow."

I offered her a choice of beverages, then waited and sipped a Diet Dr Pepper while she loved up the pooches. "You must like animals."

She gave me the first real smile of her visit. "I'm graduating from veterinary school in May. Mind if I have a look at the Great Dane's tail?"

"No, in fact, I've got a call into the vet. I think it's gotten worse."

We walked Gracie out, and I held her head while Michelle carefully stripped away the wrappings. Her fingers moved nimbly, but Gracie tried twice to reach around and mouth the girl. That sore spot must have really been hurting my dog. Gracie is normally the most complacent creature on earth.

"If this doesn't get cleared up, you might have to have it amputated."

"What?"

Michelle nodded solemnly. "Actually, I've been doing amputations all this semester. Our school is involved in a special study about the efficacy of amputations on dogs with advanced cancer. Fascinating stuff. Of course, tail docking in certain animals is done without anesthesia, but I'd call that barbaric. In the case of a dog with an advanced infection in the tail, amputation can be lifesaving, too. A lot less difficult and dangerous than amputating a limb, of course. It's not that amputations are unsafe, but you need to plan carefully so you leave the right amount of bone and tissue behind."

"Amputation?" I stuttered. "Her sore tail could get that bad?"

"Yes, the infection can travel. Unfortunately, 'happy tail' occurs frequently with large breeds. There's so much power in that swing that amputation —"

"You can't amputate Gracie's tail!" From behind us came the deep voice of Detective Chad Detweiler. "You can't do that to my girl." He knelt down beside a joyous, slobbering Dane.

Gracie perked right up.

So did I.

"The stitches are inflamed. She's had an antibiotics shot, I take it? You might try warm compresses, but she needs to quit banging her tail around. Unfortunately, that's like telling her not to smile. It's her nature. There are waggers and non-waggers. I've had dogs wag at me even as they take their dying breaths. So even though this must hurt her a lot, she can't stop," Michelle stood and stared down at the sore and angry area. "Too bad no one makes an Elizabethan collar for tails."

"You mean one of those plastic bell-shaped things that keep them from chewing on themselves?" I put my arms around Gracie's neck. She responded by licking Detweiler. I still adored her, even if she didn't love me best.

"That's right. I've heard of people using plastic piping and duct tape to create an ersatz cocoon around the area. That might work. First you'd need to shave off all the nearby hair."

"I have a couple of disposable razors in my car. I keep them for when I need to appear in court." Detweiler rubbed his chin as he spoke.

Michelle nodded. "I could shave around the stitches so the bare area extends farther. That way if you can figure out some sort of a cushion or a protective device, you can tape it to her skin."

244

I took them up on their offers. Anything, anything at all to help Gracie.

Detweiler paused on his way out the door. "Mind if I get my dad? He's in the car. He's good with projects."

A few minutes later, Louis Detweiler extended a rough hand to shake mine. "Pleased to meet you." His eyes took in everything about me; there was a compassion in his expression that nearly brought tears to mine.

"Tell me about this animal, son."

I remembered then that Mr. Detweiler hadn't wanted his son to have a dog. Even so, the older man's voice implied that he was genuinely interested in my pooch, even if he didn't pat her or love her up. Detweiler introduced his dad to Michelle. The two put their heads together and discussed various options. Mr. Detweiler asked for a piece of paper and a pencil so he could sketch an apparatus. "Of course, needs to be lightweight. Waterproof?" he asked the younger woman.

She concurred. "That's exactly what might work. The problem is where do you get some sort of casing?"

"Ee-yeah," said Mr. Detweiler. "I have a few ideas."

Detweiler the Younger helped me hold

245

Gracie's head as Michelle applied a soapy mixture to the skin and shaved off more fur. Our hands touched several times and the electricity was intense, causing me to lose my balance as I squatted on my heels. At one point, Detweiler sort of twisted so he could see the vet student's work. As he did, his jacket fell open. Michelle's face froze as she noticed the gun.

"Y-y-you're a cop!"

Detweiler nodded, but before he could introduce himself, Michelle Gambrowski raced out of our stockroom.

# FORTY

"Ee-yeah," said Mr. Detweiler stroking his chin like his son often does. "That young lady knows a passel about what happened to her mother. I expect you know that though, right?"

Detweiler nodded. "But she's not talking. Her father has her lawyered up. He's tighter than a clam, too."

Before I told him what I learned at the auction, I offered Mr. Detweiler Senior a chair. "I'm fine," he said as he leaned against the wall, opposite of his son. The two of them were nearly mirror images, a younger and older version of one man. You could see that Detweiler the Younger would age well. In fact, if anything, he would be one of the lucky few who actually grew better looking with time.

I recited what I'd learned about Ross Gambrowski beating his wife. Mr. Detweiler glanced from me to his son and back and then stared at his feet. "Hard to credit. How can a man call himself a man when he hurts a woman? Son, you know, sometimes I wonder about this job. You sure do see the worst of what humanity has to offer."

I tried to think about Detweiler's day-in and day-out existence. The people he collared, trailed, and put away. Mr. Detweiler Senior managed — in a few short sentences — to bring my concerns to the fore. What if Detweiler and I got together in the future? What would it be like to have a partner who faced down danger daily? Who carried a gun?

Could I live with that?

Whoa, I told myself. You're on a crazy crash course here. Stop this fantasizing about Detweiler. Stay in the moment!

I cleared my throat. "Um, I need to get back to work." I showed him the books Cindy had given me and explained, "I planned to phone you. Here's the place she signed this to me."

"Any idea what she means?"

"No."

"I assume you are planning to attend the memorial service."

"Yes, I'll be there. How can they have it now? I mean, doesn't it take a while for

248

someone to be declared dead if there isn't a body?"

Detweiler's father got a disgusted expression on his face, twisting his mouth as though he wanted to spit. "If you're shamed into showing that you cared, you don't wait. Or if you feel guilty ten ways to Sunday, and you're trying to scrub the slate clean. There's a reason they're having the memorial so soon. Might be money, or shame, but it's sure not because of respect or love. If that were your mama, Chad, I'd travel to the ends of the earth before I considered her dead and gone. I'd have to see it myself. You could put me in my grave before I'd give up hope. What a disgusting excuse for a helpmate. And his daughter? She looked just like a baby rabbit being teased to death by a durned cat. No girl should have to shoulder a burden like that. You could tell it was eating at her. Delivering her mama's gifts? What an odd errand. Doesn't make a bit of sense."

Detweiler the Elder was right. I couldn't imagine what Michelle was going through, but I also couldn't see myself or my daughter carrying on as she had. There'd be no way I could have walked into a store, handed over a gift, and not burst into tears.

Still . . . who was I to judge?

People thought poorly of me for taking the job here after George died. They didn't realize I didn't have a choice. Maybe Michelle didn't have a choice. Maybe she was acting the way her mother would have wanted her to act. Or the way she'd been raised to act. Thanks to my volatile father, I'd learned early on to hide my emotions.

There was also another possibility. Perhaps Michelle believed her mother was better off. There were some — and I wished I could join them — whose faith was so strong that the afterlife enchanted them. They weren't a bit scared. Oh, to be a person with such a belief! What would it be like to hold such a conviction that the next world appeared as clear and certain as this one?

I wished I could feel that way, but I didn't. Not yet at least.

However, that might be exactly how Michelle felt. Perhaps, given the horrific circumstances of her mother's daily life, her daughter felt relief. That made sense to me. That I could accept.

All this raced through my mind.

I photocopied the inscription inside my book and wrote down the book titles for the detective. "As I said, if this is her version of

*The Da Vinci Code,* I'm out of luck."

"I better get this to the station," said the detective.

"I imagine you all knew about the beatings?" I asked.

Detweiler the detective was too cagey for that. He didn't answer me directly. "Even if he did beat his wife, it doesn't necessarily follow that he killed her. We're talking murder and dismemberment. Besides, he has an alibi for most of that weekend."

"But wouldn't a wife beater keep upping the ante? I mean, think about O.J. Simpson. When she took up with another man . . ."

"Suppose Mr. Gambrowski does — or did — beat his wife. Suppose he killed her. Why now? That's what the defense would argue. They would say it doesn't necessarily follow, particularly since he's been doing this — allegedly — for years."

"Does it matter if he's the person who cut her up?" asked Detweiler the Elder, his tired eyes reflecting disgust. "Maybe he killed her, and he paid someone to get rid of the body. So what? He ought to be locked up forever just for beating her!"

"Dad, if he did this, and note carefully the operative word 'if,' we're talking two levels of penalties. I mean, sure, a guy could get sent away for killing his wife, even if the body is missing. But once you factor in dismemberment, especially when she was alive —"

"She was alive? He cut her up while she was alive?" My voice hit a high note Beyoncé would envy.

"You must not have read this morning's paper," said Detweiler. "Someone leaked this to the press." Rubbing his hand through his hair tiredly, he heaved a sigh. "Probably someone who wanted the world to know what a creep this guy is."

"Cut off her leg while she was alive?" I teetered for a moment, before Detweiler shoved a chair under me.

"It would certainly meet the criteria of outrageously or wantonly vile," said the detective.

I couldn't form words. My mind struggled to grasp what Cindy endured those last moments of her life. I found it difficult to breathe.

Good old Detweiler. That's what Anya calls him, and she's right, because the man's no dummy. He took a look at me, told me to put my head between my knees so I could count dust bunnies, and reached into the frig to pop the top on a Diet Dr Pepper for me. "Take a drink. I opened it so you don't ruin your nails."

"They'd gas him? Even without a body?"

"Since 1977, Missouri has administered lethal injections. For the forty years prior to that, the state sent criminals convicted of capital crimes to the gas chamber, which oddly enough was actually a chamber and two cells in Jefferson City."

"But without a body?" Detweiler Senior repeated my question.

Detweiler took a long deep breath. "If there's proof Mr. Gambrowski threatened to dismember her, or threatened to do away with her and hide the body, the odds would increase that he'd be convicted even if we don't find Mrs. Gambrowski. The amount of blood in the car precludes anyone living through the attack."

Laurel stuck her head in the door. "I hate to interrupt, but I have a question."

This is exactly why Detweiler makes me swoon. As gorgeous as Laurel is, he didn't even stop to stare. His eyes passed right over Miss December and stayed focused on me!

"I'll be right there," I said to her. I cleared my throat. "Gentlemen, you'll have to excuse me."

Detweiler the Younger gave Gracie one final cuddle. "Stop wagging your tail. Please?" Of course, she didn't. Detweiler turned to his father. In the younger man's eyes was hope, the sort of pleading that a child offers up to a parent, infused with the belief that the parent, being the all-powerful creatures we are, could make everything all right. "Dad, think you can help her?"

"Ee-yeah. I expect so. I'll give it a whirl at least." Mr. Detweiler Senior gave his son's shoulder a squeeze and stared at my dog thoughtfully. "I'll stop back by tomorrow or Sunday at the latest with a gizmo to help your dog. Can she hold out that long?"

"I have a call in to my vet. Maybe a stronger antibiotic will help. But really, Mr. Detweiler, I know this is a busy time of year. Don't put yourself —"

"Young lady, it's no bother. Not for you. You're my son's friend."

I held my breath, wondering if he knew what sort of friend I wanted to be to his married son. While I turned blue from lack of oxygen, Detweiler Senior continued, "And friends and family mean the world to us Detweilers. That's the way we are."

I didn't dare look at Detweiler the Younger as his father spoke. I was too scared my face would show my emotions. Instead, I kept my eyes on his father, the man Chad Detweiler would someday become.

"Sir, that's my philosophy, too. That's why I love what I do here. Maybe on your next

254

visit, I'll have the chance to show you around."

"I'd like that. Heard a lot about scrapbooking. Seems to me a mighty pleasant way to spend your time. By the way, young lady, folks quit calling me 'sir' when I left the military. I'm Louis to you, if you please."

With that, both the Detweiler men stepped out of the back door and my life. As it happens when you're all alone and the power suddenly goes out, the world seemed a lot lonelier and darker.

# FORTY-ONE

Rita Romano, one of our long-time croppers, handed me a Cricut cartridge. "Is this yours? This doesn't make any sense. Your inventory sticker is on it, but I bought it online. I would have gotten this from you, but you were out of this particular model."

I stared at the cartridge with the sick realization that it had probably been shoplifted from our store.

Rita handed over all the transaction details from Mommy's Memories to Go. I photocopied them, thanked her, and gave her a $25 Gift Certificate.

"Don't, please! I should have asked you to order this for me. We all need to support our local small businesses, especially our local independent scrapbook retailers, so I feel a bit silly. In fact, I debated about whether to bring it in, but I used to work in retail, and I figured you needed to know about it. I'm not sure what it means, but it can't be good news."

I pressed the gift certificate on her. "You don't realize how much money you've saved us."

Rita wouldn't take it. "Do you really think I could live with myself knowing I purchased stolen goods?"

Clancy shook her head. "I put a call into Detective Hadcho earlier."

I nodded. The Richmond Heights P.D. is small, so I wasn't surprised that he'd be handling a case of theft as well as checking up on our stray body part.

"I'll try Hadcho again now. Clancy, can you start setting up for the crop?"

Bama showed up at the same time Detective Hadcho did. He held the door open for her, but she didn't bother to thank him. "What is it with you and cops?" she muttered darkly. "You have some kinky thing going on? You get off on the uniforms? Handcuffs? The guns? Or the violence?"

"We think we found our shoplifter." I was not going to let her bait me into being nasty. Not today. On the spot, I decided to wait until after the holiday season and then confront her. I just wasn't up for a confrontation, not now.

"Really?"

Detective Hadcho cocked his head. "Why don't we go in the back? We can talk privately. I can take all this down."

"Bama, can you get the supplies out for the crop? Laurel left five minutes ago. She carried all the boxes up to the front. I only need help setting things at the stations."

She grunted at me. I took that for a yes.

Hadcho declined a cola, requested coffee, drank the murky instant with resignation, and whipped out a Steno pad. I handed over the cartridge, plus its paperwork, and pointed out our sticker.

"First of all, how does this gizmo work?"

I explained that the Cricut was a die-cutting machine. Each cartridge held a library of fonts and shapes. I handed over the information Clancy found as well as everything Rita Romano had given me.

"We've got someone who can trace the URL for the website. Should be able to shut this down quickly."

"Good. I appreciate the help."

He grunted. "That's my job. By the way, thanks for keeping Detweiler in the loop with that stuff about Gambrowski. You get an idea about what that message in those books means, if it is a message, you let us know. You going to the memorial service?"

I nodded.

"You got plans for tonight?"

"I'm working here until eleven and then going home. My daughter's at a dance, and then she's spending the night with a friend."

"A few of my friends are getting together over at Lumière Place. What do you think about going over there?"

I didn't catch his drift.

He added, "With me."

I picked my jaw up off the floor. Hadcho was asking me out to the newest, hippest casino in town! Wow. His steady dark chocolate eyes stared at me as he waited for my answer.

What could I say? I'm dating Ben Novak, but I'm madly in love with your married co-worker? I sometimes go out with my best friend Mert Chambers' brother, who happens to be a convicted felon?

Hey, with a love life like mine, the producers at the Bachelorette should be knocking down my door.

"I know it's last minute. Just a bunch of friends hanging out," he repeated. "Tell you what. Why don't I swing by the store and pick you up? Quarter after eleven? That way I can also keep an eye on you. You probably shouldn't be wandering around in the parking lot here alone."

It didn't sound too daunting. 'Tis the

season and all that. Wasn't like he called ahead and asked me to get gussied up to go to a nice restaurant. His invitation was spontaneous. Last minute. I hesitated. He just wanted company. Didn't want to walk in alone to a gathering of his friends. It wasn't about me. Really, it wasn't.

And why shouldn't I say yes?

Anya was off at CALA's holiday dance. A pang reminded me I hadn't even gotten to see her all dressed up. Sheila had picked my daughter up after school, helped her get ready, and done taxi cab duty. More and more, my mother-in-law was my stand-in, my parenting partner. I couldn't decide whether to feel lucky or miserable about that.

I hoped Sheila would remember to take photos. Too late for me to call and remind her.

I wouldn't see Anya after the dance, because she was having a sleepover with Nicci Moore.

I was going home to an empty house.

Detweiler wasn't going home to an empty house.

It was the holidays, after all. Other people were having a good time. Why should I go home and dog sit? Why should I spend my evening doing laundry? All I ever did any

260

more was work, work, work! Why not go out
with Hadcho?

"That'd be nice," I said.

# FORTY-TWO

I didn't have to phone Mert in a panic about my decision, because she came to the crop early. She pranced in wearing black tights and boots, a tiny black skirt, and a tight red tee-shirt with the words "Ho, Ho, Ho" printed across the bust in sequins. I wondered if she saw the irony. I decided to keep my mouth shut.

"How's Laurel doing?"

"Best gift you ever gave me. You just missed her. She even apologized because she couldn't stay longer to help."

"Yeah, she's pert near terrific, isn't she?"

I nodded. "I need to talk with Mert, the agony aunt, please."

She grinned. "Mert's Advice to the Love-lorn at your service. What's wrong? Has the season got you all mushy? Johnny gave me a piece of mistletoe to tack up over your stockroom door. But I bet you ain't thinking about my brother. You pining for that married detective? Mind you, I owe him one. Thanks to him, I won my court case."

Great. Here was a good reason to stall instead of spilling my news. "Tell me about it!"

Mert chewed on a piece of celery as she explained, "Seems my customer, one Sandra Franchino, was breaking stuff and turning in claims for the insurance. Other stuff, she done took and hocked it. When her hubby noticed all his toys was missing, he started to get suspicious-like. That's how come she blamed me. But Detweiler hooked me up with a pawn broker who testified how Sandra was this regular customer. He had video from his CCTV and ever thing. Paperwork, too. See, they gotta keep really accurate records of what comes in 'cause they don't want to be accused of fencing stolen goods. So we nailed her. That old Sandra was just lying like a cheap hairpiece."

"How come? Why'd she do it?"

"Cause she needed herself some spending money."

"I thought Nick Franchino owns that big car dealership over on Olive."

"He does. But he don't give her a cent. Makes her perform certain marital duties in payment for whatever she wants."

"Eeee-uck."

"No kidding. She ain't nothing but a high-paid prostitute, and she knows it. Heck, now the whole world knows it, too. In fact, as her sad story all tumbled out I felt bad for her skinny white butt. She started talking about how he wouldn't let her visit her dying mother, and she begged him to let her go. How he monitors her phone calls, got this high-powered monitoring system on their Internet. Even reviews the security cameras in their home."

"Why?" I straightened after slipping two dozen deviled eggs into their perfect plastic cradles. I make a mean deviled egg, even if I say so myself.

Mert continued to press cookie cutters into the soft sandwiches that Clancy had brought. The resulting star-shaped treats were absolutely adorable. Especially since their filling alternated egg salad, ham salad, and cucumber with cream cheese, and the bread alternated whole wheat with white. I unpacked a tri-level *petit four* serving tray and carefully transferred the delightful tiny treats that Mert's brother Johnny had baked.

"Did you know French bakers created *petit fours* as a way to use leftovers?"

Mert never ceased to surprise me. Most people never guessed she graduated cum laude with a degree in history from Southern Missouri University. When I asked her why she chose to clean houses, she answered, "I set my own hours and my own pay. If the boss is an idiot, I tell her off, and she straightens out."

I steered us back to the subject at hand. "You never answered me. How'd her husband react when she told the court all this? About keeping her under his thumb?"

"What do you mean?"

"Wasn't he embarrassed?"

"Heck no. He's a Bible thumper who thinks women ought to be punished for what Eve did."

"Talk about holding a grudge."

"You got that right. It's enough to make you swear off of applesauce forever. And he has to pay her court costs and everything. I'm just thankful my reputation was cleared."

"So am I."

"Now what's worrying you, girlfriend?"

"Um, Detective Hadcho dropped by. He's meeting some friend over at Lumière Place, and he asked if I'd like to go with."

"And you're asking me what?"

"Do you think I should?"

"You got a reason not to? Sounds like a good time to me. Heck, if you don't want him shoo him my way, won't you? Those pretty brown eyes of his'n make me want to melt like a candle on a birthday cake."

"It's not like that. It's just a friendly invitation." My face grew hot.

Mert crossed her arms over her chest. Only one little "Ho" was visible. She tilted her head and a tiny jingle bell tinkled. But her expression contrasted with all this merriment. Her brow puckered and her mouth went flat. She might seem all girly-girly to outsiders, but I knew her to be a tough-skinned survivor with a keen understanding of human nature. She proved this by pinning me to the wall, figuratively: "You been sniffing the Copic markers?"

"Copic markers?" I struggled to act innocent. Copic markers are alcohol-based, but sniffing Sharpie markers is even more of a trip.

"He's a man. You're a woman. An invite to drinks is a date in my book. Should be in yours, too." She narrowed her eyes, and I got real interested in arranging napkins. "We need to have ourselves a conversation, girl. How many men have you dated?"

"That's none of your bees-wax."

"Right."

"Hey, I'll have you know that I was dating a guy before I met George."

"So one boyfriend, one husband, and two on the fence? I ain't sure how to count Detweiler and Ben Novak."

"What's your point? That I'm lucky to have a guy interested in me?" I rearranged the napkins for the umpteenth time.

"I hate to think where that comes from. I surely do. My point is simple: You ain't had a lot of experience. Ain't nothing wrong with taking a car for a test drive before you buy. Provided, of course, you don't head out on the highway and act like a crash dummy."

I wasn't sure how to feel. Protected? Loved? Nurtured? Angry?

"Lookie here. I think that dating is a good way to learn about yourself. You learn what you like. What you don't like. You learn how people make you feel. Good, bad, or indifferent. And you ain't had much chance at an education, girlfriend. Taking this guy up on his offer to get together don't obligate you to nothing. Nothing. That's important to know. So what can you lose, huh? You might discover that Detweiler ain't the only tool in the shed. Or you might discover that he's the best fit for you. But you cain't know that from sitting around at home, can you?"

I nodded, slowly, as I raised my eyes to meet hers. Compassion was there, bright and shining with a full measure of honest caring that eased the tension in my shoulders, the tightness in my jaw. "I guess."

She smiled. "If you want to believe it's not a big deal, you go right ahead. That way you don't have to get all nervous-like. But you need to get honest with yourself."

"I am honest with myself. I'm not the kind of woman men find attractive. I'm not tall, I'm not thin, and I'm not young."

"Oh, really? That so? Then somewhere's along the line, you must have gotten bird poop in your eye."

"Bird poop in my eye?"

"That's right. Because the rest of the world sees a good-looking, single woman. Even iff'n you don't."

## JOHNNY'S SIMPLE *PETIT FOURS*

**For cakes:**

1 box Betty Crocker super moist cake (or any other cake mix)

**For icing:**

1 1/2 c. confectioners' sugar
1 tbsp. light corn syrup
1/4 tsp. vanilla extract (clear is best)
2 tbsp. whole milk
Food coloring
Hershey's chocolate syrup

Bake cake mix according to package directions in a 9 × 13 inch pan. After it cools, turn the cake out onto a flat surface. (A piece of corrugated cardboard covered with tin foil is perfect.) Using dental floss, cut the cake into 24 rectangles.

For icing, mix together confectioners' sugar, corn syrup, vanilla and milk, alternating sugar and milk at the end to get proper consistency. Divide icing into as many bowls as you want for different colors and add one drop of food coloring, then mix.

Spear each piece of cake with a wooden skewer and dip into icing. Drizzle top with Hershey's chocolate syrup or add sprinkles.

# KIKI'S DEVILED EGGS

One dozen eggs (at least two weeks old)
Honey mustard
Mayonnaise
Bacon (at least 3 pieces, maybe more like 6)
Green onions (1 or 2)
Olives

Put eggs in large pot and cover with cold water. Bring to a rolling boil. Cover the pot, turn off the burner, and let sit for ten minutes. Meanwhile, fry bacon to a crisp. Let it cool and crumble it into small pieces. Remove eggs from burner. Rinse eggs well in cold water. Crack shells by rolling under your palm. Let eggs cool, then cut in half and scoop out yolks.

Mix yolks with honey mustard and a dab of mayonnaise to desired consistency. Add crumbled bacon to desired consistency. Spoon yolks into a zippered plastic bag. Cut one end off of bag. Squeeze yolk mixture into eggs.

Decorate eggs with sliced green onions and olives.

# FORTY-THREE

We had a full house for the crop. Most of the croppers were our regulars. Daisy Touchette took a spot at the far end of the table. If I puffed up with pride because she was sticking with the craft, I hope I can be forgiven. After all, sometimes you work hard with a customer and never see her again. But the extra effort I'd given to Daisy that day she showed up with her fussy kids really seemed to be paying off.

Several people brought wrapped gifts for me, which surprised me to no end. I make no bones about the fact I adore presents. I managed not to squeal with joy, but it was hard. I nearly bit my tongue working the restraint angle.

Bonnie Gossage handed me a large blue shopping bag with instructions, "It's for the last night of Hanukkah. We're going out of town so I wanted to get you this early." I thanked her and spirited the sack away to the backroom. There I stopped to retrieve the gift I'd purchased for her.

At an online crafts site, I spotted a tiny pair of hand-crocheted baby slippers. They were yellow and white with tiny pompoms. They were so adorable they made my heart ache. In fact, I also bought a pair and put them in the bottom of my underwear drawer. Someday I hoped to have another baby. Maybe these booties would bring that blessing into my life. These were so tiny, I had to dig through my purse to find them. Finally, I emptied my wallet, tissues, keys, and makeup onto Dodie's desk to make my search go faster. I made a special note that I needed to go through the accumulation and get it organized.

"Kiki? Are you ready?" Bama stuck her head in the office and glared at me. "Get that mess picked up."

"I'll do it later," I said just to irk her as I'd already put a few things back. "People want to get started."

I raced out of the backroom to the crop area.

Miriam Glickstein handed me a small wrapped box and a plastic container of iced sugar cookies shaped like dreidels. "I figured you wouldn't have time to bake. You probably barely have enough time to light candles, much less buy them, so there's an extra package of candles here." I felt tears come to my eyes. "That is so very thoughtful of you," I said, and I meant it.

Jennifer Moore pressed a package on me. "I saw this and knew it would work with your long black skirt and turtleneck. Open it now, won't you?" Inside was the most darling poncho. A cable stitch design was knitted with a beige Angola-type yarn. Around the edge was faux rabbit fur. I pulled it over the brown turtleneck I'd paired with my jeans that morning. Everyone assured me the effect was stunning.

While the croppers were busy, I slipped my wrapped gift to Jennifer inside the craft tote bag she always carried. Jennifer was more than a customer. She'd been incredibly kind to Anya and me. So when the beautiful leather albums with the CALA logo came in, I set one aside. I knew she hadn't bought one, and with two kids at the school, I knew she'd put the album to good use. I also added a handwritten coupon for a couple hours of quality scrapbooking time together.

Bama and I took turns introducing and explaining the projects. She was quieter than usual. A few of our customers expressed surprise at her "new look," but she

273

clearly wasn't interested in their remarks. If there's a line between rude and not rude, she took her toe and smudged it.

Clancy left a little early for a neighborhood party back in Illinois. "Sorry, but I never miss one. Usually at least one husband gets soused and acts inappropriately, and at least one wife threatens emasculation with blunt objects. What is it about free booze and mistletoe that turns normal, God-fearing conservatives into wild-eyed, sex-crazed zombies?"

I sure couldn't answer that one. I remembered my dad getting lit on many so-called festive occasions. Sometimes I wondered if I'd married a Jew because my parents had done such a thorough job of making Christmas miserable for me and my sisters. But I didn't go into all that with Clancy. I have to admit I was sort of happy to see her go before the crop ended. If she'd hung around, I would have been forced to explain about my date. Clancy totally agreed with Mert that I should go out more often. She'd said so on numerous occasions. I didn't need to hear it again.

The gift making went quickly. We cranked up The Manhattan Transfer on an old boom box. The tiny sandwiches, deviled eggs, and petit fours were a hit. Everyone pitched in to help with the clean up. Afterwards, I hugged my customers one-by-one as they left the store. They were more than patrons to me; they were my support system.

Mert offered to drop the dogs off so I wouldn't have to run home. I thanked her, helped her get all the fur children in her truck, and waited nervously for Hadcho to show up.

"How's Gracie's tail?" she asked.

"The vet told me to bring her in on Monday if it isn't better."

"Just send Roger the bill."

I shook my head. "He's paid his dues, Mert," I said as I hugged her goodbye.

Bama puttered around the store.

"Aren't you leaving?" I asked.

She shook her head. "This is the only place I can wrap gifts without the kids seeing them. I carried most of what Santa's bringing them in from my car. The craft table is a perfect surface."

I remembered when Anya was little, and I stayed up late wrapping surprises for her. I envied Bonnie the joy of another little person in her life. Would I ever be pregnant again? I always hoped to have another child. If I closed my eyes tightly, I could imagine holding one in my arms.

*Don't go there, Kiki,* I told myself as I

dabbed at my nose. My cold was waning, but I still had a red nose and watery eyes.

A sharp rap at the front door brought me back to the here and now. I adjusted my new poncho and told Bama, "I'm heading out."

She narrowed her eyes as I let Detective Stan Hadcho inside. I could see her mind working. Those nasty comments — the ones about me having a weird predilection for cops — would all spill out if I hung around.

"Let me grab my purse. It'll just take a sec," I said to him, and I took off at a trot. I actually snatched it up, did a U-ie, and never stopped moving. That's how worried I was about Bama and her big mouth.

Bama met me as I was halfway to the front of the store. She grabbed me by the elbow. I tried to yank away from her. She just tightened her grasp. "Listen. These guys in uniform? Don't be fooled. It's not about helping people. It's a control issue."

This time I jerked my arm hard enough that she lost her grip. "I don't know what's wrong with you and I don't care. Stay out of my business!"

To my shock, her eyes filled with tears. "It's . . . I'm . . . trying to warn you. I know you don't like me. I know you don't believe me . . . but . . ."

I backed away from her. Her lips curled down, and her shoulders drooped. I rubbed my arm where she'd grabbed me. Unpleasant memories of Brenda Detweiler pranced through my head. "Don't ever touch me like that again."

Tears glistened in Bama's eyes. "You take care of yourself, Kiki. Just take care."

# FORTY-FOUR

Hadcho stood at the front door, jingling the change in his pocket, showing no indication that he'd heard Bama. He held the front door for me and gave a nod toward a sleek black Mustang parked in the back of our lot. "My personal car," he added.

Hadcho unlocked the passenger door for me. I started to climb in when a dark-colored panel van pulled into a nearby space. The driver's door flew open.

"Hey, you closed?"

I squinted. It was the man who'd dropped by the other night looking for Bama. In one hand he held another big bouquet of red roses. The fragrance drifted over the wet smell of impending snow, and the bright crimson blared like a trumpet blast in the narrow illumination of our security light. I smiled to myself.

Maybe that's what Bama needed: Someone to woo her.

Maybe that was why she was so nasty to me.

Maybe this was just a variation on a timeless theme, jealousy.

"Bama's still in there. She might not have locked the door yet. You better hurry!"

"Thanks!" he said and took off at a trot.

Towering over the riverside landscape, the Lumière sign dwarfs its neighboring buildings. It is nothing more or less than a monolithic slab of winking, strobing, twitching, crawling, blinking lights. What a bold contrast this high-wattage commercial signature makes to the Arch, that simple silver ribbon with a skyward sweeping reach! The two could not be more different. The Lumière sign crooks a finger, beckoning fun seekers. It comes alive at nighttime. The Arch stands aloof, a silent sentinel. It's closed in the evening. The Lumière sign promises you-can-be-something-you-probably-aren't. The Arch mirrors the city's own reflection, distorted and broken, but heartbreakingly honest. Taken together, these monoliths represent the dual nature so unique to St. Louis. Here is a city with a cathedral with doors once sealed by a pope, a world-class botanical garden, and spectacular free attractions including an art museum, a science center, and a zoo. It also boasts one of the country's highest murder rates and an STD rate second to none. As the Gateway to the West, St. Louis defines the crossroads of the nation. Here in the Northernmost of Southern cities, and the Southernmost of Northern cities is the meeting ground of secularism and religiosity, racial strife and harmony, beer barons and art patrons.

I stopped on the sidewalk to gawk at the huge signboard soaring up, up, up into the night sky. It's a wonderous sight, even if it is a bit gaudy for my tastes.

"Something, isn't it?" Hadcho cranked his head back.

We stared up like two corn-fed bumpkins.

"It sure is," I chuckled. The drive over had been mostly awkward, but now, as we stood side-by-side gobsmacked by the same monstrosity, the tension between us eased.

He took my arm, and we walked companionably into the casino. More than a few heads turned. As usual, Hadcho looked great. Perfect, really. I think my poncho must be awful flattering because a couple of guys eyed me with frank appraisal. (Either that or they were batting for the other team, and they wanted Hadcho on their bench. Who knows?)

We were in line to be admitted when I discovered I'd left my wallet back at the store.

I must have apologized five times when he said, "Just stop it. Everyone makes mistakes. It's no big deal. What are we? Five minutes away? There's no traffic on the road. Lumière is open all night."

Then, "What the heck?"

"That van's still there!" I said.

We pulled into Time in a Bottle's parking lot and stared at the black van. Bama's car was still in its parking spot as well.

"We haven't been gone that long, really," I mused. "And he was delivering flowers from a secret admirer. I guess he's the admirer. She's an awfully private person."

"You say he stopped by before?"

I nodded.

"Didn't seem like he was trying to hide anything, did he?"

"No. He didn't. Several of us saw him. He wore a floral delivery cap. I hate to break up Bama's hot date," I said, finally.

"Tell you what. How about if we go in together and make plenty of noise?"

"Or I could go in alone and try to sneak into the backroom. Unfortunately, that's where I left my wallet."

281

Hadcho laughed. "Right. Good idea. I'm an officer of the law. You found a body part in your dumpster. I'm going to let you walk by yourself in the dark into a building."

"Oh . . . right." Boy, did I feel silly.

We opened the Mustang doors in tandem and started toward the store. (I didn't wait for him to run around and open mine. I already felt dumber than a bucket of aquarium gravel.) My key outstretched, I tried the front door, only to discover it was still unlocked. That surprised me. I gave Hadcho one of those open-handed "what-you-going-to-do" gestures. He nudged me aside and stepped in.

The place was eerily dark. I guess I held my breath, thinking I didn't want to disturb any nighttime hanky-panky. I felt around for the light switch, but Hadcho clamped his hand on mine. We both froze.

From the back of the store came a rhythmical thump-thump-thump.

# FORTY-FIVE

It was the sound of a fist slamming into flesh.

"Stay here. Call nine-one-one," Hadcho said, and he took off running toward the sound.

I nodded and started dialing.

"Stop! Police!" he yelled. "Put your hands in the air!"

A low moan, and an inhuman cry came from the backroom. A calm voice answered my call. I managed to spit out our address to the dispatcher and to tell her a beating was in progress. "Send an ambulance. I'm here with Detective Stan Hadcho."

*Bam!* Hadcho kicked open the stock room door. The light illuminated the back of the store.

"Police! Put your hands in the air!" Hadcho yelled. "Stop now! I said now!"

A whimper and another wet thump. Then an almost inhuman moan of pain.

"I said put your hands in the air!"

I hesitated. Hadcho told me to stay put, but this was my store. Whatever happened was my responsibility. Besides, maybe I could help.

My legs moved leadenly, but I trotted toward the stock room. I know our store so well, I could zig and zag around our display units. I paused when I got to the door.

"What you going to do? Shoot me? You'll hit her!" came a maniacal cry.

I had to see what was happening. I eased the door open. I momentarily recoiled from the light. I struggled to take in what I was seeing, struggled to make sense of a seemingly incomprehensible scene.

Stan Hadcho stood there, weapon drawn and pointing at the floral delivery man who was hiding behind Bama. Her face was so swollen and deformed that her features were indistinct.

"This is between her and me!" yelled the man. "Get out of here. It's none of your business. It's a domestic case! Leave us alone!"

"Calm down and let her go," said Hadcho firmly.

"She deserves this." The man let Bama slide closer to the floor, a bloody streak marking the path down the front of his shirt and jacket. "It's not about you. I got no quarrel with you."

"Step away from her," repeated Hadcho. "Put your hands in the air."

"Your call." The man laughed and let her drop. She fell with an "oomph." Her assailant stepped to one side and smirked at her bloodied figure.

A thick and wet gurgle came from Bama's throat.

I started toward her.

Quick as a rattlesnake strike, Hadcho reached out with his free hand and stopped me.

"But she can't breathe!" I couldn't stand there and let her die, but I knew from her posture and the noise that she was choking on her own blood.

"Kiki, I told you to stay away," he said tersely.

The man used his foot to give Bama a shove. "She'll be fine," said the man. "I was just teaching Althea not to disrespect me. This is between husband and wife. It's none of your business. You and all those busy-body meddlers. We were doing fine until people like you stuck your noses into our business."

Althea? That must be Bama's real name.

"Put your hands in the air. Step away from

her," repeated Hadcho.

Glaring at Hadcho, the man slowly pushed his hands skyward while taking another small step away from Bama. She gave a shuddering, liquid clogged sigh.

I couldn't help myself. I rushed to her side, sliding my hands under her torso. "Bama? You'll be okay. I'm here. Help's coming."

"Try to turn her onto her side," said Hadcho. At the edge of her mouth, a small dribble of rusty blood bubbled. I worked at rolling her onto her shoulder. I moved very slowly, fearful of hurting her more. Her face swam before my eyes. The texture of her skin was ground up like so much hamburger, as a warm trickle of liquid came from where her nose, eyes, and mouth should be and spilled over my fingers. The feel was sticky and hot and slick.

I was there, concentrating on my co-worker when a hand grabbed my clothes and lifted me to my feet. My fingers flew to my collar, trying to loosen it, trying to get some air. The man shook me like I was a small kitten. My feet danced along the surface of the floor. He set me down a little and I staggered like a drunk. Taking advantage of my unbalance, he threw his arm across my throat to cut off my wind. I panicked, gasping, starving for oxygen, my mouth opening and closing like a beached goldfish. Then I remembered what an instructor said in a self-defense class. I turned my throat toward the crook of the man's elbow and instantly felt less pressure. I couldn't breathe deeply, but I could manage some air.

Then I felt a pinprick of pain under my chin.

"I'll slice her from ear to ear with this box-cutter," Bama's assailant said to Hadcho. "Back off or I'll let her bleed out. See? You want her dead? I didn't think so. Now set your gun down on the floor nice and slow."

I watched Hadcho lean over, his eyes never leaving the man's face, as he gently set his gun on the floor near his own feet. The detective's face was tight, but non-threatening. I could see him making minute calculations, tiny decisions, under a surface that only seemed yielding. Hadcho's warm chocolate eyes had turned flat and cold like frozen rocks.

"Kick your gun over to me." My assailant gave me another upward heave to prove I was under his control.

Hadcho did as he was told. The tip of his burgundy loafer gave the gun a slow, leisurely shove. The weapon glided my way, but stopped a good twelve inches from my toes, instead of my assailant's.

I knew that Hadcho was calculating on the misdirection to buy time. Time for me, time for him, time for this creep to make a mistake.

"Stupid! I told you to kick it to me." With a shudder of rage, the man shook me and poked me with the knife tip. A warm trickle started along my neck. I sputtered, gasping for air, shocked by this violence. The knife tip strayed from my skin. His lips pressed up against my ear and I could smell his sickeningly sweet cologne. "Listen to me, girl. I'm going to give you enough slack to pick that up. Grab it by the barrel. When you've got it, I'm going to have you hand the gun over to me by the muzzle. Try anything and I'll slice your throat before I shoot your friend."

# FORTY-SIX

"Okay," I managed. "I'll do whatever you want. I'm going to get it, but I'll go slowly."

The man had no choice but to move with me. His breath was on my neck, the cloying scent of his fragrance turning my stomach. His weight rested against me so that I could feel the expansion of his lungs. Beating another human being to a paste takes a lot of energy. This man was panting like a boxer who'd gone ten rounds. Except this hadn't been a fair fight. The other "fighter" was a slip of a woman whose life now rested in the balance. A staccato mix of coughing and gargling reminded me, if we couldn't get Bama out of here fast, she'd surely die. No one could survive such a mauling and . . .

I swallowed hard and told myself, concentrate, Kiki. You have to fix this. You can't let this guy have Hadcho's gun! He'll probably shoot Hadcho and take you along for a hostage!

Bama was lying there in a growing puddle of liquid. If she didn't pull through, if she bled to death, how could I live with myself? This was why having her photo in the paper had terrified her. This was why she was so hateful toward men. This was why she'd changed her look.

And I'd told this jerk how to find her. Told him when she worked. Explained he could find her alone!

Why hadn't she told me she was on the run? Why hadn't she warned me?

Then another thought: This was why she never wanted to be friends. She wanted to keep her distance. She wanted to remain a cipher. She had been trying to fly under the radar, trying to stay anonymous so this man couldn't find her.

What was he to her? A husband! How sick was that?

The pool of blood around her was steadily growing. My collar was damp with my own blood.

"Get the gun!" screamed my assailant in my ear.

"Okay, okay," I soothed him.

I started a slow bend toward the gun. This jerk was pressed up against me so tightly I didn't have to use my imagination. I could tell how exciting all this was to him. While I was terrified and sickened, he was thrilled! His body actually trembled as he pulled me closer. This was his idea of a good time.

What would he think of next?

I had one choice and one chance. If I picked up the gun, Hadcho would be defenseless. Bama's husband would be in total control of the detective, Bama, and me.

A soft rattle came from the figure on the floor. Bama's irregular breathing sounded more and more labored. She hadn't moaned, hadn't whimpered. The sticky scent of copper filled the air.

The man changed his grip to accommodate my bending. Now he used his left hand to twist my collar to one side, while he held the knife in his right hand. "You're going to grab that gun, then all of us are taking a little ride."

I reviewed my options. He couldn't have that gun. We couldn't get into that van. I knew the statistics. Knew our chance of survival would diminish dramatically. Whenever a crime moves away from the original site, the victims are more at risk. The perpetrator has more control, but also has more problems, problems that are easy to eliminate.

If we left here, Bama's husband would more than likely kill us and dump our bodies. Our remains might never be found. Poor Anya! She'd go through the same misery as Michelle Gambrowski.

I had to shift the odds. My eyes flickered toward Hadcho's. I think he read the determination in mine not to yield, not to follow directions, and not to give in.

With a blink at the detective, I lowered my head, but I jutted my hips out and away, so that I folded over stiffly at the waist. This forced Bama's attacker to curve his body awkwardly over mine. His left hand kept its purchase on my clothes, but the boxcutter had strayed from my neck. The reach position was ever more difficult for him. As I dipped lower, I subtly shifted my weight from both legs to one. At the low point of our journey, I used my peripheral vision to see where the gun was.

Still ahead of us.

Still beyond my reach.

I moved a smidge lower, absorbing the attacker's weight on my back.

My right leg was slightly off the floor, counterbalancing our weight like a fulcrum.

Thank goodness Bama's husband wasn't a heavy man, and I was strong from all my dog walking and carrying boxes. My back muscles hurt, but I continued my slow progression closer to Hadcho's piece.

Time slowed. I concentrated.

"I'm going to grab for the gun. Just like you told me to do." My voice sounded appropriately terrified, and I mixed in a lot of submission. I came across as meek and cowering, which is exactly what he wanted from me.

I extended my fingers, as if reaching for Hadcho's weapon. But instead of making the grab, I quickly balanced my fingertips on the floor while simultaneously sweeping my free right leg back and sideways. I threw my leg out and wide, as hard as I could.

I surprised him.

I heard a snap.

# FORTY-SEVEN

He screamed.

He lost his grip on my collar.

Out of my peripheral vision, I saw Hadcho make a dive for his gun and pull another piece from somewhere. His pocket? His jacket? It all happened so fast!

Bama's husband collapsed behind me. I was already halfway to the floor so I tucked my head and pulled it tightly to my belly to complete a somersault. I finished by rolling into a tight ball, coming down hard on the back of my shoulders. The move hurt like heck. So much so that I saw stars. But I continued my roll and scrambled to my feet, jumping away from my attacker.

My middle-school gym teacher would have been so proud.

Bama's attacker was on the floor, grabbing his leg and howling. Hadcho raced to his side. The attacker grabbed Hadcho around the feet and knocked him down.

There was a brief scramble for the gun. For a second, Bama's husband had the gun and was shakily pointing toward Hadcho.

I couldn't let that happen.

I was on my knees, by our returns shelf. I jumped up, picked up a large Fiskars Paper Trimmer and bludgeoned the man over the head. I hopped from one side to the other of the struggling men. I scanned the shelves. There was a Crop-a-dile within reach. I grabbed it and smacked the bad guy up the side of the head.

The force sent him reeling backward.

Just for good measure, I smacked him again with the Crop-a-dile.

Those Crop-a-diles are built tough.

The attacker roared in anger. He covered his face with his hands. Instead of coming toward me, he limped toward Hadcho like a mad bull charging.

But Hadcho was ready for him. "Uf," he grunted as he rocked back on his heels. In a neat move, my date sidestepped the attacker, whirled him around and forced him up against a wall. The takedown was almost balletic in its grace.

"You're under arrest," said Hadcho, snapping handcuffs on the man's wrists. The detective cranked the guy's arms up behind him so hard, his shoulder sockets popped.

The guy howled in pain. "You hurt me. My face is bleeding! I think she busted my knee! You dislocated my arms!" he whined.

That was fine by me. He deserved everything he got and more.

I squatted at Bama's side. Her reddened face was still swelling, turning its contours into the smooth surface of an inflated balloon. Her nose was flattened and her lip was split. All distinctiveness blurred as her features were absorbed by the puffery of her wounds.

Fearful of hurting her, I slid my arms around her shoulders and again tried to roll her onto one side so her airway was clear. I worried about her spine, but I figured breathing was the first priority. As I gently turned her, I heard her sigh and stiffen. For a cruel second, I thought she died. I leaned my ear to her lips, "Hang on there, Bama."

"I hate you, Kiki Lowenstein," she whispered.

# FORTY-EIGHT

Well, good. She was alive.

"Hold on, help is coming," I said, patting her shoulder with my free hand. I would have stroked her hair, but there was so much blood I couldn't be sure I wasn't touching split skin. "I called nine-one-one when we came in."

Hadcho talked on his cell phone, with a voice both even and authoritative. I heard something about units en route, and a bus was coming, and something about the front door being unlocked. He also explained they'd be transporting one of us to the emergency room, and he wanted a domestic violence team to meet Bama there.

He said all this as he rested one foot on the back of the attacker. Hadcho now had the attacker on the floor, face down, and the detective was using the sole of one elegant loafer to keep the man prone.

"I'll be out of jail tomorrow," the man on

the floor lifted his head and screamed. "I'll find Althea and finish the job! She can't hide from me! That witch took our kids! She stole my boys from me! And my girl! I'll kill her, I tell you. I'll kill her."

Hadcho squatted low, put one hand between the man's shoulder blades and talked in his ear, "Forget about it, buddy. You are down for the count. You aren't going anywhere. Your social calendar is completely full. Except maybe for a trip or two to solitary confinement and back. I'm going to have you locked up like the sick animal you are. You assaulted a cop, you realize that? You're on the ropes, pal. Beyond the violence you did to that poor woman, you choked Mrs. Lowenstein. You pulled a gun on me. That's not cricket. You're doing major time, pal, major time. See, I know a judge who just hates wife abusers, because she used to be married to one herself. She'll see to it you never see the light of day. Never as in not ever. Look around, pal, because this is the last time for a long time that you're on the outside."

"I've got a jacket in my locker. I'll get it for you." Hadcho helped me remove my once-gorgeous poncho and hand it over for the clerk to book into evidence.

I shivered as I stared at my wrap. Bama's blood had dried on the fabric and turned the once soft knit stiff and smelly. I signed the personal property form, musing how weird this was. A few hours ago, the poncho brought me a measure of happiness. Now, I never wanted to see it again. Things are things, and the joy they bring is incredibly fleeting. What adds to our happiness is the imprint of lovely memories. What blots out our happiness is the lasting stain of tragedy.

"Will she be okay?" I flicked away tears with the back of my sleeve. Bama's ex-husband, Jerald McCallister, had already been processed.

Hadcho's hand was deep in his pockets, turning over his coins, playing his own loose-change version of Jingle Bells. I knew he'd been in contact with the ambulance drivers.

He shrugged. "Depends on what you mean by okay. She'll live through this. I'm pretty sure. The EMTs had her stabilized. The docs are working on her. As for her face, well, who knows? If there's a good plastic surgeon on call, he might be able to patch her up good as new. But, that's no biggie. Not compared to what that creep planned for her. She's got you to thank for being alive. That's all that counts. You did a good job of tossing him to the floor."

"But it's my fault the guy found her!"

Hadcho shook his head, raised an eyebrow, and gave me a gruff, "Huh?"

I explained about the man approaching me in the parking lot a few days earlier. "Then, tonight, I told him the door was unlocked."

"Do you know for sure that it was unlocked?"

"No-oo," I admitted.

"Did you know he was her ex and that he wanted to beat her up?"

"No."

"Did you know she was running from him?"

I shook my head.

He gave a disgusted little "harrumph."

"Look here. First thing I learned as a young cop, perps do what they do because they are bad. They're always looking for an angle, see? A way to cheat? Always. They are predators. They lie in wait while the rest of the world plays by the rules. You can't be blamed because you don't think like Mr. McCallister. Normal people don't. Heck, sometimes we cops don't, either. Remember, I was standing right next to you tonight when this creep asked about her. If I hadn't been so nervous about taking you on a date, maybe I'd have realized there was something hinky going on."

He was nervous? About taking me out?

I rubbed my eyes hard. This was too much for me to absorb. I slumped against the hallway of the jail processing area while he grabbed the jacket for me. He helped me slide my arms into it. "How about we go get that drink? I think we both need it."

The detective and I chatted more on the drive to the casino than on our initial journey. He was upset with himself that he'd given up his gun. "They drill us on this stuff all the time. Never let a bad guy get your weapon, even if he has an innocent in custody."

I noticed his hands were shaking.

"But he had a knife to my throat."

"Right. I made a judgment call. I figured I could get the gun back or use my backup piece, but I had to get that blade away from your skin. All I could think of was Detweiler."

I absorbed this with a bit of shock. "Detweiler?"

"Yeah. He would have killed me if anything happened to you. As it is, he's going to be really ticked."

At Lumière we had one quick drink along with a couple of thick burgers. I asked for a

Seven and Seven. I hadn't had one in years. Hadcho downed two glasses of Jack Daniels, but he showed no signs of being inebriated.

When the waitress came for our food order, I wasn't ready. I usually avoid meat. I wish it didn't come from animals. (I know how silly that sounds, but it's true.) I hate the look of flesh in a skillet. (After Bama's beating, it might be a long, long time before I could see raw hamburger without getting queasy.) I'm not much of a carnivore in the best of times. No matter how I rationalize the act of eating another living creature, it still upsets me. But, at this particular moment I really craved the burger, and at certain times of the month, my body needs the iron.

Hadcho saw me dithering. "You need a decent meal. You look wiped out. Get some protein. Besides, you lost a little blood with that cut on your throat."

I fingered the plastic bandage and gave in. When the food came, I was glad I had. I inhaled the rich aroma of the burger, the heft of it in my hands and relished every morsel. I also enjoyed the surroundings, especially the people watching, although I admit, I could have appreciated it more had not a blanket of exhaustion crept over me. Between the adrenaline fade and the alcohol fog, I was definitely winding down.

Hadcho called the hospital. Bama was in stable condition. They would be moving her into a regular room tomorrow. Relief swept through me. I'd worried through our meal, but hadn't realized it until the tension fell away from my body.

On the way back to my car, which was still at Time in a Bottle's parking lot, Hadcho turned absolutely chatty. He mused aloud about why any man would beat up on a woman. "Of course," he sighed. "It's no excuse but there are times when a spouse really pushes your button. There's no misery like family misery, my dad used to say. Funny how a family member can get under your skin."

I nodded. I thought of my mother and my sister. They both knew exactly how to hurt me, how to turn the tiniest pinprick into a stab wound. "I guess we're the most vulnerable to the people we love. I always think about Star Trek and how they'd lower the shields on the *USS Enterprise*. Once they did, pow! — they could be attacked. Maybe that's how it works with family. We lower our shields. Offer no resistance. They zoom in and . . ." I didn't finish the sentence because I was lost to bad memories, nightmares I worked hard to suppress.

Hadcho was quiet for a minute. "I've been thinking about telling you something, something that's probably none of my business. Certainly not in my best interest."

This piqued my interest. I roused a bit from my stupor. "What?"

"It's about Detweiler."

I snapped to attention, but I tried not to show it. "Okay."

"Not exactly about him, more like about Brenda. See, he was my first partner. Did you know that? I figured you didn't. So he and I have been like this," and he held up two crossed fingers. "I've known Brenda from the start of their relationship. They met when she was an ER nurse."

I said nothing. I figured he was about to lecture me about staying out of their lives, about how I was making trouble in their marriage. To compensate for what I knew was coming, I stared resolutely out the side window. I didn't want him to be able to see my face. I wanted to keep a bit of composure, if I could, and certainly I hoped to hang onto my pride.

What was left of it.

"I still can't figure out why he married her. I think it was because they got thrown together the way people do in our line of work. When she started having trouble with drugs —"

"Drugs?" I was so tired that I had trouble following.

"Right. Brenda's into drugs. Has been for quite a while. She turned herself in once, and the nursing union has this program where if you turn yourself in, they will help you get straightened out. No harm, no foul. But druggies usually take several tries at rehab to get it right."

The night was so dark, the lights so sparse. A world of shadows, of hidden intent and obscured shapes, was right outside my window. How indistinct. How unknowable. Hadcho shed a light on one portion of this puzzle. One portion of my own corner of the world, a place formerly occluded from my vision. I thought I knew what motivated her. I thought I understood why Chad Detweiler had been so concerned about his wife abusing me.

Maybe Brenda Detweiler had been high when she shook me. I hadn't exaggerated the situation. In fact, I'd minimalized it. She could have killed me or any other patient in the hospital. She hadn't been in her right mind! She shouldn't have been walking around, seemingly giving us care. Having access to more drugs! No wonder Detweiler had told me I shouldn't have covered for her.

I hadn't done anyone any favors.

Not myself. Not Brenda. And certainly not Detweiler.

# FORTY-NINE

*Saturday, December 19*
*3rd Day of Hanukkah*

Monroe and I definitely were falling in love. The big-eyed donkey nickered appreciatively when he saw me coming. In turn, I always took the time to scratch him around his long ears. This morning, I'd visited him before the sun was up. He pressed his forehead into my hand and snorted. I took that for a "Glad to see you. How's tricks?" I told him all about Bama and the horror of the night before. I lay awake most of the night rehashing the fight. The effect of the alcohol wore off quickly, leaving me despondent and headachy.

Hadcho had lingered at my doorstep. Not willing to encourage him, I hurried inside after mumbling a "thank you." Only after his car roared away did I remember I was wearing the man's coat.

*Stupid, Kiki*, I told myself. *Here you were*

*thinking he was angling for a kiss and all he wanted was his jacket.*

I arrived at Time in a Bottle early. After I got the dogs settled, I cracked a can of Diet Dr Pepper and tackled the bloodstains in the backroom. I had to stop a couple of times and splash cold water on my face so I didn't upchuck. I was there on the floor on my hands and knees when Horace walked in. He studied what was left of the stain, covered his eyes, pinched his nose, and said, "Cleaning up after Bama, right? I told Dodie she needed to tell you of her situation. We argued about it. My darling won, but now Dodie's embarrassed to face you."

"Tell me what?" I rocked back on my heels. With scrub brush in hand, the scene brought to mind that one from Snow White. All I needed to do was burst into that "ah-ha-ha-haaaaaa" aria, and I'd be mimicking one of the most disastrous heroines of all time. I mean, really, she's the heir to a throne and instead of hiring a good lawyer, she scrubs and sings in the courtyard. Foolish, foolish girl. I have a hunch she encouraged a whole generation of women to act like victims.

Horace pulled up the stock stool and perched on it. "Dodie is part of a network called WAR, which stands for the Women's

308

Aboveground Railroad. These volunteers help abused women find new lives."

"Bama was one of their, um, projects?"

"Oy, vey." His tears were wet. "This monster has pursued her throughout five states. Threatening their children. Beating her and leaving her for dead."

So I was right. RJ, Harley, and Virginia were Bama's kids, not Katie's.

"Dodie gave her a job and helped her settle here?"

"Yes. My darling did all this. I told her that you deserved to know. She felt it was risky."

"She worried that I'd let it slip. That I'd blab about Bama."

He turned his gaze away, and he twiddled his thumbs, rotating them rapidly one around the other.

I started to get angry. I could see where this was going. "Or worse. Dodie thought that because I didn't like Bama, I'd be careless. That I'd tell others about her fix. Isn't that it, Horace? Dodie didn't trust me!"

He spread his fingers wide. "She took the situation very seriously. They all take a vow not to share details, because a leak could be fatal. These are women in flight, women whose lives are overshadowed by relentless pursuit. Families at risk. Endangered by the very men who are supposed to cherish and care for them!"

The implication was clear: I couldn't be trusted to keep my mouth shut. Heat spread around my collar. I pulled at it with my fingers, parting my blouse where today's collar rubbed against the abrasion from the night before.

"What happened to you?" Horace said. "Your neck, it is hurt?"

"What happened to me was Bama's husband."

Horace muttered in Yiddish. I didn't understand most of it, but I caught *meshugana* and a few other words. "Tell me what happened last night. All we know is that Mr. McCallister attacked his wife again. That a detective happened upon the scene. You were here? Involved?"

As calmly as I could, I rewound and replayed the scenario. With each word, Horace's shoulders drooped more heavily. Finally, he covered his eyes and shook his head. "A nightmare. A catastrophe. Kiki, I am so sorry that you were involved."

"If I had known, I might have prevented it. I might have called the cops the first time he came by. Horace, if I hadn't left behind my wallet, Bama would be dead today. This mess? You can't tell it now, but there was a lot of blood. All over. And the situation could have been even worse. Her husband turned Detective Hadcho's gun on him!

"Yes, my neck is hurt. He tried to slice my throat. I guess you two didn't hear about that, did you? Well, that was what happened before Jerald McCallister tried to load us in his van and take us goodness knows where. Great plan Dodie had. You can tell her I said so. We could have all been killed. But trusting me was a problem? Let's recap here: I can be trusted with your business, I can trust you with my money as a minor partner, but I'm not to be trusted about Bama's past. Nice!"

He stood to apologize, his hands waving in the air, but I couldn't take any more. "Please go," I said. "I have to finish cleaning up this mess, and I'm responsible for the store today, of course. I appreciate that you are trying to be kind to me, Horace, but I'm pretty upset and I'd like some time alone."

Two years ago when my husband died, I would have never had the courage to ask someone else to leave. I guess I've learned a bit about taking care of myself. I've learned that it's my duty to say when I've had enough, when I can't go on. It was smarter and better for me to ask Horace to leave

311

than for me to struggle any longer.

I kept my head down and concentrated on the stained linoleum. When I stood up again, Horace was gone.

# FIFTY

Clancy came in an hour after we opened. "Dodie called me," she said. "You okay?"

I gave her a curt nod. "I guess."

Clancy reached for me and gave me a long hug and whispered, "You saved her life. Bama should be thankful to you."

That almost brought me to tears. "But I told her ex where to find her!"

"No, you didn't. He was searching for her, and when her photo appeared in the paper, he knew where she was. That photo wasn't your fault. You didn't dump a body part in your own trash, did you? So you're okay, and she's alive. Thank goodness for small favors, right. Now, what I can do for you? Make you coffee? Brought you a Kaldi's vanilla latte."

"That's perfect. I could use a heaping dose of caffeine to help me make it through the day."

"So will a spoonful of Sally Sunshine.

Laurel's on her way. Your phone must be turned off. She wanted to come help out. I filled her in on what happened."

Dressed in black jeans tucked into tall black boots and topped off with a cherry red turtleneck, Laurel looked like the type of helper Santa would have if the North Pole switched places with the Playboy Mansion. Threaded through her earlobes were tiny gold bells, much like Mert always wore. In fact, she was a lot like Mert in her mannerisms as well. Laurel gave me a more restrained hug. "It's going to be all right. We're here now."

The three of us worked as a well-oiled team. Both Laurel and Clancy proved resourceful and good at up-selling. At 1 p.m. we took a quick break for lunch. Clancy passed out sandwiches she made at home the night before. I sure appreciated her thoughtfulness. We caught each other up on what we'd sold, and Laurel took a quick inventory. "I'll restock the shelves, but I figured it's best if we direct people to the items we have plenty of."

Smart thinking. She came back right away with bad news: Two Cricut cassettes were missing. Clancy muttered a curse word, then called Detective Hadcho. "They have a warrant for the stolen materials," said

Clancy as she hung up. "Sounds like they'll be picking up our shoplifter later today."

"Not a moment too soon," said Laurel. "I could have sold one of those cartridges an hour ago."

When the mid-afternoon lull hit we were back on the floor, working hard. I was restocking paper when Detweilers Junior and Senior walked through the front door, with Anya in tow. I was shocked to see my daughter with them, but I didn't get a chance to ask what was up.

The first words out of Detective Chad Detweiler's mouth were, "Stan Hadcho said you were all right. I wanted to see for myself. That was a close call."

"I'm okay," I said tentatively. My neck was getting stiffer by the hour, and my shoulder muscles were starting to hurt where I'd hit the floor hard. Clancy had learned that Bama was in a regular hospital room, which indicated she was on the road to recovery of sorts. Her sister Katie was with her. I took all that as a good sign.

The nearness of Detweiler suddenly caused me to feel weepy. I wanted to throw my arms around his neck and sob, to tell him how scared I'd been and how bad I felt about the beating. But the presence of Detweiler Senior and my own child fortified my own sense of propriety. Whatever I knew about his wife, it didn't give me permission to overrule their marital vows. Sure, he had a problem. A problem named Brenda, and she was engaging in risky, illegal behavior. But that didn't mean I could throw caution to the winds and assume he'd leave her.

In fact, knowing Detweiler, it meant he'd stay until the bitter end. He wasn't a quitter. His loyalty was both his strong suit and his stumbling block. If she was getting help — and I prayed she would because I'd seen firsthand how an addiction could ruin someone's life — he owed it to her to be supportive.

So instead of following my heart, which hung on his every glance, which waited for a sign that he'd welcome my hug, I straightened my shoulders and took a step away from Detweiler.

I was processing all this when I realized that my daughter was also hanging back, looking everywhere but straight at me. Usually she greeted me with a hug.

What was going on?

"Anya, I thought you were with Nicci Moore," I said. "When I called earlier, Jennifer said she'd dropped the two of you off at the mall."

"May I speak to you in private?" asked

Detweiler Junior.

Uh oh. I recognized his tone of voice. We had a problem.

Anya's lower lip stuck out a good yard and a half. She cast a baleful look his way. "Let me come, too."

"I want to speak with your mom away from her customers. Since this concerns you, you are welcome to listen in," said the hunky detective.

We all marched back to the stock room. Detweiler Senior followed in tow, carrying a large white plastic garbage bag with a cylindrical bulge. "I have this gizmo for your dog's tail. Could one of your friends hold her head while I tape it on?"

I stuck my head out the stock room door, waved Laurel over, and asked her to help him.

Inside the small office with the door closed, Detweiler seemed uncomfortably large, his long legs bumping the front of the desk as he sat down. He wore a cranberry red v-neck sweater and a pink button-down collar shirt with a simple pair of slacks. His expression was anything but cheery.

What in the world was up?

Anya took a seat next to him, but I noticed she leaned as far from him as was humanly possible while defying the laws of gravity. I swallowed hard. Any problem involving my kid worries the heck out of me.

"Dad and I were shopping at the mall when I saw Anya. She and her friend Nicci were being teased by a group of boys. I know it's not really my place to interfere, but the boys were being inappropriate. They might have been teasing, but they were disrespectful and —"

"Excuse me? You're talking about disrespect? You're the one who's married and who kept hanging around my mom!" She hopped up out of the chair and pointed at Detweiler. "You're telling me how to act? Huh? That's a good one."

I gripped the arms on my chair to keep from falling off. I couldn't believe what my daughter had just said. "Anya, apologize right this minute. You don't speak to an adult like that."

"I won't apologize!" she yelled.

Merry Christmas. What a nut cluster this was turning into.

"Kiki, this is my fault." Detweiler rubbed his chin, as a tired expression crept over his face.

I have to admit, I was a bit shocked and curious about what he meant. I leaned forward as he continued, "Anya's got a point. Sit down, Anya, because I owe you an apology first, then I owe one to your mom. You see, my wife had left me when I met your mother. I intended to tell your mom what was up, but I lied to myself. I kept my mouth shut and I should have been more honest. That was disrespectful, and I'm sorry for it. Your mother didn't tell you what happened because she was keeping a confidence after I explained it to her. That put her in a tough spot. You both have every right to be upset with me. That said, Anya, I hope you'll still think of me as a friend. I wouldn't let anyone talk that way to one of my sisters, and it made me mad to hear them talking that way to you."

"You think of me like a sister?" Anya's eyes were bright as she sank back down into the chair. With her gangly legs in purple tights, her cute black mini-skirt and her big turtleneck, she seemed more like an adorable pixy than a real, living child.

"Of course, I do. I've always been overly protective of my sisters. Listen, kiddo, you can't let guys talk that way to you. Even if they are seniors and have cars. Make them treat you right. Guys will like you more for it. Trust me. On this, I'm an expert." With that he threw up his hands in a gesture of surrender and gave her a goofy, heart-melting grin.

"I'm not sure that I agree."

"That's fine," he said. "You think about it. And pay attention. You'll see that I'm right."

She smirked that devilish smirk of hers that always preceded a smart remark. "You sure put a scare into those seniors."

He hooted with laughter. "I sure did. They'll think twice about talking to any girl the way they did to you and Nicci."

She drew a line on the floor with the toe of her new Uggs. "I have to say, I didn't like it much. I mean, I didn't like the things they were saying. I think they were just showing off to each other. That's how rappers talk. But when you really, really listen, it sort of gives you the creeps."

Detweiler reached for her hand and gave it a squeeze. "Trust your gut, Anya. There's a reason you didn't like it. If stuff doesn't feel right, pay attention. Now, let's see how my dad is doing with Gracie."

# FIFTY-ONE

Detweiler the Elder stepped back to admire his handiwork. A length of white plastic tubing about a foot long covered the sore spot on Gracie's tail. The edges of the plastic sheath were taped to her skin with duct tape.

"Eh-yeah, inside there's sort of a lightweight foam donut serving as a bumper or spacer. I taped those down first. I split this old wiffle ball bat I found in the grandkids' toys lengthwise and wrapped it around the tail. I think it'll absorb the banging and give the skin a chance to heal. The young lady here —" and he gestured toward Laurel "— cleaned up that nasty spot with warm towels. She was a big help holding your dog's head so I could mess about with my invention."

Laurel smiled, looking every bit as beatific as an angel on the top of a tree.

I thanked her and Louis Detweiler profusely. Like his son, he was wearing a v-neck

sweater, but his was navy. When the two Detweilers stood side-by-side, you could tell
they were father and son, an older and
younger rendition of the same basic facial
features.

Laurel excused herself to wait on customers.

Detweiler Senior cleared his throat. "You
know, Anya, I've got a granddaughter same
age as you. Her name's Emily. She's having
a sleepover tonight at the farm. I took the
liberty of asking, and you'd be welcome to
join her and her friends. In fact, we could
even bring your friend Nicci if you'd like. I
checked with my wife and she said the more
the merrier. Since my little girls have grown
up, I miss the sound of their laughter in our
house. My wife does, too."

Anya hesitated. She's not really shy, but
she can hang back as I often do.

Louis Detweiler noticed her reticence and
threw in the coup de grace: "My wife said
one of our barn cats will probably have her
kittens tonight. You don't suppose you'd like
to see those babies, would you? They're
small as mice and blind as fence posts, but
they're still pretty dang amazing."

That was all she wrote. If Anya noticed
the bandage on my throat, she didn't say
anything. I was grateful. She didn't need to

know what had happened here the night before.

I imagine she was just self-absorbed. That was certainly age-appropriate behavior. It was also a reminder that someday soon, she would be grown up, off to college, and no longer a part of my daily routine. I fought back those thoughts and listened in as Anya called Nicci to issue the extended invitation. I spoke to Nicci's mom, Jennifer Moore, and everything was settled. The girls would go home to Illinois with the Detweilers this evening and come back to town late tomorrow night. Chad Detweiler would be attending the memorial service for Cindy Gambrowski, but Louis Detweiler was coming back to St. Louis anyway and would be happy to drop Anya off.

There was just the matter of a change of clothes for Anya. The Detweiler men would take Anya by our house to pick up a few things and then drop by the Moores' house to pick up Nicci.

"Mr. Detweiler, tonight's the third night of Hanukkah," said my daughter. "Would you mind if I lit the candles and said a prayer at your house? I mean, you don't have to pay any attention, and I could just go off on my own. I missed doing it last night because of the school dance, but my dad and I always did it together, and . . ." her voice turned husky, "I miss it."

My throat tightened with an indescribable pain wholly unrelated to the rough treatment I'd received last night from Jerald McCallister. In the hustle and bustle of working so many hours, I'd let my daughter down. I'd lost track of the days, and I hadn't set aside time to light the candles. This was one of the traditions she and her father loved most, and I had dropped the ball.

I'd been too busy earning a living to live my life.

I covered my mouth with a trembling hand. How long could I go on like this? My kid needed me, and I was spending every waking hour trying to hold body and soul together. Dodie's illness, Bama's injuries, the holidays, all combined to keep me here selling supplies for other people's memories. Meanwhile, I was neglecting making my own.

I felt indescribably sad. My child needed me and I was missing in action. Detweiler the Elder's smile toward her was so kindly, so genuine that I knew he was speaking from his heart when he said to Anya, "Young lady, I've always wanted to know more about that holiday. I'd be proud for you to tell us all about it. Can you do that?"

# FIFTY-TWO

The rest of the day went by quickly. Clancy noticed the stiffness in my neck and said, "You probably should see a doctor or a chiropractor. Bama's ex sure gave you a mean fake sunburn, and I can see you're in pain."

I thanked her, but that wouldn't work. I mean, seriously, what were my choices? To go home alone and let our recent hires run the store by themselves? To take time off during the busiest season of the year? If I made a trip to a hospital, my first priority should be checking up on Bama, but I couldn't muster up the courage. Not yet at least.

As for getting my neck looked at, it was simply out of the question. I don't have health insurance. My budget couldn't stretch to cover more medical bills. Without Bama's input, I had no idea how we were doing as far as our bottom line.

I remembered a Vicodin in a drawer in Dodie's desk. She'd tucked it away after having a root canal. "It's a good thing to keep it handy," she'd announced. "Half a pill is just enough to take the edge off of pain."

Downing that pharmaceutical along with a can of Diet Dr Pepper, I returned to the business at hand. If we were going to close part of the day tomorrow for Cindy Gambrowski's memorial service, I had a lot of work to do.

There was a lull in the evening, so I asked Laurel to see where we were with the votes for our "All about Me" pages. This proved utterly unsatisfactory because we had a three-way tie. Our winners were Rita Romano, Harriet Sabloski, and Cindy Gambrowski.

"I guess you get to cast the deciding vote," said Laurel.

"How about you and Clancy vote."

Clancy groaned. "All three of us can vote. Here, write your choice on a slip of paper."

We each did and pushed the torn pieces into the center of the table. Laurel opened them one at a time. "Still a three-way tie."

She smiled at me, showing that lovely dimple. "Guess it's up to you, Kiki."

My neck hurt too much to shake my head.

Instead I heaved a mighty sigh and said, "Isn't it always? Lately?"

Clancy patted my shoulder. "Feeling a mite sorry for ourselves, are we? I suppose that's to be expected. You're having a tough holiday season, but then aren't they all? I get sick of this 'fa-la-la-la-la' attitude and the fantasy that the holiday spirit will make everything perfect. Certainly, you hope people will rejoice in the spirit and be extra kind to each other, but I suspect the elevated stress levels counterbalance any and all attempts at goodwill toward men."

"In other words, ho-ho-ho-humbug?" Laurel teased Clancy gently. Turning to me, she added, "Considering what you walked in on last night, I think you're handling yourself pretty well. That must have been gruesome."

"I can't get the image of Bama's beaten face out of my mind. She was so pulverized. I mean, that's the only word that adequately describes what that monster did to her."

"And to you," said Laurel. "I propose a new rule. We lock up all the boxcutters when we aren't using them."

"Here, here," said Clancy. "What happened last night would be enough to make you swear off men for good."

"Not me," said Laurel. "I love men. But

I'm a big believer in being picky."

She had that right.

Ten minutes later, the Vicodin kicked in. My neck quit hurting and my body surrendered to a lovely, careless, floating feeling.

*No wonder Brenda Detweiler does drugs,* I thought. I could get used to this.

# FIFTY-THREE

"Mom, we got here just in time to see the kittens being born. They are so cute! One is all gray with a pink nose. Can I have him, huh? I mean, he's not old enough yet, but in six weeks, maybe? Please?"

I couldn't remember when I've heard Anya so excited. "Could we talk about it more when you get home?"

"Mrs. Detweiler said I needed to think hard about it. I know pets are a big responsibility, but Mom, he's so cute! The mama cat licked my kitten all over. His fur is sticking up so he's got this awesome Mohawk. And his eyes are closed so he can't see how adorable he is."

I laughed. "Use your best manners, sweetie. I'm glad you are having a good time."

"Oh, Mom, this is just the best. When I grow up, I want to live on a farm. The Detweilers said I can visit anytime I want!"

I hummed a Christmas carol as I organized our shelves. After six o'clock, the place was nearly empty. Laurel had gone home. Clancy was collecting her things, and I was ready to step out with her. "After last night, I'm feeling a bit spooked," I admitted.

"Not that anyone in his right mind would attack a woman guarded by all those dogs," said Clancy with a snicker as Jasper and Fluff ran around us in circles.

They were a pretty rambunctious lot, I had to admit. Petunia's shyness was slowly dissipating as he played with her friends. Fluff was getting tired out by Jasper. Izzy had taken to riding around in the pocket of my craft apron. His head bounced along as he took in his surroundings. He was such a good boy.

Gracie was her placid self. I resisted the urge to peel open her wiffle bat tail cover and see how she was doing. I sure hoped Detweiler Senior's gizmo would help her heal. I could love her with or without that big tail of hers, but I hated the thought of her going through surgery and more pain.

*Sunday, December 20*
*4th Day of Hanukkah*
The next day was busy. Even so, I closed the store early so we could all go to Cindy

Gambrowski's memorial service. We piled into Clancy's Mercedes sedan. Since my poncho was still at the police station — and it might never come clean — and my winter coat stunk like cat pee when it got overheated, I grabbed a sweater, tossed a warm shawl over my shoulders and hoped the trek from parking lot to funeral home wouldn't be a long one.

Our feet made muffled sounds on the way to a designated room. At the front was a collection of obviously very expensive photo portraits on easels. None of them were of Cindy alone. All of them included Ross.

Several of our store customers had arrived before we did. How odd it seemed to see so many of our clientele dressed in such somber colors. Most of our customers love the bright shades of card-stock and patterned paper, and their choice of clothes reflects the same. Today, these women had donned subdued colors. Mainly black, but a sprinkling of gray or navy showed up, too. It occurred to me that this wasn't so much a celebration of Cindy's life as heavy mourning for the torture she'd endured. By now, the newspaper articles hinted at Ross Gambrowski's beatings, citing "domestic disturbances." A few family friends had come forward to admit they'd seen Cindy with black eyes and bruises. Another friend spoke anonymously about calling the police once after watching Ross drag Cindy out of a car by her hair. Slowly, the public was turning on Ross in the manner that a pack of angry wolves surrounds a former alpha male, taking a nip here and there, drawing blood, slicing through tendons, and waiting for the perfect moment to finish him off.

Ross and Michelle walked in seconds before the service began. The young woman stood several feet away from her dad. She angled her body away from his, too, by slightly turning her back on him.

Detweiler slipped into the pew beside me. Out of the corner of my eye, I saw Hadcho squeeze into a seat a couple rows up.

Detweiler and I sat with a respectful distance between us. Even so, his presence comforted me. We listened to one woman after another eulogize Cindy. They spoke of her love of cooking, the joy she took in decorating her home, and her affection for her daughter. The twelve-thousand-pound elephant in the room was her relationship with Ross. No one mentioned that Cindy was married. No one suggested that Cindy loved her husband. The minister chose readings about life after death and about life's seasons. If the crowd had gathered to see high drama, it wasn't happening. People began to shift around, nervously, as time wore on.

A woman with a striking resemblance to Cindy walked to the podium and opened a sheet of paper. She started reading from it, never lifting her eyes. "I'm Cindy's sister Mindy. Ross Gambrowski was Cindy's first love. He was a good provider and husband. Ross helped my husband get started in the roofing business. Ross also gave our daddy a job when he needed one. Ross has been very generous to our family. When our brother Jason lost his job, Ross put him on the payroll as a contractor. So, um, I wanted to tell all of you that Cindy was really lucky. She didn't want for anything. Ross was the best husband she could ever hope to have."

With that, Mindy looked up from the paper toward Ross, clearly asking for his approval.

He nodded.

She sat down.

A chill settled over the crowd. That was quickly replaced by a hush of excitement as Michelle walked to the podium. Once there, she withdrew a piece of torn notebook paper from a pocket and smoothed it flat with shaking hands.

"My mom loved me. She did everything

she could to keep me . . . to take care of me. She supported me when I wanted to go away to college. She told me how important it was to have your own career. She said education and a good job meant freedom. No one will ever know . . ." Michelle started to sob.

A young woman about Michelle's age hopped up and ran to the girl's side. She hugged Michelle, crumpling the jacket of Michelle's navy-blue suit, and took the sheet of paper. Once the friend found her place, she continued on Michelle's behalf, "Mom would do anything in her power to have me live a better life. Anything. She would give up anything. I know that now. She was the best mom anyone could ever have. I will miss her more than I can ever say. But I am comforted by the fact that Mom's in a better place. A place where no one and nothing can ever hurt her again!"

With her friend's shoulder to cry on, Michelle drew in a shuddering sob, and then righted herself. She managed to choke out, "Thank you all for coming. Mom would have been surprised to see so many of you. She didn't realize she had so many friends."

That last comment sat like a big stinker over the group. I could see people drop their heads in shame. The message, though veiled, was obvious: Where had all of us been when Cindy was alive?

# FIFTY-FOUR

I swallowed a lump in my throat. I wondered if Cindy had dared reach out for help. If so, who among these people had turned away?

What had I missed? I read her journaling, and she always wrote about how perfect her life was.

Then it came to me: That was the irony. She was writing about the appearance of her life, not about the reality.

I hadn't understood. If I had, could I have helped her?

At least Dodie knew how to help a woman in need. I surely didn't! Dodie had given Bama a new start and a new life. I wondered how my boss had become involved in the rescue organization? I wanted to know more. Scratch that: I needed to know more. I vowed to learn more about the signs of abuse, to put up posters about it in our store bathroom, and to find out what I could do to help. In fact, I would start by adding information to my "All About Me" class handouts. That way, as women reflected on their lives, they could decide for themselves if they were victims of abuse, and certainly they could note the warning signs.

Michelle started to shuffle away from the podium, and the minister rose from his seat to replace her. But before the man could take his spot at the lectern, Ross Gambrowski leaped to his feet. The man next to him grabbed at Ross and said, "Sit down," loudly enough for most of us to hear. We watched the pantomime as two men in impeccable suits struggled with each other.

Ross angrily brushed the man's hand aside.

Detweiler leaned close to me and whispered, "That guy? With Mr. Gambrowski? He's Thomas Collins, a criminal defense attorney. The best in town. He's representing Gambrowski."

Collins put a staying hand on Ross Gambrowski's forearm. The attorney glared at Ross and repeated, "Sit down!"

Ross shook him off like a horse does an irritating fly. "Leave me alone! I'm going to speak my piece, and you can't stop me!"

Collins said, "As your counsel, I warn you —"

Ross didn't care. A big man, almost a giant, he took up a lot of space there in the front of the room, as he turned to us and bellowed, "I loved Cindy very much! She was mine! She would never leave me! Someone did this to her, and I'm going to find him! I want her back! You hear me? She was my woman, mine! I made her everything she was! I kept her in line, and we were married for all time. None of you understood that. None of you! You were all just jealous. Jealous because you couldn't have her! We had our problems, but it was her and me against the world! She knew that!"

"Come on, let's go," the attorney nodded to another man. Together they strong-armed Ross Gambrowski, one on each side. Ross was still shouting as they pushed him down into his seat.

I thought I was going to be sick. I put a hand up over my mouth and concentrated on keeping my lunch down. I'd heard all this before. Years ago, O.J. Simpson spoke about Nicole Brown's murder: "If I did it, I must have loved her a lot, didn't I?" Here we were, nearly twenty years later, listening to the same self-absorbed, petulant, narcissistic rant of ownership.

At least, that was my take on it. Maybe the other mourners saw it differently. The rest of the crowd put their heads together and murmured. Whether they truly felt sympathy or they recognized his comments for what they were, I don't know.

Ross Gambrowski's speech wasn't a eulogy; it was a tantrum.

# FIFTY-FIVE

I shivered uncontrollably.

The minister read one more prayer and then, with a glance at Ross, he read Psalm 45. Maybe it was my imagination, but he seemed to stumble over a few of the lines:

*Forget your people and your family far away*
*For your royal husband delights in your*
*beauty; honor him, for he is your lord.*

The mood in the room shifted from uncomfortable to disgusted. I twitched with restlessness. Did the other mourners hear what I had heard? Could they also pinpoint the obsessive strand of ownership that ran through Ross Gambrowski's speech and other elements of the service?

I hoped so. I hoped the community would turn its collective back on Ross.

But I doubted it. Society has a very short memory. Besides, now Ross had a new role to play: grieving widower.

Unless the law enforcement community

could nail his butt to a tree, Ross would move on. Probably even find another "Cindy" that he could mold, abuse, and discard.

Really, the only difference between Ross and Jerald McCallister was money. Because Ross had money, he had been able to keep up his abuse and control his wife. Jerald simply lacked the resources to keep Bama — Althea? — under his thumb.

Bile rose in my mouth.

I wasn't a sworn officer of the law. I wasn't an attorney. Or a social worker.

How could I make sure that Cindy's killer didn't get away with her murder? What weapons did I have in my arsenal to turn Ross Gambrowski's self-serving speech about his love into my personal call to action?

There was one other consideration: What if Ross didn't do it? Maybe he was a wife-beater, a narcissistic jerk, but was he a murderer?

I didn't know.

"It's okay," Detweiler said, reaching over to give my hand a quick squeeze. "We're going to get him. We're onto his tricks. He won't get away with this."

"What's stopping you?"

"Concrete information. We can't depend

341

on country club gossip. We need proof. Dates of beatings. Photos of Mrs. Gambrowski's injuries. Doctor's records. Emergency room visit records. Right now all we have is hearsay."

"Is this because you don't have a body? *Corpus delicti?*" I recalled the term from a mystery novel. "That means you can't charge him, right?"

"No. *Corpus delicti* means the body of the crime, not a human body. But, yes, we have a *corpus delicti* problem, because we don't have evidence that a prosecutor could use to prove the murder beyond a reasonable doubt."

We filed out the back of the room. The funeral parlor's staff tried to direct us into a receiving line. They set up stanchions with velvet ropes, leading to the spot where Ross Gambrowski reached out to shake hands and corral supporters. But the greater mass of mourners walked around the man, like pedestrians maneuvering around a drunk on a sidewalk.

By the time we were even with Cindy's husband, Ross Gambrowski stood alone, avoided by the press of visitors. He reached out to people, called out names, and pushed forward with his hand outstretched, but the mourners surged away from him en masse as if he might contaminate them.

Except for his hired help or those who were direct recipients of his largesse, everyone was onto the man. Ross Gambrowski might claim publicly to love his wife, but he didn't. That wasn't love. All of us knew it, even if Ross had confused possession with affection. Ross wasn't mourning. Oh, no. He was ticked over the loss of his property. Cindy was nothing more to him than that. Nothing. Ironically, the speech he'd given to proclaim his innocence had done exactly the opposite; it had exposed his guilt.

All Detweiler needed was evidence. Who among us could supply that?

I thought about the message sent to the police. Somewhere out there was a sender who believed I knew more than I did. I played with a button on my sweater. Or could it be that the sender had also supplied me with information, but I'd overlooked the hints?

After all, wasn't my attention divided sixty-zillion ways?

I gritted my teeth. At the foot of the steps leading from the funeral home to the parking lot, Laurel and Clancy waited.

"We'll see you tomorrow, bright and early," said Laurel. She was wearing a sleek mid-calf leather duster and a fluffy scarf.

Clancy added, "I'll bring in a crockpot of chili for our customers. In fact, I was thinking about sending out a Constant Contact blast announcing that we'd serve lunch if they wanted to hang around and shop."

"Brilliant idea," I said. Honest to Pete, these two were dynamos. Their new energy had to be helpful to our sales.

Hadcho caught up to us. "A couple of officers just arrested your shoplifter. Caught her with merchandise from two other local independent scrapbook stores as well. Does the name Daisy Touchette sound familiar?"

I gawped. "I can't believe that! She has kids! I helped her by watching them, and how'd she repay me? By stealing our stuff! I'd like to wring her neck. That's so unfair."

Hadcho and Detweiler exchanged looks. Hadcho said, "Yeah, it's a cheap shot, but she must have thought she could get away with it. I'll get the merchandise back to you next week."

"Drat. Not in time for us to sell it," I mused.

"Nope."

"Let me know what you need me to do, if anything."

"What's the situation with Jerald McCallister?" asked Detweiler. "You have an airtight case against him?" There was a challenge in his voice, a sort of "why didn't you protect Kiki?" tone to his voice.

"The dope pulled a gun on me. Kiki witnessed it. He also took a swipe at me. He'll be sitting out the season for sure, and if I can get Judge Van de Wenter to hear the case, McCallister will be sitting in the penalty box for a long, long time." Hadcho raised an eyebrow. "You made any progress on the Gambrowski situation?"

"We're building a solid case. I don't intend to let him slip through our fingers. We're doing the grunt work, following up on all our leads," said Detweiler coolly. "As you probably noticed, several of us were here to check out the crowd."

Right. What was the deal with these two? They were acting like two stray dogs staking out their territory.

Hadcho's eyes narrowed. "I showed up to make sure Mrs. Lowenstein was okay. If Mr. Gambrowski didn't put that leg in their trash, someone else did. Until you can prove he did it, she's at risk."

"Laurel? Clancy? You ready to go? I promised to pick up my daughter in half an hour," I said.

Whatever problems these men were having, it was none of my business or concern. There was nothing more I could do for

345

Cindy Gambrowski right now. First thing tomorrow, I was going to look at her scrapbook pages in a whole new light. I planned to take the layouts apart, to tear the whole store to pieces if necessary, looking for evidence that would send Ross Gambrowski away.

# FIFTY-SIX

I picked up Anya from her grandmother's house. Because I had a car full of dogs, I called from the driveway and asked my daughter to come outside.

Okay, I was also dodging Sheila. I figured she'd give me an earful about letting Anya go to the Detweilers' farm. I could do without the hassle.

I rested my forehead on the steering column, closed my eyes and waited for my child.

A sharp rapping woke me up.

"Roll down your window," shouted Sheila.

Her wish was my command. I struggled to put a pleasant smile on my face.

"Heard you tangled with Bama's ex-husband," said my darling m-i-l. She stood all cozy and comfie in her full-length brown mink. Harry gave it to her years ago, and I must admit, Sheila could double as an aging movie star in that big pelt.

I only hoped that the minks had been suicidal before they were turned into outerwear.

"Yes," I said.

"Yes? That's all?"

"Yes," I said.

"He cut your neck?"

"Right." Wasn't the bandage obvious? I sighed and bit my tongue before wiping my nose. Dang, it was like my cold briefly went on holiday and came back bigger, stronger, and meaner. I did not have the energy to tangle with Sheila. Not today.

"I saw Dodie at temple Friday night. She plans to help out at the store this week."

"Good." Honestly, I hadn't kept up with Dodie's schedule. I was still miffed at her for keeping Bama's little "problem" a secret from me. In the end, it was better not to plan for her help than to hope for it.

"Your daughter can't stop talking about those fool kittens in the Detweiler's barn. You aren't going to let her have one, are you? I told her she couldn't. Told her it would be just one more mouth for you to feed. Ridiculous! Besides you already have problems with cat pee and clothing."

*Thank you, Sheila,* I said to myself. *I love how you leave the big decisions to me.*

"You've got a date on Tuesday with Ben

Novak, right?"

"Yes." I blew my nose. I figured it might make Sheila back away.

It didn't.

"I don't need to tell you he's going to move on if you don't give him some encouragement. You'll lose him, Kiki, and he's a fine catch."

*Oh, good, just what I need. I can't add a cat to our lives, but I need to scoop up this "fine catch." I bet Ben'd just love to hear himself described like a jar of gefilte fish.*

"I don't think that will happen." I saw Anya stop on her way to my car as Linnea, Sheila's maid, called to her. I watched the chocolate-skinned elderly woman hand over an insulated grocery bag and give Anya a hug. With pride swelling inside me, I saw my daughter hug Linnea back and give the woman a peck on the cheek. I raised my hand and waved at Linnea.

"Thank you," I called to Sheila's maid. I had a small gift wrapped for her, a photo of her and Anya, heads bent over a cooking project. I planned to bring it over later this week.

Maybe Hillary Clinton was right: It does take a village to raise a child. Linnea, Mert and Roger, Dodie, the Moores, Clancy, the Detweilers were all part of Anya's personal village. As much as I missed George, I enjoyed the sense that my daughter's world had grown significantly since his death. After George's murder, I was forced to reach out to others. I couldn't do everything on my own. What seemed at the time to be an admission of my incompetence, now proved to be the best move I ever made. Where one of the villagers was weak, another was strong. In all colors, backgrounds, shapes, sexes, ages, and sizes, they formed our very own familial Rainbow Coalition, and the pot of gold into which they poured all their love and affection was my daughter.

Sheila poked me with a finger to stop my woolgathering. "Pay attention, Kiki. What do you mean when you say you don't expect Ben to move on? Are you planning to make a commitment? I don't want a double-wedding, thank you. I have my own plans."

Brother, did she ever. Poor Robbie Holmes was going to be dressed in a monkey suit, trained like a chimp in a zoo, and paraded around like a pet ape. Heck, I bet all the police working for him didn't give him near the headaches good old Sheila inflicted.

A little of my mother-in-law went a long way. Robbie was a good sport, but I worried that he would get his fill of her.

"What is your plan?" Sheila repeated. Louder. She must have thought I was hard of hearing. More like sick of hearing. *Yada, yada, yada.*

I decided to give her an earful. As Anya climbed into the car, I said, "For your information, Ben Novak is plenty interested in me, Sheila. See, I have this belly-dancing routine I do for him, with a jewel in my navel and all these veils. I shake and I shimmy and I rotate my hips. I do the bump and grind, and then I let the veils fall, one by one by one, and gosh, Sheila, I'd say from his enthusiastic response, he's PLENTY interested. You should try it on Robbie sometime. Ta-da, now!"

I slammed my car into reverse and left her standing there, scraping her jaw up off the driveway.

# FIFTY-SEVEN

"Everyone at the Detweilers' liked lighting the candles," said Anya, right before she burped. Linnea had sent her home with slices of brisket, carrots cooked with honey, and a fruit salad. I made my famous latkes, which we paired alternately with sour cream and applesauce. Both of us were stuffed.

My daughter's face glowed in the light of the menorah. She'd opened the iTunes card from me with a whoop of joy. I opened a gift package of body wash and body lotion in Gold Leaf, my favorite scent from Thymes.

Izzy sat on Anya's lap, drowsy because of his own full tummy. Gracie leaned against me, encouraged by my scratching around her ears. Jasper and Fluff curled up, spoonlike on the rug, and Petunia was displaying his round tummy so I could tickle it with my toes.

"Tell me everything," I said. I hoped I

didn't sound desperate, but I was. In my more dreamy moments, I fantasized being a part of Detweiler's family, having the type of relationship with his mother that I never had with Sheila, and enjoying his dad the way I never could mine. Life on a farm sounded infinitely appealing to me, even though I was smart enough to realize it was a harsh, unforgiving way to make a living. Still, Detweiler once told me that the farm had been in their family for generations. It was a Centennial Farm, a designation given by the Illinois Department of Agriculture for those properties with straight or collateral lines of ancestors that could be traced back a hundred years. The state boasted about eight thousand such homesteads.

"Came through my mother's family," said Detweiler. "My dad's parents moved here from Germany, and my dad worked for Mom's family. He fell in love with her and the land at the same time."

"It's really sick," said Anya, using the latest teen slang for "great" or "cool." "They have this white house with dark green shutters. Sits on a hill. Out back is a big tree with a rope swing. Their barn is red, like Old MacDonald's. Mrs. Detweiler has a huge herb garden and a vegetable garden, too. She's really into canning and making preserves. There's a creek running through the land. It dumps into this totally awesome pond where you can fish in the summer. We piled onto a wagon that Mr. Detweiler loaded with bales of hay. Mrs. Detweiler covered us with quilts she'd made and gave us each flashlights. She gave Emily a picnic basket for us to open later. Mr. D. drove us really carefully along the county road where they live and onto a neighbor's land. There were two of Emily's friends, Sophie and Kendra. Their parents had built this bonfire so we could roast hotdogs. Mrs. D. packed potato salad and buns and hot cider for us. I never ate so much food in my life."

I wanted to ask what Detweiler's sisters were like, but I didn't want to seem as nosy as I felt. Instead, I skirted the subject by asking about the kittens.

"Totally cool. See, the mama had six. She was fine with us touching them. Mrs. D. had her in a big wooden box in their kitchen. So Mama Cat was lying on all these towels and surrounded by all these teensy, tiny squirmers. They went, 'Meeeyou,' in the smallest little voices. Can I have one, Mom, please?"

"Let's get through the holidays, okay?" I knew she'd be asking me daily, but this would buy me some time.

"Grandma says we don't need another financial drain. She says that unless you hurry up and get married, we'll be broke forever."

"I see. Does that scare you?"

"I get tired of seeing you worry. I wish you didn't have to work so hard. But I don't want you to marry anyone you don't want to. I mean, Mr. Novak — Ben — tries really hard to be nice to me. I can't imagine him as a stepfather though."

I nodded. We'd make short work of cleaning up the kitchen. The short, fat Hanukkah candles were almost burned down to nothing.

"How about if we declare this a 'no worries' night? Just for tonight, we'll make like the Australians and say, 'No worries, mate.' I think we need a bit of fresh air. How about if we drive over to Santa's Magical Kingdom?" I waved two tickets at her. They were a bit crumpled from being squished in my back pocket.

"I'm too old for that," said Anya, cautiously.

"That's right, you are. You're too old for fun, too old to get excited, too old to have a good time with your mother, right? Better go to sleep right away because tomorrow you have to go out and get a job. All those adult responsibilities, whew."

One side of her mouth hitched up in a smile. "Oh, Mom. You are so weird."

I giggled and she did, too. "By the way," she added. "Do you really have a belly-dance outfit with lots of veils?"

# FIFTY-EIGHT

The line into the park was long, but the cars moved quickly. We followed the wonderful light displays, oohing and ahhing over all of them. My favorite was the dancing elves. Anya loved the river of lights. On the way home, I pulled off the highway into an empty store parking lot. We sipped our hot chocolate and ate the sugar cookies Linnea had sent home for us. She cut them into menorahs, dreidels, and stars of David before icing them in blue and white. Anya shared more about Emily, Sophie, and Kendra. "Emily's, like, really smart. Cute, too. You can tell she's, like, the leader of them all. Sophie is more quiet and totally pretty. Kendra is a tomboy, but she still likes girlie stuff, too. Even Nicci admitted they were neat. That sort of surprised me because Nicci can be a snob," Anya said.

I smiled to myself. Yes, I figured that about Nicci. I was glad Anya noticed it, too.

"I'd like to visit the girls again. Better yet, could we have them over here for a scrap-booking crop? None of them know much about scrapping. I told them I could show them. I think they'd be totally, like, amazed at the store. They can't believe you're a part owner."

I told her we'd make plans to reciprocate after the first of the year, and she started ticking off all the fun things the kids could do on this side of the river. On the way back from Santa's Magical Kingdom, which was over in Eureka, I brought up the topic of boys and respect, but things definitely had not gone as I had planned. My nimble daughter danced around exactly what happened and who was involved. I got the distinct feeling this hadn't been a chance meeting. Dollars to donuts, Anya and Nicci were using the mall as a rendezvous spot. I made a note to myself to discuss this development with both Sheila and Jennifer Moore.

I also suspected that Anya harbored a crush on one of the seniors.

Was he one of the mouthy boys? I couldn't tell.

I desperately wanted to hammer home the importance of R-E-S-P-E-C-T, really I did. In the end, however, I decided that Detweiler had made his point — and that Anya had gotten the message. Additional harping by me might actually do more harm than good.

How I wished he were sitting here now! How I missed having him drop by! We'd often talk about kids, about the problems involved with raising them, and the best ways to help a kid stay on the right path. Even though he was childless, I valued his input. He had learned a lot by watching his sisters. As the only boy in a house full of sisters, he seemed to understand how girls think.

I turned the cell phone over in my hand. My fingers hesitated over the keys. In the end, I decided to wait. Tomorrow, I would search for proof hidden in Cindy Gambrowski's scrapbook pages. That would give me a good reason to call. While we were on the phone, I would ask for his family's address so I could send a handwritten thank you note, a "bread-and-butter" note, as my Nana always called them.

Detweiler's family. That was a subject I wanted to explore further.

Anya grew excited as she talked about her new friend Emily, but she became confused as she tackled the names of Detweiler's sisters. Anya was getting muddle-headed as she grew sleepy. She skipped from one topic to the next. From the Detweiler neighbors to the kittens to the girls and then she rambled on about places they could visit on this side of the river. My sweet kid was clearly running out of steam. First, she'd talk a minute, then be quiet for several more, then mumble a disjointed word or two. By the time I pulled into our driveway, she was fast asleep.

I managed to rouse her and guide her into the house. She plopped down, face first, onto her bed. I pulled off her shoes and tucked her in before I went about my end-of-the-day chores. Monroe was standing at the fence, searching for me, waiting patiently. Might have been my imagination, but when I told him that Leighton would be home tomorrow, he seemed inexpressively sad.

"Monroe, darling, now that I know what a complete lover-boy you are, we're friends for life." I rubbed the insides of his long ears. To return the affection, he fluttered those long gray lips and tried to smooch me.

Stroking the big, mute beast soothed me.

There was an aspect of Anya's reportage that niggled, that I couldn't shake off. One of the Detweiler sisters had said, "So your mother is the famous Kiki Lowenstein?"

"But she didn't sound mean or nosy. Not really. More like she was thinking hard, you know?" Anya rushed to clarify.

"Yes," I agreed, not wanting to make a mountain out of a molehill.

But that "yes" was a boldfaced lie. I worried that either or both of Detweiler's sisters were Brenda Detweiler fans. A panicky voice inside me obsessed over the small bother, the way your fingers worry a scab.

I gave Monroe a final pat and headed for the house. If his sisters hated me for Brenda's sake, there was no help for it. Certainly, nothing I could do tonight. In a fitful effort to banish my worries, I washed and folded two loads of clothes. I ironed a blouse for Anya and one for me. I mixed up banana bread, poured it into loaf pans and stuck it in the refrigerator, so I could bake them tomorrow.

I was worn out and coughing by the time I decided to call it quits. This had been a long and tiring day.

I turned the thermostat down as low as I could. I set my alarm clock.

I stared at my bed. It seemed too vast and too empty. I shrugged. Once in a while, it hits me that I might be alone for the rest of my life. That's when moving on becomes a struggle. And facing that empty bed was more than I could handle tonight.

I put on my jammies, a pair of knit pants, an old white tee-shirt of George's, and a faded sweatshirt. Then I headed back into my living room.

The dogs were snoozing happily on my sofa. Martha Stewart might want to smack me around a little, but I quit tossing my furry friends off the sofa years ago. Instead, I cover the cushions with old beach towels. After all, the dogs aren't trying to be bad; they just want a soft spot on which to rest their weary bones. I understand; I do, too.

Before I settled down, I checked on Anya one last time. She was curled up in a ball while Izzy was sleeping in the crook formed by the hollow behind her knees. He raised a pair of bug-eyes to me, growled a sec until he realized who I was, wagged his tail, and whimpered a distinct, "Uh, sorry about that!"

I laughed and petted him. "Hey, a guard dog can't be too careful, can he?"

He wagged his tail harder to indicate his total agreement.

I closed Anya's door and asked God to protect my baby.

I sighed, nudged the dogs to one end of the sofa and settled down with my library book. A rumble shook the window panes. I listened for a second and went back to the latest Duffy Dombrowski mystery *Out Cold.* I love Al, the basset hound in the series, and even though I don't like boxing, I think Duffy is fantastic. The thunder outside crescendoed into a low, dish-rattling threat. Petunia sat upright and sobbed. "Come here, little boy," I said, lifting him into my lap. "It's okay. Just one of those weird Missouri midwinter thunderstorms. You'd think Mother Nature would have sense enough to hit the snow switch, but no. She sends us a totally inappropriate thunder-boomer of a rainstorm."

He shivered and stuck his head under my armpit.

I pulled him closer, tucked my feet under us and rested my head on the sofa arm.

It was good to know that one of God's creatures — small and miserable as he was — could look to me as a tower of strength. Petunia slowly backed out from under my armpit and shivered up at me. I cuddled poor Petunia. "Buddy, I know you are scared, but it's just a big noise. Sound and fury signifying nothing. Sometime tonight the rain will turn to snow. Tomorrow, you'll be romping in the flakes with your friends. Close your eyes and dream of Milkbone biscuits and chew toys."

He relaxed a bit in my arms.

In return, I snuggled deeper into the sofa. Soon he was snoring, and I was more asleep than awake.

Tomorrow I would tackle nailing Ross Gambrowski's tail feathers to the wall.

But tonight was a "no worries" night. I had declared it so. Behind my closed eyes, I conjured up the Mary Engelbreit poster, "Queen of Everything."

"Petunia, I am the Queen of Everything. Did you know that? You are my loyal subject, Tunia-Boy." I rubbed his velvety ear, and he rewarded me with a loud snore. That made me smile.

My kid was safe, I had food in my tummy, a roof over my head, and a dog in my lap plus three at my feet. Oh, and there was that donkey in my stable. Just like the one that the blessed Mary had trusted to carry her and her baby to safety.

"God, please, carry us to safety." That was the prayer that ended my day.

# FIFTY-NINE

*Monday, December 21*
*5th Night of Hanukkah*

Overnight my daughter morphed into Snarkerella, the princess who couldn't be pleased. She snarled about the bagels, devoured all the cream cheese, complained about the banana (too ripe!), and stamped her foot with impatience when I explained I forgot to buy more orange juice.

"Gran is never out of orange juice! Never! She knows how much I love it," howled little Miss Drama.

I mumbled to myself, "That's because Linnea does the shopping. Your Gran wouldn't know where to buy o.j. if she lived in Florida right next to an orange grove."

"What?" Her hearing was perfect even if her mood was bad.

"How about if we stop by McDonald's on the way to CALA? I'll get you whatever you want." Okay, so I capitulated. I prefer to think that I know how to choose my battles wisely.

Grumpy Girl stomped her way toward the front door, paused after she yanked open the door and shouted, "It snowed! It snowed! Wooopppeee! Is today a snow day?"

I'd already been out taking care of Monroe and playing doggie doo-doo handmaiden to my herd of hounds. "No, sorry. But there is an early dismissal. Your grandmother will be picking you up."

"Sick. Totally sick. This is, like, awesome."

Right. Easy to say when you don't have to drive in it.

The drop-off line at CALA moved more slowly than ice melts off your windshield. Most of the other moms wore their Blu-Tooth attachments. I wondered who they were speaking with. I knew most of them were SAHM, Stay-At-Home-Moms, so I couldn't quite understand the urgency that compelled them to chat nonstop in their cars. When one of them cut me off in her humongous white Escalade, I laid on the horn.

"Mom! Geez," Anya scolded. "That's so not necessary."

Maybe Anya's bad mood infected me. Or maybe I was twitching because of the restless urge within me to get to the store and find proof that would send Ross Gambrowski to jail. Forever.

The moment we pulled up to the curb, my mood shifted to poignant. In another two years, Anya would be driving herself to school. Chauffeur duty would end, and endless vigilance would begin. How silly I was to wish her up, to try to speed up time rather than to enjoy each minute.

After all, she might be my only child. I might never have another chance to savor all this mystery, mayhem, and moodiness.

"Anya," I grabbed the edge of her backpack. "You know I love you?"

She rolled her eyes. "Yes, Mom. Can I go? My friends are waiting."

"Of course." I watched her race off to where Nicci stood with two other girls. Girls I didn't know. I chided myself for not being better aware of whom my daughter was palling around with.

I added that to my personal worry list and headed toward our store.

The dogs raced around me in the parking lot, tangling their leashes so that I shuffled into the store. Once I got them settled, I headed for our store computer, where Dodie stored the class data. In that file I found the list of all the classes I'd taught and all the students who had signed up and/or attended.

Fortunately, Dodie alphabetized the names. Unfortunately, I teach classes nearly every month. I sipped a cup of Lipton's tea, ran my finger along the screen, and settled into the search.

Fifteen minutes later, I discovered Cindy Gambrowski as an attendee for my "Hidden Journaling Class."

This surprised me. I couldn't recall having her in that class, and usually I remember my students.

I couldn't recall Cindy ever attending that class.

In fact, I was sure she hadn't.

I sat back in my seat and stared at the list.

I resumed my search. Cindy's name appeared on two other class rosters. Again, I couldn't recall her being my student. She signed up for "Writing about the Sad Times," and "Journaling Your Journey." The only class I recalled her attending was the last session we offered, "All about Me," the class that spawned the page contest of the same name.

My cell phone sat within inches of my hand, but I had trouble dialing Dodie's number. She owed me an apology for not telling me about Bama. Phoning her would seem like a capitulation. Not phoning her would keep me stuck here at the computer. Twenty minutes until opening time. Twenty minutes I didn't have to waste.

I couldn't change what happened to Cindy Gambrowski. I couldn't miraculously heal all of Bama's wounds, either. But I might be able to put a wife-beater in jail for the rest of his natural life.

I phoned Dodie. She picked up on the first ring.

# SIXTY

"Sunshine, how are you?"

A million responses zipped through my head. Dodie's joy was so genuine that it angered me. How could she be so flipping happy to hear from me when I was so bummed to be talking to her?

"Fine."

"I've heard you are doing great at the store."

"Things are selling."

"Yes, that's to be expected, but I've heard you are having a really profitable last quarter. I hope to stop in tomorrow or the next day and see the displays you've put up. Maybe I'll even be able to help out a little."

"Oh." I sat there flummoxed. How did she know about our sales figures? Every time I asked Bama how we were doing, she'd stonewalled.

"I think you'll be banking a nice bonus," Dodie continued.

"Oh," I said again. A bonus sure would go a long way toward making my season merry. "How do you know all this?" I couldn't help it if my tone was peevish.

"I've done a shadow set of books while Bama was learning the accounting system."

"I thought Bama knew all this stuff."

Dodie chuckled. "She was learning as she went along."

"How is she? Do you know?"

"Better than I expected. We visited her yesterday in the hospital. A good plastic surgeon was on call, and he actually fixed her deviated septum when he set her nose. Luckily, she didn't lose any teeth."

"No thanks to you." I couldn't help myself. I was ticked, and her comment about Bama's teeth set mine on edge.

Dodie sighed. "I did what I thought was best. The rules of the group demand we keep our travelers' identities safe. I took a vow. An oath. The other women have been doing this for years, and I adhered to the policy they've developed. Most of the time, it's proven a valuable safeguard. This time . . . perhaps not so much. In retrospect, I should have asked you to take the WAR oath. I just didn't want to drag you into this. Especially since you and Bama weren't exactly getting along. Which, by the way, was more her fault than yours."

I didn't know how to respond to that.

"Bama's ex-husband is a cop. Law enforcement officials have a high propensity to be abusers. When Detweiler visited you at work, his presence frightened Bama. Instead of dealing with her own fears, she chose to blame you. No matter how often I discussed the matter with her, she persisted in being upset. I actually arranged a session for her with a counselor, hoping they could discuss the matter. Bama refused to go. I guess on a deep psychological level, she believed her fears worked to protect her. She was afraid that if she let her guard down, she'd be at risk."

"They didn't protect her. Not at all! You do know that a cop saved her?"

"Not by himself. You also took a licking when you helped her. Kiki, I am so sorry. It must have been awful. To have him hold a knife to your skin?" Then she mumbled something in Yiddish.

When I didn't respond, she translated, "The cholera on him!"

Even though she couldn't see me through the cell phone, I nodded. That morning I caught a glimpse of my shoulders. On the blades I sported twin bruises, almost like a matching set of purple angel wings. Under the bandage, the cut was scabbed and angry. My nose was red from being wiped. I was a colorful, painful mess. I hoped Jerald McCallister met a bunch of new friends in jail. I knew they could be particularly tough on cops. I hoped they'd show him how much fun it was to be beaten to a quivering pulp.

"There are wounds on Bama's outside, but far worse are the scars on her mind. Bama's struggled with Post Traumatic Stress Disorder for years. She's come a long way, but she's not capable of thinking rationally. You must be familiar with Maslow's hierarchy of needs. He theorized that every human being has basic needs which must be met in order to graduate to higher levels of functioning. The most simple need is that for safety. If a person lives in a war zone, she doesn't concern herself with hygiene or social niceties. She puts all her energy into survival.

"Bama is like that. She's stuck at the lowest strata of the hierarchy. She couldn't respond to your overtures to be friends. She couldn't shed that war zone mentality and see you as an ally. She was minimally functional in a lot of ways. Jerald had been beating her for fifteen years. That's a long time to suffer abuse."

"Why didn't she leave? She has an MFA!" I nearly shouted into the phone.

Dodie chuckled. "That was part of the back story we created for her. In actuality, she has a GED. Jerald forced her to quit high school. He controlled every aspect of her life, including the purse strings. One of the reasons I wanted her to do the books was so that she could develop a sense of appropriate income and outgo. He terrorized her by making her account for every penny he gave her. To her, money was power."

That explained why she had been such a witch every time I handed a customer a cola and forgot to write it down.

"Yes, until this disaster, she had changed a lot, and for the better. For example, her vertigo had mostly disappeared. Thanks to the move here, she was no longer getting hit in the head on a regular basis. She had time to heal."

I blushed, remembering how I first thought Bama's dizziness came from drug use. I studied my feet, thankful that Dodie wasn't here in person for our conversation. I felt lucky I didn't have to look her in the eye.

I was still irked, but not as much.

A glance at the clock told me I needed to wrap up our conversation.

"Dodie, the real reason I called is Cindy Gambrowski. I noticed she signed up for several classes, but I don't recall seeing her take them. Am I just being forgetful?"

Dodie sighed. "I guess it doesn't matter since she's . . . dead. Poor Cindy would sign up for a class, but Ross would refuse to let her attend. I told her we'd keep trying until he got sick of saying, 'No,' which he did. I left her on the roster, and I paid you, because I shared your handouts with her. I would drop by the house, show her the pages you made as samples, give her the materials, and answer any questions. Often Ross would come into the room to check up on us."

My lower lip trembled. Dodie had actually figured out how to take my class to a needy student, without alerting me. I wasn't sure what to make of that.

"That was really nice of you," I said finally. My voice nearly failed me, but I croaked it out. "Really nice." I nearly blurted out that if she'd told me what was up, I would have happily visited Cindy myself. Or expanded on my handouts. Or anything!

"Fat lot of good it did her," said Dodie. "She had pearls around her neck and his foot upon her heart."

# SIXTY-ONE

I brewed myself a strong cup of tea, added Stevia to sweeten it, and opened a three-ring class handout binder. Spreading the resources in front of me, I carefully reviewed the course material Cindy would have received from Dodie. Somewhere, out there, was a clue I'd missed. What else could I do but retrace all my steps? And my handouts were steps, even if their impact had been unknown to me.

I read and re-read all my journaling handouts. Then I sat at the desk and stared off into space. What was I missing?

Nothing came to me. Nothing at all.

Whenever I'm creatively blocked (or just plain blocked), I resort to good old-fashioned walkies to get my juices flowing. I snapped leashes on my crew, slipped Izzy into the front of my zip-up sweatshirt and took off at a brisk pace, slipping and sliding my way down the street. Our shop is on one side of a city block. The other three sides are private residences, once upon a time they must have been adorable houses. Most of the owners have since retired, and the houses have seen better days. Still, out of courtesy to our neighbors, I clean up after my pooches. That can be tough in the late fall with leaves on the ground. Brown is brown is brown, and when you have two dogs pooping, keeping track of their droppings can be a challenge. In the snow, it was much easier.

That's when the epiphany hit me: Cindy sent me books about hidden images.

She had taken my class on "Hidden Journaling."

I raced the dogs back to the store, gave them treats, and took out Cindy's page once more. After carefully washing my hands and pulling on latex gloves, I slipped the page from the plastic protector. In all my classes, I harp on the value of hidden journaling. That's scrapbook speak for creating secret interactive places where a scrapper can hide her writing. See, not every part of our story is for public consumption. Hiding parts of our written history is a cagy way to save our tales without putting all our "dirty laundry" on display.

Here's an example: Anita Folger worked

with me on her wedding album. Anita's mother-in-law nearly ruined the day by showing up in a cream-colored, floor-length gown, and repeatedly drawing attention to herself throughout the event. She insisted on standing between the bride and groom for the formal photos! Anita rightly wanted to blast the woman in her writing. "She made me miserable. I'm not going to lie about it by writing about what a wonderful day it was," Anita said with a pout.

"You could do that, but if you do, everyone will focus on her . . . again. Instead, why not journal the hurts and scrapbook the highs? Remember? The winners write the history books. Write down what happened. We'll create a hidden pocket behind a photo. You can slip your narrative inside that pocket. You'll know it's there. You can share it with your girlfriends. But you won't have to hide away your wedding album," I said. "Instead, you can be front and center."

"I don't intend to hide my wedding album." Anita frowned at me. "I'm putting it out on the coffee table."

"What about your husband? How did he feel about his mother's behavior?" I probed.

Anita colored. "He was upset. He begged me to overlook it. Ever since his dad died, she's been a whack-job."

"So every time he sees this album, he'll have to deal with her bad behavior all over again, right?"

"Yes." She sighed. "You're right, Kiki. I can write it out, get it on paper, and he won't have to know, will he?"

"Not unless he pulls the page out of the plastic protector, and he searches for it. Most people wouldn't go that far. Most guys focus on the pretty pictures, and that's it. At least, that's the excuse I've always heard for buying girly magazines."

All this came back to me as I studied Cindy's layout, a pretty scene showing her and Ross arm-in-arm, standing in front of their fireplace. Pulling my magnifying glass from a drawer, I examined the image closely. I could see where his fingers dug into her arm, wrinkling the fabric of her blouse. I put the glass aside and held the page at arm's length. The pose struck me as unusual. I realized why.

Cindy was leaning slightly away from Ross, trying to free herself from his grasp.

Using the tip of a bone folder, I tried to lift the largest page element — the focal photo of Cindy and Ross — to test the adhesion. I held my breath as I slipped the ivory instrument under the picture's matted edge. Maybe Cindy told her story. Maybe she'd recorded her abuse. There was only one way to find out.

The bone folder slid under the photo. I slipped it deeper, weighing how much pressure I could apply without causing damage. Turns out, the folder met little resistance at all. With a flick of my wrist, the happy photo flipped over on the page, exposing another photo underneath.

That picture sent me running to the john to upchuck.

# SIXTY-TWO

Detweiler rubbed his hand across his mouth. I warned him on the phone about what I'd found, and he'd stopped to buy himself a large bottle of Diet Coke. He had also called Hadcho with the news. I think my liquid drug of choice — cola — was rubbing off on him. He shook his head in amazement at the image before us. "I'm glad you didn't go any further. I'll need to take these layouts with me."

"I want to see what's here."

"You don't need to see this. You don't need this seared into your brain."

"I'm responsible for returning these items to Cindy's family. I can't vouch for their safe return if I don't know what's here," I argued. "These are store property. Fortunately, the rules say that upon submission, the pages belong to us. I'm sharing this with you as a courtesy. We agree to return them to the submitter as a courtesy, too."

"But there's more there. You think she hid something else on the page."

"Yes."

"Hang on." He phoned Hadcho again, and this time told the other detective to bring a search warrant. Hadcho was already on it.

"Otherwise, we could run into problems. A smart attorney would try to suppress this," said Detweiler as he stroked his chin. "Whatever 'this' happens to be."

I went about my work in the store, while Detweiler sat on a stool and waited. It seems like it took Hadcho forever to show up, but my watch said he'd made good time.

The two men stood on either side of me.

I was both sick at my stomach and insanely curious. My body was recuperating from the impact of the first photo. With Detweiler at my side, I thought I could handle whatever came next. Hadcho stood poised with a digital camera to record what I'd found. The three of us stared at the horrific image on the table. Our eyes kept returning to it the way you can't help staring at the aftermath of a car crash. Your common sense tells you to turn away, but tragedy is magnetic. Perhaps that's God's way of reminding us how incredibly fragile we are. We hurtle ourselves through life at a breakneck pace, confident we are invincible. But we aren't. And when we see death or destruction we are forced to recalculate, to reassess the thin silver thread of life that ties us to this existence.

Before us was a photo that turned my stomach. Cindy labeled it: "Miscarriage at four months." The image zoomed in on a pair of tiny hands and feet resting on a bloodied scrap of newspaper. On the back of the photo was a shrunken hospital bill for a D and C from a clinic in a nearby suburb. Behind both of those was a photo of a battered Cindy — obviously a self-portrait given the camera angle. On its back was a bill from a doctor for wiring her jaw.

I turned my attention to another embellishment, a photo of the Gambrowski's home. From behind it, my tweezers pulled a list of dates and injuries. Another list detailed appointments with doctors, chiropractors, and physical therapists.

"Smart lady," muttered Detweiler. "I can corroborate these appointments and the dates of her treatments. In one domestic abuse case in Virginia, a supervisor used her calendar to track the days her employee missed work or showed up with bruises. That informal record was entered into evidence, proving that the dates of the beatings dovetailed with visits to local emergency wards. It goes a long way toward showing a continuing pattern of abuse. That husband was convicted, and he's still spending time behind bars."

He rubbed at his eyes. "It'll take us a while to hunt down these people and get them to talk. We can do it, though. We'll subpoena them."

Detweiler bagged the photos, labeled the evidence and jotted notes on an official-looking form. His skin usually radiated a healthy glow from working outside at his parents' farm, but this morning, he was pale. I probably looked a little green around the gills as well. "How hard do you have to hit a woman to make her miscarry?"

"There are a lot of variables. It depends on the woman and on her pregnancy. And on how hard and where the man hits her."

"How common is it? I mean does this happen often?"

"One study done in the UK in 1997 identified domestic violence as the primary cause of miscarriages or still-births. Another study noted that 30 percent of the time, physical abuse first occurred after the woman became pregnant."

"You're saying the pregnancy becomes the catalyst for the violence?"

"Evidently."

"So Cindy is telling us she lost this baby because Ross beat her?"

"This baby and maybe others."

"Others?"

Detweiler looked away from me. A tiny muscle along his jaw line twitched. "Sexual abuse has been proved to have a strong correlation with fetal loss overall, but emotional abuse has the strongest association with multiple stillbirths. Once a woman experiences domestic abuse, she is 50 percent more likely to lose a pregnancy."

"So, maybe she lost other babies?"

"It's certainly possible. She must have had Michelle, what? Twenty-two years ago? Considering Mrs. Gambrowski's age, it's feasible she could have gotten pregnant and lost the babies many times."

"Lost multiple babies . . ." I whispered.

I had to know. I hastily pulled apart the page, separating the largest background of 12 × 12 inch paper from an interior mat approximately 11 1/2 by 11 1/2 inches. Out tumbled four more grisly photos. On the back of each was a date. By my count, Cindy had lost at least five babies.

I gritted my teeth and clutched at the table edge. After a moment, the hot spate of anger abated.

Detweiler said nothing, his beautiful green eyes assessing me. His hand moved toward mine slowly. An inch away, he hesitated, withdrew.

Tears filled my eyes, my throat squeezed shut and I cried for those poor little ones. Slowly, gently, Detweiler pulled me into his arms and held me. Hadcho looked away. I rested my face against Detweiler's shirt, soothed by the steady lub-lub-lub of his heart.

Leaning there against him, I wondered if he knew how much I'd like to have another child. Was it palpable, this feeling of desire? Did we women send out Morse code, dot-dot-dash, I-want-a-bay-bee, S-O-S? Wasn't it feasible that a silent hormonal signal passed between potential couples, signaling in the same way you stand up in a crowded stadium and wave to a friend, "Come sit by me"?

I think so because I felt a roar within me, a supersonic buildup of pressure, and my mouth opened as if to cry out. A tiny, "Eek," escaped, but I pulled away from him. I slapped my fingers over my lips real quickly and forced myself to back away.

Grounding myself in the here and now, I reached down and squeezed the inanimate wood tabletop hard as I could. Once I'd bled off that excess energy, I grabbed a tissue and dabbed at my eyes.

A thought came to me.

Clenching my jaw shut, and stiffening my spine, I lifted the page with both hands to the level of my eyes and took note of the thickness of the piece.

An embellishment is to a scrapbook page what a scarf, a pin, or a belt is to an outfit. These small additions add visual punch and emphasis. They tie together colors and patterns. They direct and sometimes fool the eye. Since most are add-ons and not printed directly on the paper, nearly every embellishment adds depth, even if it's just a smidge. In addition to the thinnest layer of the paper, there's also a thin layer of adhesive. Taken together, there's always an elevation.

But usually, a canny scrapbooker will accentuate an embellishment even more. It just adds a whole new level of "oomph." Most of us favor raising a tag or an accent with 1/8-inch foam tape or foam dots.

As I rotated the page, I could see that the entire 4 × 3 inch page title was elevated on Cindy's layout. But the lettering was flat. I wondered why she would go to the trouble of raising the mat and not use chipboard, glittery, or textured letters?

That didn't make sense.

Unless she was sending a signal.

I peeled up the page title mat.

"What's that?" Hadcho wondered as we gazed at a rectangular plastic slab roughly the size of a credit card. A small label dated it a month before Cindy's disappearance.

"It's a recording device," I said. "We don't sell them but you can get them online. It's self-contained. This model both records and plays back. See? There's the play button."

"I'm going to kill you and chop you up into a hundred little pieces," growled Ross Gambrowski. "See if I don't, Cindy! I'll cut you up into hamburger and throw you in the trash where you belong. No one will ever be able to find all of you when I'm done!"

## SIXTY-THREE

Detweiler handed over a receipt and promised me the department would send another receipt for the scrapbook page to Michelle Gambrowski. But first, it would be entered into evidence.

"The lab will have to go over this." Hadcho's eyes were brittle as two pieces of ice. "Mrs. Lowenstein, I need your signature and statement to attach to my chain of custody."

I nodded. "Laurel and Clancy can also verify the provenance of the page. We were looking at it earlier because it was a contest entry. They know I didn't find the hidden info because if I had, we'd have all seen it. We were looking at all the pages in the contest trying to decide on a winner."

"But you missed this information?"

"I'm embarrassed to admit I didn't look for the hidden journaling — and she did an ingenious job of tucking it away. The idea the page concealed information came to me after I reviewed a list of the classes Cindy had registered for."

I left the office to round up my two co-workers who had come in a little before Detweiler arrived. While they wrote up brief statements, I watched the floor. Fortunately, only one customer stopped by, a husband who wanted a gift certificate. Minutes later, Clancy and Laurel took my place up front, and I typed up a brief statement to accompany the scrapbook page. "There's no way any of us could have inserted these photos or written this script," I explained to Hadcho and Detweiler. "We'd have had to tear apart the whole page. But you'll be able to verify that at the lab, I assume."

Hadcho shrugged and his eyes caught Detweiler's. "Probably this won't matter much to convince the prosecutor to file charges. Instead we can use it to get collaborative statements from doctors, family friends, and so on. We can get subpoenas. It would be pretty tough to stay silent with this sort of proof tossed onto the playing field."

"I wonder if the daughter will talk," Detweiler mused.

"You never know in these domestic cases," said Hadcho as we tucked the page and the statements into a large shopping bag.

"I'm not sure how Michelle will take this," I said to the detectives. "After all, Ross is her father. Now that Cindy's gone, he's all she has. This information will make her an orphan, sort of."

The two detectives both stared at me, wordlessly. The quiet discomforted me. Despite my attempts to hold their gaze, I looked away. "You know, you only get two parents. No matter what they do, or how they treat you, you . . . you always love your family." That last word flew out on an exhale. I knew it sounded lame, but I also knew it was the truth.

"Michelle Gambrowski won't have a choice about talking to us. The law is the law. We'll take this to the lab, talk with our boss, and then decide how to proceed," said Detweiler. "We need to get right on this."

The two men took their leave, their heavy footsteps reflecting the long hours of work ahead.

I stood over the sink, rinsing and sloshing and washing my hands repeatedly, trying to wash away my feeling of guilt. Honestly, though, the more I thought about the situation the stupider I felt. Michelle had been trying to tell me where to look all along! I mean, wasn't that "gift" set of books from

Cindy all a hoax? A big road sign pointing to hidden meanings? Wasn't it possible that Michelle was counting on me finding the evidence? I sighed and considered slamming my head against the wall.

What a dope I'd been.

And I knew why. I just couldn't face my part in the deception.

I raised my head and stared into my own eyes. I noticed the tiny scar splitting my right eyebrow. I thought about where and how I'd gotten it.

My lower lip trembled. Had I missed Cindy's hidden pain and Ross's cruelty because violence had once been a daily occurrence in my own life? My mother never needed medical attention, but there had been plenty of shoves and slaps from my dad. For the most part, my sisters and I knew how to keep a low profile. Especially when Dad was in what we euphemistically called "one of his moods." But the summer before I left for college, he'd raised an angry hand to my face and his wedding band split my eyebrow.

Had Michelle suffered worse than I? At the memorial service, she stayed clear of her dad. I recalled how frightened she looked when I mentioned her visit to the store.

"Oh, no," I moaned. Was she all right? Would Ross hurt his own child?

*He murdered several of his own children, didn't he?*

I raced out of the bathroom and dialed Detweiler.

"Michelle! I'm worried about her!" The words rushed out.

"I know. We sent a car to sit outside the house. Gambrowski called his attorney and we had to move the officer. Until we process this, we're stuck. We can't drag him in. We can't do much of anything! We've got to interview people and back up her story before we can move ahead." Detweiler let loose with a string of curses.

Usually, he hid his frustration from me. Not this time.

"Do you think he'll hurt her?"

"We have no evidence of that."

"But you have evidence of him causing the miscarriages!" My voice rose a notch. "Men like him settle all their arguments with their fists. They think it's their right! They justify —"

Detweiler cut in. "There's nothing more I can do for Michelle tonight. Not yet anyway. I have to go."

His voice was curt, and his dismissive tone chilled me. I nodded (although he couldn't see my response) and stumbled through a goodbye.

I'd had about enough from Chad Detweiler. His light switch behavior — on/off, on/off — grated on my nerves and tore down my ego. While I appreciated the kindness his family had shown Anya, that was a separate issue. His wife had threatened me. He had led me on. I was sick of being played as a patsy by other people.

"You okay?" Clancy put a hand on my shoulder. "You look unwell. I know that album was upsetting, but thank God you found those photos!"

"Thank God," I whispered. (Although privately I thought, "God where are you in all this? Huh?") I had to keep moving. I got up and started pulling out the special make-and-take tag that was our gift to all the crop attendees. Pulling another bottle of Stickles from our store stock, I found myself face to face with a display of holiday layouts. We'd challenged our customers to use the Stickles when creating pages that celebrated family. I knew most of the women, but not all of them.

Or did I really know any of them?

How many more of them lived in fear?

# SIXTY-FOUR

Clancy, Laurel, and I confabbed. We decided that hands-down Cindy Gambrowski was our grand prize winner. She'd followed my directions to a "t." Her nimble pairings of happy, overt images and a quiet detailing of her "real" life proved extraordinary, to say the least.

I sat down to pen a note to Michelle, one that would be mailed along with her mother's prize. What could I possibly say? I set down the pen and confronted a new problem: How could I explain who won to our croppers? How could I tell them why we'd chosen Cindy's page?

I couldn't.

But we always did.

Early on, we'd decided on a policy of explaining our contest picks. Everyone knew this was what we did, and how we did it.

I motioned to Clancy and Laurel. "I can't very well not give Cindy the prize, even posthumously. But I also can't explain why she won."

"You're right," said Clancy. "Being transparent about winners is important."

There was no help for it. "We'll have to have an alternate grand prize winner." We quickly decided Harriet Sabloski, an infrequent customer, was our champ. I sighed. The extra prize might well come out of my pocket since I hadn't cleared it with my co-owners. This holiday was fast turning into a real drain on my finances. I also needed to reimburse the store for a "get well" bouquet I'd sent over to the hospital for Bama. She wasn't answering my calls. I couldn't very well claim to be family, so I was stuck in that ugly limbo where you want to apologize to someone and you can't.

Fortunately, I didn't have time to brood over my money problems. Our Monday night croppers burst through the front door chattering and laughing as they took their places at the craft table. This evening was planned as a combination holiday party and dash for the gift-giving finish line.

Bonnie Gossage put the final touches on a recipe album for her younger sister who was off to college. Debbie Chabot finished an album for her grandbabies. Jen Farber completed an album detailing the construction of a one inch to one foot scale historical house that her family was presenting to the St. Louis Miniature Museum. Meg Hutts put labels on "treat buckets," those cute faux paint cans that you decorate and fill with goodies or what-nots. She was making some for her fellow teachers and a couple for the other Sunday school teachers at her church. Jane Campbell finished "Sleep Tight" boxes, a gift she cleverly devised. She filled decorated shoe boxes with oil of lavender, CDs of ocean waves, an acupressure chart, a pair of earplugs, a journal, a recipe for several soothing nightcaps, bath salts, and a brochure on progressive relaxation. Gina Lopez assembled kits of greeting cards, twelve different designs suitable for most occasions. Harriet Sabloski was finishing small Hanukkah albums to give her grandkids.

I broke out a couple of bottles of sparkling cider, set out finger sandwiches, and tiny sugar cookies. Most of the women brought food to share. Our "goody" table groaned with the weight of all of it. I'll admit my all-time favorite was the Fool's Toffee Susan Lutz made for us each year. She found the recipe years ago and tweaked it to perfection. You would have never, ever guessed the foundation was Saltine crackers. The combination of salt, caramel, and chocolate was so good I couldn't help myself. I ate three pieces, and I enjoyed the lovely after-taste so much that I would have eaten more. I restrained myself because I knew any minute someone would notice what a total pig I was being. Who cares? I thought. My body is mine and mine alone these days. As long as I can button my pants, it's all good.

Besides, with my flaming red runny nose, the bandage on my throat, and the bruises on my shoulders, I wasn't exactly angling for a spot in any beauty contest.

Throughout the festivities, I caught myself staring at Bonnie Gossage's softly rounded belly. I guess she'd given up trying to hide the pregnancy, or maybe she reached that spot where suddenly, no matter what she wore, she showed. Bonnie's face was glowing with the serenity of knowing she carried a new life. I wondered if the halo depicted on Mary was actually an outward expression of this inner joy. All I know is that I envied her fiercely. With every fiber of my being, I longed to have another child. When I closed my eyes, I conjured up the downy fuzz of an infant's head. I recalled the sweet smell of their untarnished breath, and the firm grip a tiny hand could wrap around a finger, thereby totally embracing a heart.

I explained to the group that Dodie would return soon, Bama was recovering, and I hadn't been seriously hurt by my co-worker's ex. As for questions about Cindy? I answered them as Detweiler had answered me: There's an ongoing investigation.

Our winner's name was announced, and Harriet jumped for joy (literally). Later, she sidled up to me and whispered, "You don't know what this means to me. It's the sort of encouragement I've needed."

As Dodie would have said, our choice was *bashert* or fated.

By the end of the evening, I teetered on the precipice of exhaustion. Mert stopped by at the conclusion of the crop. My best friend helped me clean up after the croppers left. She listened to my description of Cindy's "All about Me" message. The normally chatty Mert said nothing as she wiped down tables and swept the floor.

"You okay?" I asked.

She turned sad eyes on me. "You ever lost a baby?"

"No."

"I did. People tell you that it was God's will or even that something was wrong with it, and you should be happy 'cause you wouldn't want it to suffer." Mert paused to wipe her eyes. "Used to be, they took your

399

baby away first thing. You couldn't even see it. Made it disappear. Couldn't even take the baby home to bury it. They made like nothing ever happened, except you got yourself this aching hole in your heart. And then the doctor? He'd tell you jest not to worry about it. Jest to try again."

"Mert, I didn't know! I'm so sorry."

"Don't know why I'm bothering you with all this. Especially seeing the time of year it is and all."

"It's the time of year when a very special baby was born. A baby whose mother watched him die at the hands of an angry mob. I can't imagine a better time for two friends to talk about having and losing a child."

"If'n there's a special hell, that Ross Gambrowski ought to go there. Making a woman lose her babies, and then getting her in a family way again? It's a crime against nature."

## SUSAN'S FOOL'S TOFFEE

*No one can resist this! Susan has perfected this recipe — and you'll never guess what the main ingredient is — Saltines.*

Pam Cooking Spray
Original Saltine crackers
1 c. butter
1 c. brown sugar
1 bag Hershey's chocolate chips
1 bag Reese's Peanut Butter chips

Prepare a 12 × 18 inch cookie sheet. Cover it with foil and spray with Pam Cooking Spray.

Lay out Original Saltine crackers end to end.

In a sauce pan, melt the butter.

Add the cup of brown sugar. Boil hard for 3 minutes, stirring constantly. Mixture will become frothy looking. Pour it over the crackers and bake at 350 degrees for 5 minutes.

Bring the cookie sheet out of the oven and pour one bag of Hershey's chocolate chips and one bag of Reese's Peanut Butter chips evenly over bubbly crackers.

Use a wooden spoon to spread the chips around until you have a gooey, yummy mess of peanut butter and chocolate. Put the pan back in the oven for 3 more minutes. (Lick the spoon! It's a mandatory part of the cooking process.)

Pull the cookie sheet out of the oven and put it in the refrigerator for several hours or overnight.

When hard, break into fist-sized sections and put them on a plate. They won't be there for long!

## SIXTY-FIVE

Mert offered to help me load the dogs into my car. I discovered a missed message from Dodie on my phone, but I didn't want to answer her. Not yet, at least. Anya was at Sheila's, spending the night and I could sense that Mert wanted to talk. I hugged my friend tightly. "I'm sorry that this might have brought back old memories."

"This here time of year, I get sad. It's dark and cold and I miscarried on the twenty-third, so it ain't exactly my favorite day. But hearing about Ross Gambrowski, it's just the capper. You and I need to find some time to catch up, proper like." She wiped her eyes.

"I know we do. Honestly, Mert, these retail hours are brutal."

"Try being in the domestic janitorial business. Everybody and his second cousin's inviting company over, and sudden-like they all want their house scrubby Dutch clean."

I grinned at the term "scrubby Dutch." This was an old St. Louis expression, one frequently used. As best as I could tell, it was a mispronunciation of "Deutsch" and complimented the fastidious Germans. "Scrubby Dutch" standards were legendary, taken from the fact that these women literally scrubbed their front steps clean.

"Look, we need to make time for our friendship. You're important to me. I squirreled away a bottle of red wine in the back, behind a stack of albums. Would you like a glass?"

Mert smiled at me. "A small one won't hurt. My tummy's full, and I can take my time sipping so I'll be okay to drive."

I uncorked the bottle, and we toasted ourselves. For about half an hour, we chatted about this and that. I told her how much I liked Laurel. She told me that Johnny was nearly through with the community college class he'd been taking for landscaping. Johnny and I dated off and on, but never seriously. He'd become about as good a friend to me as his sister. I missed seeing him.

I told her about Anya's visit to the Detweiler farm and about the incident at the mall.

"Good thing you got right on that. It starts

thataway, you know? They talk bad to you. They tell you how stupid you are or laugh at you. Keep you away from your friends and family. Cut you off, kinda like a dog nudges that one sheep until it leaves the flock."

An undertone to her voice told me she spoke from experience.

"But Detweiler intervened."

"He's a good man. Too bad he's already taken."

"His wife's an addict. Hadcho told me about her the night we went to Lumière."

"She's still his wife. A what-cha-ma-call-it. Legal impediment to another marriage."

Brenda Detweiler was certainly that.

We finished our glasses, rinsed them out, and loaded the dogs into my car.

"The best-est gift I ever got was you," said Mert. "You remember? You was standing in the aisle at Lowe's trying to find a sink cleaner."

"You suggested Zud and handed me your card."

"Three days later I was scrubbing your floors. Lordie, how time does fly."

I hugged her again. "We've been through a lot together," I whispered in her ear.

"I'm in this here friendship for the long haul."

"Me, too."

"You know, you could do a lot worse than Ben Novak."

I stiffened, but the expression on her face was loving. "I know."

"He's a nice man, and he don't have no impediments. Nice view from the back, if you get my drift. Plus, it'd make old Sheila happy."

"I live for that."

Mert giggled.

Once I pulled out of the parking lot, I called Dodie back. Normally I would have waited until I was home, but I knew the minute I turned off the engine all the dogs would clamber to get out of the car. As it was, I could chat with her for a few minutes at least. The back way to my house gave me ample time to drive through nearly deserted streets.

"How are you?" I asked.

"Never better, Sunshine. I'm coming in tomorrow. Sheila told me you have a big date with Ben Novak. I'll be there to cover for you."

I told her what hours Laurel and Clancy would work. "By the way, we had to award a duplicate prize in our contest," I said as preamble to my explanation of our decision to have two winners.

Dodie listened carefully. "I can't argue with your logic. The store will cover the extra prize. And the cost of flowers to Bama."

"Those are more from me, really."

"The store will cover them," Dodie repeated herself. "I saw Bama today. She's probably going home tomorrow."

"How is she?"

"Better than expected. She's healing fast. Jerald being behind bars is a big relief to her. She has a full faith and credit on him."

"Huh?"

"It's a legal term that guarantees her order of protection will be valid wherever she travels. Fortunately, she probably won't need that again. After he cut you and held the gun on Detective Hadcho, Jerald McCallister sealed his fate, so to speak, and committed a felonious act. Actually, the pulling the gun on the law enforcement officer was a real stroke of good luck. Usually, a miscreant like old Jerald hits his wife, goes to jail for a couple of hours, makes bond, and walks right out through the revolving door."

"But not this time."

"Not this time."

"How are her kids?"

"Shell-shocked. A family advocacy counselor has been talking with them and plans to talk with Bama tomorrow."

"She still mad at me?"

By way of answer, Dodie said, "I'm going to send you a link for the Kaufman Drama Triangle. Check it out tomorrow if you get into work before I do."

"Why?"

"Once you see it, you'll understand Bama better. People stuck in unhealthy relationships tend to go around and around, never getting healthy, just trading off roles. First they are victims, then persecutors, and then the rescuer. Bama has been a victim for years. This sick way of seeing the world is familiar to her. Right now she's trying on the role of persecutor."

"Why?"

"Because she doesn't have good coping skills. Because her ex-husband brainwashed her. More than likely, she grew up in an abusive home, and she's got a skewed view of reality. Most of all, she hasn't learned to be honest with herself."

"Who will she persecute?"

"That's 'whom,' not 'who.' And the answer is probably you."

That was just ducky. Just super-fine, hunky dory, ducky.

# SIXTY-SIX

*Tuesday, December 22*
*6th Night of Hanukkah*

My herd of hounds spent twenty minutes sniffing around to find the exact right spot for bowel and bladder evacuations the next morning. I remembered seeing a Consumer Reports survey showing that "dog poop" was #6 among the top ten things Americans griped about. Maybe that's why dogs are so picky about where they pooh.

All I can say for sure is that my canine crowd obviously put credence in that old real estate saying: Location, location, location.

After everyone's tank was on empty, I fed and loved up Monroe. His agile lips fluttered my cheeks with a kiss. "So you hate anything white, buddy. Must be a real panic for you when it snows. Hmm?"

Finally, I checked Gracie's tail. I'll admit I held my breath while I unwrapped the wiffle bat casing, but then I exhaled with gusto and a whoop of joy. The sore spot definitely showed signs of healing. I made a mental note to send another thank you card to Louis Detweiler.

Upon arrival at the store, I checked the clock and seeing I had time, I pulled out the shawl I was crocheting for Dodie. I sat at the crafts table and finished it by working in the loose strands before tucking it into a gift bag. All the books suggested blocking my work, but I didn't have time for that. I held up the piece, and admitted to myself Dodie would probably like it a lot. Not bad for a beginner!

My face fell when I recognized Horace's voice coming from the back. (I felt a little bad about our last interaction.) But he greeted me happily and handed over a nicely wrapped box. "It's rugelach for you and Anya. Don't share it with Sheila. She has her own box."

"My friend Stacey's grandmother's recipe," Dodie explained. "There's a secret ingredient — cream cheese. Here take a piece."

The pastry was flaky and rich, in contrast to the sweet filling of raisins and cinnamon. In short, heaven in my mouth. "Wow," was all I could manage. Any vestiges of upset with Horace or Dodie disappeared quickly as I took my second bite.

If world leaders sat down over rugelach instead of booze, the world would be a much nicer place. We'd have world peace licked in no time. Trust me on this.

"Bama showed me the financial statements," said Dodie as she sank down into a chair. My friend's color was pale and her voice raspy, but the bright light of her eyes told me that Dodie was on the mend.

"How are we doing? You heard about the shoplifter, right?"

Dodie nodded. "Good job catching her. I saw that you gave Rita a gift certificate. I'm thinking we might post a sign to the effect that anyone turning in any shoplifter will be rewarded."

I nodded. "Actually the pilfering is much worse than I expected. I mean, I never knew so much stuff walked out of here. I thought all our customers were our friends!"

Horace shook his head and said something in Yiddish.

"Beware of your friends, not your enemies," Dodie translated.

"What's the bottom line? I know we've had to hire more hourly people. I think our classes have gone well, and the crops have been full. How're we doing?" What I didn't say, specifically, was the uppermost question in my mind: "Are you sure we made enough that I'll take home a bonus?"

Horace and Dodie shared a smile. He reached into a pocket of his jacket and pulled out an envelope. I opened the flap and the tight band around my heart eased. The extra amounted to an entire month's salary.

"That's the upside. Here's the downside. Bama and her sister have decided to move back to Huntsville, Alabama. They have family there, and only left because they were trying to run from Bama's ex. Since he's in jail and he's assaulted another law enforcement official, they don't need to worry about him following them."

"So her portion of the business is for sale."

"Yes."

I said nothing more. There was no way I could conjure up another portion. I was still building a savings account. My car would need to be replaced soon. I needed to repay Sheila for the security deposit she had given Leighton for my house. "So, like, can just anyone buy her share?"

"No. We have to have a co-owner we can work with. One who understands this business." Dodie smiled. "I have a few ideas. Don't worry about it, Sunshine. You have a big date today, right?"

I nodded but I had one more question for my boss. "Do you think . . . I mean . . . You suppose I could see Bama? I want to tell her I'm sorry."

"I'm not sure that you have any reason to apologize," said Dodie. "But I'll talk to her. If she doesn't want to see you, don't take it personally. Remember, Sunshine, just as you were jealous of her, she was jealous of you. In fact, she was more jealous of you than you were of her by a long shot."

I sighed and got up to begin my chores straightening up the store. While my hands rearranged stock, my mind skipped around. "Maybe if she'd known me better," I muttered to myself. Of course, she had pointedly shut down any attempts I'd made to become friends. Maybe, just maybe, the whole situation was doomed from the start.

After Dodie settled into a chair at the front of the store, I went to the back, ostensibly to check stock, and called Detweiler.

"What's up with Ross Gambrowski? Is he in jail yet?"

"I can't comment on our investigation other than to say we don't have enough information to make an arrest."

That put me in my place, and strengthened my resolve. This relationship had hit its final bump in the road. I was ready, willing and able to type "THE END" across Detective Chad Detweiler's forehead.

"Thanks. Thanks a heap. Merry Christmas to you, too, bucko!"

With a quick punch of my thumb, I severed my relationship with Detective Chad Detweiler.

# STACEY'S GRANDMOTHER'S RUGELACH

*This treat is pronounced "ruh-guh-luch."*
*That last "ch" is sort of a gurgle. Fortunately,*
*you don't have to pronounce it correctly*
*to make it!*

**Basic rugelach dough:**

1 bar of cream cheese, room temperature
2 sticks of butter, room temperature and
  cut into small pieces
1/4 c. sugar
2 c. flour

**Filling:**

1/2 c. of walnuts, chopped fine
1/2 c. of golden raisins, chopped fine
1/4 c. granulated sugar
1/4 c. packed light brown sugar
1/2 tsp. ground cinnamon
A jar of any preserves or jam (apricot or
  raspberry are nice)

Plus: A plate of cinnamon sugar for rolling the cookies in before baking

Process the butter, cream cheese, and sugar either in a food processor or with a stand mixer. Add the 2 cups of flour after the dough starts to come together. Make sure all of the ingredients are incorporated. You will have an *annoying,* sticky, thick buttery dough.

Make 6 individual balls with the dough. Flatten them by hand into 8-inch discs and wrap each disc in plastic wrap. Refrigerate for 2 hours.

Take out of refrigerator. Slice into 8 wedges, just as you would divide up a pizza.

Mix together the walnuts, raisins, sugars and cinnamon.

Spread some of the preserves on the slices. Sprinkle with chopped walnut, raisin, sugar, cinnamon mixture.

Roll each slice into a crescent shape, starting with the large end and ending with the point. Roll each little crescent (rugelach) in the plate of cinnamon sugar to coat. Place on parchment-paper-lined cookie sheets.

Bake around 25–30 minutes at 350°F.

# SIXTY-SEVEN

What more was there to say? Detweiler had his job to do. I wasn't a part of his life or his world. It was time to move on. Maybe even, past time. In my case that meant going into our tiny bathroom and alternately crying and splashing cold water on my face. Not a smart idea because I ended up looking like a pink raccoon with a red nose. Sort of like a kid might color at a restaurant when he's only given two crayons. I stepped out of the john to grab my purse and my makeup kit. Since Ben was meeting me at five, and since customers might take one glance at me and run for the hills, I needed to make repairs.

I bumped right into Laurel. "Whoa doggies," she said, in a voice I could have easily mistaken for Mert's. There we stood: the beauty and the beast.

"I was just going for my makeup kit."

That was really a bit of a joke. I carried a

lip gloss and under-eye concealer. Big whoop.

She tilted her head to survey me. "Hey, how about if I do your makeup? I once worked at a cosmetics counter. And I've got a bottle of Visine in my purse. A new one, unopened. We'll start by getting those red eyes cleared up."

Whatever. I mean, I frankly didn't care but she seemed excited by the prospect. Besides, with her standing over me I couldn't burst into tears, right?

I took a seat on a stool and Laurel set to work. In ten minutes, she was done. A quick trip to the bathroom with its big mirror told me I'd made a wise choice. Laurel had skillfully brought out the best in my features. By filling in my eyebrows, Laurel added symmetry and emphasized my eyes. They sparkled. (Thank you, Visine, Goddess of Red-Out.)

"That lipstick shade you've been wearing is all wrong," said my new stylist. "Try this one." She pulled out a small tube, slicked it on my lips and admired the change.

Again, she proved right.

"Take it. I get free samples all the time."

I just bet she did. If I sold cosmetics, I'd want Laurel handing out my stuff. She was the next best thing to a walking, talking sales pitch for better beauty through chemistry.

The rest of the day passed quickly. Dodie called old customers on the phone to say, "I'm back," which resulted in a steady flow of people through our front door.

"I guess I'll have to sign up for chemo and radiation again next year," she laughed.

That wasn't funny at all.

Precisely at five, Ben Novak waltzed through the door with Anya in tow.

"I called Sheila and offered to pick up your daughter rather than have you make an extra trip," he explained. "I hope that was okay."

I could tell by Anya's posture that she'd been fine with the switch.

"By the way, you look great!" His eyes were approving. "I have a gift for you. You might want to open it now."

From behind his back, he pulled a large gift box wrapped in silver and blue paper with matching ribbons. On the top was a card.

"The card might be better read in private," he blushed.

Inside the box was a luxurious shearling coat (faux fur, of course!) in black with a two-way zipper down the front. It fit perfectly.

Anya stepped up and handed me another box. "From me, Mom."

Inside was a pair of red leather gloves lined in Thinsulate and a matching red scarf.

"This is from my sweetie and me," said Dodie, as she pulled a small box from behind the counter.

Inside was an enameled pin in the shape of a poinsettia.

"I know you can't have them around the house because they're poisonous for dogs, but there's no reason you can't enjoy one that's costume jewelry," said my boss. "Besides, red is your favorite color and when Anya told me about her gifts, I thought this would be a nice embellishment."

A sense of relief flooded through me. I'd worried about how I'd stand the cold while we visited The Hill. I'd brought my stinky coat in a plastic garbage bag, and I'd shoved another sweater into a second bag as well. But neither would have been attractive choices.

Ben's thoughtfulness surprised me. How had he known what I needed?

Sheila must have told him. That was it. He cast around for gift ideas, and she supplied a suggestion or even helped him pick out the coat because the size and style were perfect.

"We have reservations for dinner at Trattoria Marcella's," said Ben. "They have a fabulous dish I order off the menu, lobster risotto."

After a comfortable ride in Ben's car — his black Lexus had heated seats which were divine — we arrived, ate a yummy garbanzo bean dip with bread, and then savored the lobster risotto, which was to die for with big chunks of lobster meat and a wonderful creamy cheese flavor. Absolutely heavenly! After our meal, we wandered The Hill, enjoying the *presepios* that twenty-five shop owners and bakeries displayed in their windows. Illumination by spotlights gave the scenes an extra dose of magic.

"The Italian Club of St. Louis organizes this Nativity Walk every year," said Ben. "Most of the scenes come from Italy, but a few were made locally by Wash U instructors."

"So Washington University teachers actually contributed these?" I asked for clarity. "They're marvelous!"

Ben explained that a variety of materials could be used: clay, terra-cotta, papier-mâché, and wax. Each scene charmed me, whether the workmanship was intricate or crude.

"Elephants!" shouted Anya pointing at a window. "This scene has elephants!"

"The ones from Naples include shopkeepers, tradesmen, farmers, and children. But it only counts as presepio if images of Joseph, Mary, and baby Jesus are included," explained Ben. "The Italians tuck scenes like these into hillside indentations along the Amalfi coast. The townspeople keep the statues out all year, tending the figures and adding to them. *Presepio* comes from the Latin word for enclosure, which is what the manger did. It enclosed or protected the Baby Jesus," said Ben.

My daughter laughed. "Here we are viewing Nativity Scenes with a Jew for a guide."

Ben laughed, too, and for a moment I could imagine us as a family. If Ben was reticent around my teenager, maybe that was for the best. How many stories had I heard about stepfathers who were inappropriate? But watching these two together, I noted a new ease, a sort of camaraderie. My reverie was interrupted by Anya's cell phone ringing loudly.

"Mom, Nicci got preview tickets to that new vampire movie. Can I go? I'd have to be there in half an hour? Huh? Puh-leeze! I can spend the night at her house. We only have a half-day tomorrow, and mostly it's a school meeting in chapel. Come on, Mom!" My child hopped up and down like a bunny, temporarily forgetting her new mission in life was portraying extreme boredom at all times.

Ben smiled at me, "It's cold out here. If she wants to go, we can drop her off and go back to my place."

Sounded like a plan to me.

I'd never been in Ben's loft before. In fact, I avoided going there. Weird, I know, but visiting a guy's condo seemed like a step toward single-dom that I wasn't ready to make. Usually I used the dogs as an excuse, but this time Ben pre-empted that by offering to swing by my house and help me with them. While he watched them, I checked on Monroe. Although Ben has always been awkward around Gracie, he found three-legged Jasper fascinating. Jasper, in return, took a special shine to Ben. By that I mean, Jasper attached himself to Ben's side as though Velcroed to his pants' leg.

That solved another concern in my mind: I worried that Ben didn't like animals. Turns out, he does, he just found Gracie's size intimidating.

Ben's place astonished me. He explained

how he loves reclaiming demolition materials and using them as furniture and decorative objects. His loft used to be a warehouse, so he left the walls with exposed brick showing through. Very cool. The coffee table made from four short chimney pots totally thrilled me, as did his fireplace, an Arts and Crafts piece complete with glazed tiles.

Can you fall in love with a man because of his décor? Beats me.

"You might want to look at your card now," suggested my host.

I withdrew a beautiful full-color image of two people holding hands set against a white background. Inside the legend read: "My holidays are happy because I'm spending them with you!" And in his careful script, Ben added, "You complete me. Love, Ben."

As I swallowed the lump in my throat, Ben popped the cork on a bottle of Prosecco, poured some into a flute, dropped in a strawberry, and toasted, *"L'Chaim,"* then paused and added, "Specifically *l'chaim* with you. I want to marry you, Kiki."

They say women are like crockpots, taking a long time to heat up. All I know is that suddenly, my temperature spiked. When Ben wrapped his arms around me and pulled me close, I melted. When he kissed me, pressing against me with his whole body, my resistance slipped away.

# SIXTY-EIGHT

*Wednesday, December 23*
*7th Night of Hanukkah*

I woke up to the delicious scent of cheese and onions. Ben served me quiche for breakfast. "I knew you'd want to check on the dogs," he added, "so I didn't let you sleep late." He stepped over to his Expobar — a machine with handles and knobs galore — and made me the best latté I've ever had. Of course, he used Kaldi's espresso, so what could I expect but perfection?

Actually, I *expected* to feel embarrassed or awkward, but I didn't. My makeup smeared slightly, but whatever I'd lost on the sheets, I'd gained by a new inner glow. I decided I didn't want to spoil the mood or the day with a long dissection of the evening's Olympic marathon event. Instead, I decided just to enjoy the new sensation of being well-loved. If I had a tiny whisker-burn on my cheeks, well, who needed rouge?

Ben drove me to my house and kissed me soundly at the threshold before leaving for his work. I opened my door with new eyes. By comparison to his loft, my place reeked of shabby and not-so-chic. Yet Ben had never complained or belittled my lack of funds. He'd never acted uncomfortable about my thrift shop furniture. Maybe that was because he respected recycling, although he practiced it on a much grander scale.

I let the dogs out quickly. They all ran to the far side of the fenced yard and barked like hooligans on holiday at some unseen critter. I called for them, and they milled around but didn't come.

I guess it was their way of protesting my staying out all night.

"Whatever!" I pulled on my coat, picked up leashes, and brought them in two at a time. As I did, I realized that Ben never once griped about having to work our visits around them. Or around my daughter. He knew what he was getting into before we dated. He'd never shown the slightest regret that by taking me on, he'd also be instant parent to a hormonal teenage girl.

These were aspects of our relationship I'd never considered before.

I had pushed him away. I had accepted

his marriage proposal once and then broken up with him hours later, and he kept coming back for more.

I stared at the card Ben gave me. "You complete me." How curious. Here was a man who had everything — money, status, family, looks, and poise. But he pledged to me that he had nothing unless he had me. What was it I brought to his life?

I had asked that during one of the lulls in the action.

He pulled me close and whispered, "You are life, itself. There's this impossible energy and creativity and chaos swirling around you."

"But I'm not perfect!"

"You might not be perfect, but you are perfection. Never doubt that. I know you have your demons. Maybe I see in you a chance to chase those demons away? A chance to be a white knight? Who knows. All I can tell you is that my world is simpler, quieter, and a lot more boring without you."

Treating the card like a talisman, I tucked it into the pocket of my new coat and set out across the yard for Monroe's shed. A few feathers of snow drifted down around me. The forecast had been for an accumulation of six inches. With the cold maintaining the sprinkling from a couple days ago, we could count on a white Christmas.

A Christmas that might include Ben. He had offered to come stay at my house, even if that meant sleeping on the sofa for propriety's sake.

Either the man was a glutton for punishment, or he was sincerely, deeply in love with me. Or both. It sure wasn't because he lacked for other prospects. I'd noticed the keen interest Laurel showed in him. Clancy mentioned repeatedly what a gorgeous guy he was. Even Mert liked him.

Of course, there was Sheila, my mother-in-law, with her ringing endorsement.

Ben's parents liked me, too.

I opened the human door to Monroe's shed and stared out toward the paddock. Leighton was supposed to get back from a book tour the day before, but I hadn't heard from him. Our agreement was that I'd continue to care for Monroe and Petunia until I knew my landlord was safe at home. The way travel plans could change, this seemed like a prudent course. I called to the donkey and he didn't come in from his tiny paddock. I called again, more insistently. Monroe walked up to the donkey door of the shed and stopped. He wickered at something. His eyes rolled to show their whites and his eyes were set back against his head.

"Don't worry, Monroe. Your daddy will be home soon. I have an apple for you," I held up the shiny red globe. Monroe loved his apples. He stared at the doorway, at me, back at the doorway, and then he reluctantly trotted forward.

A bit of old feed stuck to the bottom of his food bucket. I didn't like that. I wasn't sure if donkeys could founder like horses did, and I wasn't sure that old feed was a problem, but I wasn't willing to take chances. Pulling off my gloves and shoving them in my left pocket, I reached in the bucket and tried to jam the edge of the scoop under the frozen mass. The container wasn't that deep, but I'm short so I had to rise up on my tippy toes and stick my head down low to get leverage. My butt was up in the air, and my back was to the opening from the paddock to the shed.

A hand grabbed the back of my coat and jerked me hard.

## SIXTY-NINE

"You witch! You sicced the cops on me!"
Ross Gambrowski shook me like a dog does
a rat.

"Let me go!"

"Let you go? I've been waiting to teach
you a lesson all night. You little slut. I saw
you! I sat outside your fancy john's condo. I
know what you are!" Ross lifted me so high
my feet were off the ground. The light from
outside silhouetted him, his beefy face and
his angry scowl. What a fool I'd been. The
dogs had tried to warn me. So had Monroe,
until his love of apples got the better of him.
Ross Gambrowski had been waiting just
outside the shed while I fiddled around with
the frozen matter at the bottom of the food
bucket.

I batted at the big man with the scoop,
but I couldn't reach far enough behind me
to do damage. "Let go! Help!"

"Stop that!" he squeezed my fingers. The

431

metal scoop made a muffled clatter as it fell through the straw and banged against the concrete floor.

"Leave me alone!" I kicked his shins, but my rubbery soles couldn't have done much damage.

If he'd let go of me, I could race out the gate and lock it behind me. That would mean Ross would have to climb over the fencing to catch up with me. With any luck, I could be inside my house and calling the cops. Surely fear of the dogs would keep Ross at bay.

Yeah, right. Like Fluffy and Izzy were going to scare him.

But Gracie might.

Ross started to drag me backward through the shed. Monroe stood beyond us, neighing and nickering nervously. I flailed at the big man, my hands sliding off his leather trench coat. His grip on my collar kept me off balance. I had no weapons. No way to save myself.

He stopped in the middle of the paddock. "Good a place as any to show you who's boss!" He brought up his left hand to join his right. With both hands around my throat, he began to squeeze. The scent of his cologne on his palms rose up and into my nostrils.

He countered this by bending over my face. I could feel drops of spittle on my skin.

"No one ever taught you to behave, did they? Huh? You need a lesson, and I'm the teacher!"

I saw his lips moving, his day's growth of beard close-up, and watched his Adam's apple bounce up and down.

"I tried to teach Cindy. She was so stubborn. I tried because I love her! I didn't kill her! I just loved her!" he wailed as his fingers dug into my flesh.

"Thanks to you, the cops are talking to all my friends. They're cracking under the pressure, one by one. They're saying things they shouldn't! Talking bad about my Cindy and me. It's all your fault!"

At first, it was the pressure on my throat that hurt. I coughed and screamed and tried to wrestle free. Then, there was the mounting sense of suffocation. My lungs ached for air! The edges of my world blackened.

I pressed my feet against the ground hard and pushed back.

Temporarily, he lost his grip.

But only for a second. Clearly, Ross Gambrowski had practice at grabbing women by the throat. He knew exactly what he was doing.

He planned to kill me.

I had to save myself, and I had to do it fast.

Ross was stronger.

My vision was blurred, but the gulp of oxygen gave me another chance. I twisted and turned, thrashing against him. My body slid against the slick surface of his coat, but his fingers continued to dig into my throat.

I had no weapons.

In the periphery of my vision, I saw Monroe's tail. His head must be facing us.

I heard him whinny. He was clearly distressed, clearly unsettled by the man in his paddock.

The edge of my hand touched Ben's card. His white card in the white envelope.

Clumsily, I pulled it from my pocket. I waved it around. I could feel the air woosh past my hand. I waved the card some more.

If nothing else, Ben would find it. He would know I thought of him.

But what about Anya?

Who would raise her?

I pressed against the frozen ground. This time, I got lucky. I managed to stomp on the insole of Ross Gambrowski's right foot. But he was wearing those heavy wingtips that men favor, and I weighed about a third of what he did. Although he yelped and lost his hold for a second, the crushing squeeze began anew.

I wondered if he'd snap my neck before I died of asphyxiation.

I kept waving the card behind Ross Gambrowski's back.

What a pitiful excuse it was for a real weapon. A silly greeting card.

Stars swam in front of my eyes. I knew I was nearly gone.

All of a sudden, a force rammed us, Ross and me.

The big man stumbled to one side. I dropped the card.

It fluttered toward my captor.

Monroe head-butted Ross again.

*Omph!*

He tripped over his own feet, but the card sailed after him. Monroe dipped his head and brought it up under Ross's jaw. Hard.

"That no good —" and Ross began to yell and curse. He reared back and struck Monroe in the nose.

The donkey responded with a scream of his own. A sort of "eeyore" with more emphasis on the "eee."

I remembered belatedly that Ross had hurt Monroe the last time he stopped by to hector me.

Monroe remembered that, too. And he was not happy. Not at all.

The donkey reared away from his attacker, then dropped his head, and ran forward. I watched in slo-mo as Monroe's forehead came up squarely under Ross Gambrowski's jaw. I heard the crack of bones. I saw a piece of pink tongue fall off the man's face.

I watched blood gush down the front of Ross Gambrowski's silk tie.

I crouched on the ground, one hand on the stiff blades of grass.

I knew I had to run. My body wouldn't obey me.

My breath came in quick little gasps.

I bounced to my feet. I raced toward the fencing.

Ross screamed in pain.

From beyond him came a figure carrying a shovel.

Leighton Haversham took aim at Ross Gambrowski and smacked the man so hard up the side of the head, making a "gong" sound so loud, you'd have thought the Liberty Bell was tolling right there in Webster Groves.

And it was. I was free.

No way was I going to spend any time at a hospital. Not after that last close call with Brenda Detweiler. I declined the EMTs offer of a ride to the emergency room.

"Good riddance to bad rubbish." Leighton

and I stood side-by-side and stared after the ambulance taking Gambrowski away. "I met him years ago and detested the man. We were at the country club, and he was drunk as the proverbial skunk. Ross reached over and pinched Cindy's arm hard. He laughed at her reaction. Everyone else at the table snickered out of politeness. I made the biggest mistake of my life."

"What do you mean?"

"I kept my mouth shut, too. I've hated myself for that ever after."

"What could you have done?"

"I could have gone up to Cindy privately later and asked if there was any help I could offer. I could have called the police to try to file a complaint. I could have said, 'It's not okay for him to treat you like that. Even if people laugh along politely, we all know it's wrong.' " He shook his head.

"What good would that have done?"

"See these trees?"

I stared up at the empty limbs on the huge maples that surrounded us. They had to have been thirty years old at least.

"Every one of these trees started as a seedling, yay-big," he separated his thumb and forefinger to indicate a narrow width. "I could have planted a seed that day. A seed that one day could have germinated.

437

When the time came, Mrs. Gambrowski would have known I would help her. She would have known what she was suffering was unacceptable. She would have known she had a friend in this big wide world."

Even with all that commotion, I walked into the store only an hour late. For this final push on the eve of Christmas Eve, Dodie and I had decided to open our doors at eight for any last-minute traffic. It embarrassed me that I'd personally weighed in for the early hour, yet here I was strolling in at nearly nine.

"Where on earth have you been?" Clancy rushed up to me. "We've been worried sick!"

"That must have been some date you had yesterday with Ben Novak." Dodie raised an eyebrow at me. "Of course, we'll expect a full recounting. There are flowers for you on the front counter."

I pushed past my co-workers and rushed to the front of the store. A dozen long-stem red roses filled a huge crystal vase. My fingers snatched the card and quickly ripped it open. "You complete me," it said. Nothing more.

I smiled.

"Gee, gorgeous, rich, and romantic?" Laurel grinned at me. "You hit the trifecta

—Whoa! What happened to your neck?"

I yanked up my turtleneck.

"Hey, that's not a hickey. What did he do to you?"

Clancy scurried to my side and pried my fingers away. "I'm calling the cops. Nobody gets away with treating you this way. No one!"

"Wait! It wasn't Ben!" I patted down the air. "Ross Gambrowski visited my house this morning. He tried to kill me."

"From the looks of your neck, he darn near succeeded. I hope you called the cops," Dodie said.

I told my friends all about my morning. I also explained that I'd been checked by an emergency medical technician, and I'd chosen not to go to a hospital. I didn't explain why, other than to say, "I hate hospitals and I'm fine. Please respect my decision."

"You didn't have to come in," said Dodie. "You could have called."

I sighed. "There's nowhere I'd rather be. Trust me."

# SEVENTY

Leighton showed up at closing time. "I wanted to check on my favorite tenant." His cheeks turned a bit pink. "If you haven't had dinner, I thought you might like company."

It had never occurred to me that a famous person like Leighton might get lonely. I also realized he was checking on my safety.

"That would be nice."

Over a lovely plate of pasta at a family restaurant on The Hill, I explained to him that Anya was spending the night at Nicci Moore's house. The Moores were leaving the next day to go skiing in Park City, Utah, and Jennifer Moore had volunteered to drop Anya off at Sheila's the next morning. That was fine by me because I'd need to get to work early for our last hurrah.

Leighton and I talked about the incident with Ross, who was now safely behind bars. Then I encouraged him to talk to me about his life, which was fascinating. When we got home, he checked my house for me and waited while I let out the dogs before telling me goodnight.

*Thursday, December 24*
*8th Night of Hanukkah*
*Christmas Eve*

The next morning was Christmas Eve, as well as being the last night of Hanukkah. While there weren't a lot of customers, a steady flow stopped by, mainly to tell Dodie hello and to wish us "Happy Holidays."

Around eleven, Dodie excused herself. "I promised Bama I'd go say goodbye to her. She and her sister plan to leave town right after the kids open their gifts tomorrow morning."

This hurt. I'd hoped my co-worker would forgive me. Now I realized she'd never get over being angry with me. Horace stopped by and helped his wife into the car. As the two of them drove off, Clancy came over to hug me. "Get over it, Kiki."

"I saved her life!"

"I know you did. She does, too. But she has to have someone to blame."

"Why me?"

"Why not you? Look, in actuality, she should blame herself."

441

"Huh?"

"Don't you think there were warning signs she ignored?"

"Such as? I bet old Jerald didn't go around with a neon sign flashing 'potential wife abuser.' "

Clancy laughed. "No, but I bet he started with coercive behavior. He probably told her she was stupid or belittled her and made fun of her. Later, he might give her a little shove or hold her down and tickle her."

"Those are signs of abuse?"

"Yes, and they escalate. A man like that will be bossy and demanding. He'll get jealous easily and tell the girl she caused his pain."

"That's a key," said Laurel, pulling up a chair and joining us. We'd started on our sandwiches without ever formally announcing it was time to eat. That was a trait I valued in my new co-workers. There was a grand congeniality I never had with Bama. She wanted me to schedule my lunches and any breaks I took. These women seemed to share my motto of "Go with the flow."

Laurel continued, "I had one friend who spent her entire freshman year in her dorm room. She'd walk directly to classes and come directly back. Wouldn't participate in study groups. Wouldn't eat at the cafeteria.

442

Her boyfriend didn't want her to 'flirt with other guys.' His words. She nearly flunked out because she wouldn't go to the library!"

"Why? That's just nuts! I mean, if you're going to live like that why not move to a third-world country where women have no rights?" I threw my hands up in despair.

"Exactly," said Laurel. "This guy went so far as to keep tabs on my friend through the GPS on her cell phone. She went to the gym one night to run around the track, and he went ballistic. Gave her a black eye. But it gets worse. Some guy in her Chem 101 lab 'friended' her on Facebook, and this girl's boyfriend showed up at the dorm. He dragged her out of the common area in the dorm by the hair. The RA called security. And guess what?"

"She refused to press charges?" Clancy suggested.

"Not only that, she apologized to him! Can you believe that?"

"Wow. That's awful."

"Oh, no, that's not awful. What's awful is how the story ends."

"Which is?" I was afraid to ask, but I couldn't help myself.

"He decided they needed to seal their 'love' forever by committing suicide. He pumped her full of Ativan and then planned to drive his car off a bridge. Only he chickened out at the last minute. She was too doped up to unbuckle her belt."

After we ate, I ran out to pick up a few last-minute presents. Between two and three, about a dozen shoppers dropped by for gift certificates. We had our own production line going. Laurel busily sealed forms worth various amounts in decorated envelopes. Clancy logged the certificates into a computer program so the recipient would get credit even if she lost the paperwork. I rang up the sales on the register.

"That e-mail blast I sent out really worked," said Clancy while Laurel ran to the back to make us all cups of hot chocolate. "Putting a list of what a person could buy for different dollar amounts really helped."

"Makes sense to me. I know that when I'm making a charitable contribution, if they say that ten dollars buys a meal, but twenty-five buys enough food for a family, I'm going to write a check for twenty-five, if possible."

"How's your neck feeling?"

"A little sore, but fine. What eases my pain is the mental image of Ross Gambrowski being carried into the ambulance."

"I think they call that rough justice," said Clancy.

Laurel held out a tray full of hot beverages. "What sort of sentence do you suppose he'll get?"

"Death penalty," said Clancy.

"You're kidding!" I nearly spilled the cocoa all over me. "I hate the death penalty. It never made sense to me. I mean, what are we saying? You killed someone and that's wrong, so we're going to kill you and that's right?"

"That's a pretty simplistic view," said Clancy.

"Maybe but recently that big think tank on the death penalty disbanded. Even the best of the best had a hard time rationalizing the way we dole out the ultimate punishment. They said it was tough to standardize the penalty and allow judges discretion at the same time."

"I can see where it's questionable in a crime of passion or a so-called 'stupid crime,' but in Ross Gambrowski's case, he's responsible for more than just Cindy's death," said Laurel. "Remember, she lost all those babies. You could argue he's a serial killer."

"Except that 'serial' is misleading and doesn't apply in this situation. It doesn't mean one murder right after another. It means 'serial' as in the old-fashioned serials on radio or TV where each episode upped the ante. The typical serial killer hopes for a bigger and bigger experience with each murder."

"How do you know so much about this, Clancy? Ugh."

"I read crime fiction." Without missing a beat she added, "That's how I relax."

# KIKI LOWENSTEIN'S LAST-MINUTE GIFT IDEAS

*One of the simplest ways to turn any ordinary item into a special gift is by personalizing it. This technique will work on serving trays, cups, clipboards, or any smooth surface. If the surface is multi-colored or patterned, so much the better.*

1. You'll need enough letter stickers to spell your recipient's name or a message. (Tip: Stickers with a clear backing or stickers that are a silhouette of the letters work best.)

2. You might also add stickers of flowers or any other designs. For example, if your gift is intended for a teenage girl, stickers showing cell phones or hearts might be appropriate. For a boy, skateboards might be cool.

3. Carefully clean the surface of your gift with a bit of rubbing alcohol on a cotton ball.

4. Adhere the stickers as desired.

5. Coat the stickers with clear nail polish. Make sure to especially coat the edges of the stickers as this is where they are most likely to peel up.

(Tip: Tell the recipient not to soak the item in water when washing it. While the nail polish makes a great seal, you don't want to risk letting water get underneath.)

# SEVENTY-ONE

Dodie walked through the back door. She was holding hands with Horace. "Sunshine, we need to talk in my office."

Even if I do own a part of the business, this still sounded suspiciously like a summons from on high. I got up reluctantly and gave my two co-workers a mock salute.

"We who are about to die, salute you," I said.

"Right," Clancy laughed. "Kiki Lowenstein, you are such a card."

I didn't feel much like a card. I felt like a little kid trooping off to the principal's office.

I sat next to Horace, and Dodie made herself comfortable behind the big desk. The day was wearing her down. Her color was fading and the dark circles under her eyes were more prominent. Still, she sat up straight and tall, so I knew she was on the mend.

"I visited Bama."

"Right." Tell me something I don't know, I thought.

"I told her that you wanted to visit her. She still doesn't want to see you. I'm sorry. Just so you know, it wasn't the photo of her in the paper that tipped off her ex-husband."

"Right." I didn't much feel like contributing to this conversation.

"No. In fact, I doubt that he even saw the picture in the paper. He was already hot on her trail because it was so unusual that three kids whose ages matched those of his children exactly were enrolled in the soccer program here about the time Bama and the kids disappeared. And his kids loved soccer. The school system actually has a protocol for protecting the children of abusers, but as a law enforcement official, he had a good idea what that protocol was. He visited one school after another and got nowhere. But then he posed as someone from a national soccer association, and well, he knew what to say and how to say it."

Dodie grabbed a bottle of water from her purse. The treatments dried up her saliva, and she was never without a liquid to sip on. "Sunshine, I asked the counselor to talk with Bama. It can be very difficult for an abused woman to see clearly who is on her side — and isn't. I probably should have pushed her harder —"

Horace stopped her. "Kiki, the truth of the matter is Dodie hasn't been thinking straight. There's an aftereffect to these treatments. They call it 'chemo fog.' The patient's brain isn't as sharp as usual. What I think my darling is trying to say is, she's sorry."

"That's right. I am. I'm partially responsible for putting you at risk, and I apologize."

This took a while to sink in. I mean, to my mind, Dodie was infallible. All wise. All perfect. Sure, on one level, I knew better, but on another, I'd pegged her as Super Woman. Even though Super Woman never existed, even in comic lore.

"Where do we go from here?"

"She gave me a note for you."

Kiki —

I'm still not letting you off the hook, but here's the deal, I can't do the cruise. My face is a mess and my fingers on my right hand are broken. The boat leaves on January 5. You know the materials. I want you to take my place.

    *(signed) Althea Vess McCallister*

Althea Vess McCallister. As I folded the

letter and slipped it back into the envelope, I realized I never even knew Bama's real name.

"She told you what's in here?" I asked Dodie as I tapped the envelope against the desk.

"Yes, and I've got the store covered. After everything you've been through recently, I thought the trip might do you good. Sheila's agreed to watch Anya, if you wish."

I nodded. How like the two of them to go behind my back.

"You'll need this. It's the contract Bama signed. She's sent them a letter designating you as her surrogate. There's a copy of that as well. Here's a brochure about the cruise."

Dodie cleared her throat. "Please, try to forgive her. And me."

Her voice sounded so raspy, I couldn't stay mad.

Looking at the colorful photos, a warm glow started inside me. I'd never been on a cruise. I hated cold weather. This was going to be cool.

I could understand Bama not wanting me to see her. After all, she had been pretty badly beaten, and I knew from working with her that she was very fussy about her appearance. But, for her to send me on a cruise was an unexpected perk. I mean, I thought to myself, she must like me, right? Otherwise she would have never shared her largess with me.

A rap on the doorframe caught our attention.

"It's four o'clock, and we're officially closed. If you don't mind, we'd like to pass out a few gifts before we hit the trail," said Clancy.

Horace popped a bottle of champagne. We all toasted the fact we'd gotten through the holiday season.

Dodie loved the shawl I'd crocheted (with a little help). I gave Clancy a cafetière because she loves coffee. Although we kept a pot at the store, we filled that workhorse with whatever brand we could find on sale. Clancy, like me, loved Kaldi's, so with the cafetière, she could brew up a cup or two for herself. Laurel had noticed my love of java, and she'd given me a gift card for Kaldi's. I'd given her a new paper trimmer by Fiskars. "If you're going to be a crafter, this is indispensable. In fact, I'm not sure how any household can be without one." (And that's the truth.)

Clancy gave me a simple but elegant pair of silver hoops. "Silver is great with pinks, purples, and anything with a blue tint," she said, by way of explanation. "You have those nice gold hoops, but these will round out your accessories."

All in all, a very satisfying exchange. My friends confirmed they knew me well, and isn't that the joy of getting a gift? I mean, it's not about the money or the item, it's the thought. Okay, that's a cliché. But the thought needs to reflect that the other person really understands you and considered what you might like, need, or use.

That circuitous path led me back to Ben. As I walked the dogs to my car, Clancy said, "You have a bit of a glow about you these days, my friend. Things go well with Ben?"

I nodded. "Very well. Better than I expected. In fact, I did something totally out of character for me."

With the tension of the work day behind me and a little bubbly in my veins, I felt positively chatty.

"Why? You're a grown woman. You've been widowed for more than a year. Nearly two. You never dated much before you married. As long as you took precautions —"

"Which we did —"

"What's wrong with getting physical? Especially if you think he might be the one." She said "the one" in a dramatic voice that mimicked Morpheus from *The Matrix.*

That sent us both into gales of giggles.

"You know, I've kept him at arm's length waiting for Detweiler. But that's silly, isn't it? Detweiler's married. I don't want to break up a marriage. I'm not interested in playing games. Besides, he's proven to me that he's not interested." I didn't go into details on that last charge.

Clancy studied me. I noticed for the first time the tiny crinkles at the corners of her eyes, those creases that were signs of maturity, not old age. "We haven't known each other long, but we've been kindred spirits from the start. I think you are wise to move on. If he does split with his wife, he'll come with baggage. You'll wonder if you were the cause. He'll wonder if you were the cause. But with Ben, you have a clean slate. True, the good detective has that 'bad boy' thing going for him because he's a cop. So what? You're not a high school girl trying to rebel against her parents. You're a woman ready for the commitment of marriage."

She pursed her lips. "Was he any good?"

I blushed. "Oh, yeah."

"All the more reason to move on down life's highway."

# SEVENTY-TWO

Before we said goodbye, I made a request. "Clancy, you're smarter about contracts than I am. Will you look this over? I want to go on that cruise, but I'm scared I'll misread the fine print. I don't want to incur any obligations I can't fulfill."

"Gladly," she said. "I'll get back to you quickly so you have time to contact them if there's a problem."

"You won't be spending tomorrow alone, will you?"

She fought a smile. "No. An old friend is back in town. He's single, and he heard about my divorce. We plan to spend the day together."

That made me happy.

I drove home, took care of my canine charges, and then on to Sheila's for the last night of Hanukkah. I can't say I was surprised when Ben answered her door instead of Linnea.

"Hope you don't mind."

"How could I? First of all, it's not my house! Once again, those roses are beautiful. I'm leaving them at the store because everyone is enjoying them so much."

"Maybe I should have sent them to your house, but I worried you wouldn't be there for the delivery," he took me into his arms and kissed me.

"I'll take delivery of that any day," I murmured.

The noise of my daughter letting the swinging kitchen door fly shut caused us to jump apart. I'm sure we had "guilty" written all over our faces because Anya froze. She stared at me and then at Ben and back at me.

"No PDA, okay? I'm not old enough to see stuff like that."

Ben smothered a laugh.

"Gran said to tell you two we're waiting in the kitchen." With an exaggerated roll of her eyes, Anya added, "She always wants to light the candles in there. She's scared silly of burning the house down."

The smell of Linnea's roast chicken hurried us along. I gave Robbie Holmes and Linnea brief hugs before I extended my arms to Sheila. I have to admit, I'm glad these days for her affection. We're not perfect, either one of us, but we both have our good points. On the balance, she's certainly fallen on the plus side of the scale more often than the minus, especially if you offer brownie points for the positive impact she has on Anya's life.

Usually she hugs me quickly as though it's a chore to check off her to-do list. Tonight, I started to pull back, but she added another squeeze just before we separated. A lump formed in my throat. My poor throat. It was really getting a workout lately.

"Properly, these should have been lit at sunset, but I'm bending the rules because surely it's sunset somewhere," huffed Sheila.

*"Baruch atah . . ."* intoned Anya and we all joined in, even Robbie Holmes and Linnea.

Sheila passed out her presents first. I squealed with delight when I opened the signed "Queen of Everything" print by Mary Engelbreit. Sheila handed Linnea a bonus check and a box of Godiva chocolate. She'd gotten Ben a new cashmere muffler, Anya received a gift card for her iTunes, Robbie also got a muffler, although he added, "I've got my love to keep me warm."

With that, Sheila held out her hand. "Observe. We are now officially engaged."

"Wow. That's quite a sparkler! You did a

good job hiding it by turning the stone to your palm."

"Otherwise I would have spoiled the surprise. It's from Mary Pillsbury of course. She does designs for all the best people."

Linnea brought out a bottle of champagne so we could all toast the happy couple.

"I want a June wedding," said Sheila. "This will be so much fun to plan."

I could almost hear poor Robbie choking on his drink.

"I need to run out to my car," I said. My presents were more modest. I'd bought Ben a big bag of Kaldi's expresso. He was delighted. I made Robbie a small album with pictures of him golfing that I'd borrowed from Sheila to copy. I crocheted a scarf for Sheila, and while I never expected her to wear it, she promptly tossed it around her throat. I was amazed at how nice it looked. Finally, I gave Linnea a tea cozy I'd crocheted.

"Been needing one of these. I saw them using these on Masterpiece Theatre, and I thought to myself, that's a smart idea. Thank you!" With that, she gave me a heartfelt hug. She added, "I know it must have taken you a while, so I'm doubly proud to own this, because when you make something with your hands you give a person a little bit of yourself."

I couldn't have said it better.

Ben gave me a lovely silver starfish necklace from Tiffany's. He gave Sheila chocolates, and to my daughter, he gave a book of passes to the local movie theatre. I could see his thoughtfulness touched Anya. She stared at the passes, then at him, and then at me. "This is really, really neat. Thanks so much."

Robbie asked if he could borrow me, and we moved into Sheila's great room. "You all right? I heard what happened with Ross Gambrowski. I meant to call you right away, but I knew you'd be busy at the store. Detective Hadcho filled me in."

"My neck hurts. Nothing I can't deal with."

"After this holiday is over, I'm taking you to the gun club. That's my gift to you, Kiki. I want to make sure you're safe. While I'm still not sure that arming citizens is the way to go, at least if you have training, we can decide later what to do."

I felt a frisson of alarm. "You think Gambrowski's getting out? Or are you worried about Jerald McCallister?"

"Neither. There have been sightings of your husband's killer. Besides, I guess a single woman can't be too careful in today's world. Used to be, men lived by a code of conduct. Today? Even men of stature like Ross Gambrowski act like thugs."

"If he hadn't been a 'man of stature,' he might not have gotten away with brutalizing his wife for so long."

"That bothers me. I've sworn an oath to protect and defend, but how many more women like Cindy Gambrowski are out there? Women whose husbands have the social clout to keep them isolated? Time was, we thought domestic violence happened in lower-class families. Now we know, it occurs in all levels of society."

"I plan to put up a poster in our store."

"That's a great idea, Kiki. Now I better get back to your mother-in-law, er, my fiancée." He blushed to the tips of his ears.

# SEVENTY-THREE

*Friday, December 25*
*Christmas Day*

Christmas came softly and bought us a present of fresh snow. Anya wasn't awake yet. I decided to let her sleep. The snowfall of a few days ago still covered the grass in spots. But mostly, the precipitation had been a stop-and-go feeble effort.

Now it was really coming down. What a picture-perfect Christmas morning!

I decided to visit Monroe before it got too deep. I'll admit that walking into his shed caused the hairs to rise on the back of my neck. I was still sore from Ross Gambrowski's manhandling me. But I had a lovely apple for my savior, and I decided that visiting him on this quiet morning would make a perfect start to the day.

I heard footsteps behind me.

"Kiki?" The voice was Detweiler's. "I

hoped I'd find you here. How's Gracie's tail?"

"Healing really well, thank you. Tell your dad thanks, again, from all of us."

"Did Anya have a good holiday? I mean Hanukkah? And Christmas Eve? I'm not sure what you celebrate." He sounded desperate. "I know some people open their gifts the night before the day."

"I try to celebrate everything. That's what life's all about, isn't it?"

He nodded. "I heard about how that donkey saved you. I found this poem for you. I thought you might like it."

He handed it over shyly.

## THE LEGEND OF HOW THE DONKEY GOT HIS VOICE

After the Christ Child was born long ago
In a stable that first Christmas night,
An angel warned Joseph to leave
    Bethlehem and
So the whole family took flight.
Then, as the three of them journeyed to
    Egypt,
They rested when stars filled the sky.
And while they were sleeping, their
    donkey's keen ears
Heard King Herod's soldiers nearby.

He tried very hard to get Joseph awake,
but donkeys were mute in
those days.
Then all of a sudden a miracle
    happened . . . he let out
Some great piercing brays!
The family awakened in time to escape
    and hurriedly
Slipped out of sight.
The donkey was grateful and quite
    humbled, too,
That God chose to use him that night.
And still, to this day, the loud, piercing
    bray from a
Donkey so gentle and mild
Reminds us again of that creature's
    devotion and love
For the dear Holy Child.

                              — Author unknown

"That's really cool. Thank you. I'll have to
share it with Leighton."

We stood there, staring at Monroe.

"If Anya would like a kitten, I'd be happy
to bring one over. If that's okay with you.
Once they're weaned, that is. But I won't
offer one to her unless you say so."

"I'm not sure how Gracie would react."

"I bet Gracie wouldn't care. She's pretty
docile. You could try a kitten and see. I think

Mert has crates. You would just introduce the cat to Gracie a few minutes at a time. She's always taken well to new dogs."

"Of course she has. Gracie's wonderful."

"That's for sure."

We walked out into the area by the fence and both of us leaned against the structure without talking. The snow continued to fall around us, a thick and fluffy blanket. I brushed a small clump off my face with my new glove.

"Are you angry with me?"

"No, I'm just confused. That last conversation we had, well, you were pretty brusque."

"Sorry about that. It was frustrating that we couldn't bring Gambrowski in. Frustrating about Michelle, too. When you called, I was in a meeting and I didn't know what to say."

I nodded.

I couldn't take the silence, so I continued, "I understand and respect the fact you are married. I appreciate you are trying to work things out with Brenda. But, life's short and I want to move on. I'm not asking you to leave your wife. I . . . I just don't know what the deal is. You're married, so I've been thinking that . . . well, I need to make a new plan, Stan."

That last part was supposed to be a joke. It fell flat. He took me into his arms. I felt a wetness on both our faces. Hard to know whether they were tears or snow. Not that it mattered.

His voice was husky when he said, "I don't want you to make a new plan. I wake up every day hoping I can find a reason to see you. I tell myself I'm wrong. I tell myself you deserve better. Don't give up on me, us, yet. Please? Brenda is finishing her master's degree. She's been in and out of rehab. I think if she gets this degree, she might straighten up because she'd have too much to lose. She's talked about moving to Colorado. Can you hang in there until the summer? Is that too much to ask?"

"And then? I mean, what specifically are you asking?" Okay, I put it all on the line. I pushed away and stared straight at him to see his reaction.

He slid his arm around my shoulders. I stiffened and then relaxed into the shelter of his embrace. I buried my face in his coat.

"I'm not moving to Colorado. She knows it. She's already had a job offer." His lips brushed the top of my ear. It wasn't really a kiss, more like a promise.

The surge of electricity made me bold. "What if . . . what if something happens

466

between you."

"Something?"

"Like a baby," I whispered up at him, as I wrapped an arm around his waist. I had to know this, too. Call it a test. How honest would he be? If they were still man and wife, there was still this possibility. I held my breath, waiting.

"That's not going to happen. At least, not with me."

There was a tone, a sureness that I've never heard from him before. We swayed together, locked in each other's arms. Two friends. The best of friends.

Or was he?

"What have you told her about me?"

He sighed. "That I love you. How lucky I was to stumble over you. How much I tried to stay away. How no matter what, you're the world to me. You and Anya."

I pulled back and studied him.

This was my moment, my dream come true.

Or was it?

But what about Ben?

I mean, Detweiler could have told me this weeks — even days — ago. But he hadn't. He'd assumed there was no hurry.

I swallowed hard. "You might be too late."

467

# EPILOGUE

I found out why Bama had been so generous to me. Turns out, the contract she signed to teach on the cruise included a default clause. If she didn't go, or send someone qualified in her stead, she owed the events manager money for lost revenue.

I shook my head at Bama's nerve when Clancy explained that to me. But it didn't stop me from going and enjoying myself. Especially when I left St. Louis right before a nasty ice storm.

I got off the cruise ship at Cozumel because I vaguely remembered Cindy Gambrowski having said once that there was a cool museum in the city. I thought that stopping in would be a neat way to pay homage to her and to learn about local history.

What happened on my way back to the tender will never be resolved. I'll always wonder what I should have and could have done differently. You see, I took a cab to the museum and then wandered along the downtown area intending to pick up a few gifts. I was holding a large pink conch shell in my hands when I spotted a woman on crutches.

A woman who looked exactly like Cindy Gambrowski.

I put the shell down. Really, I was being ridiculous.

Or was I?

What was it Michelle Gambrowski said when she examined Gracie's tail? "Actually, I've been doing amputations for the past few weeks."

I stepped away from the merchant's stall and started toward the woman on crutches. My watch said the tender would leave for my cruise ship in ten minutes. The loading area was five minutes away, if I walked quickly.

But I kept staring at the back of the blonde a few stalls over.

Cozumel was Cindy's favorite place. I remembered her talking about it with Bama.

You could give your own blood, couldn't you? It could be stockpiled. People did it all the time for operations.

What if you knew you'd never be free? That your daughter would never be safe?

Trapped animals were known to gnaw off a limb. Couldn't a human do the same?

I set down the shell. What if it was her? What if Ross had been right? What if she and Michelle staged her whole "death and dismemberment"?

The state of Missouri was sure to execute him.

I broke into a run.

"Cindy! Cindy!" I called.

For a split second, that other woman hesitated. She turned toward me.

I thought I saw a half-smile on her face.

Two tourists stepped between us, blocking my view.

By the time I reached the spot where I'd seen her, "Cindy" was gone.

# ACKNOWLEDGMENTS

Thanks to Tom Morrow and Judge Bill Hopkins for legal advice. Sharon Hopkins was a brilliant helper with the legalese. My deep appreciation goes to Marjorie Morrison for her invaluable information and insight into domestic violence. Hugs and thanks go to Dana Churovich for information relating to nurses and substance abuse. Jane Campbell and Gus Castellanos provided insight into all things medical. Any mistakes I made in these areas are mine alone.

Susan Lutz has been making her Fool's Toffee for my husband David and me for years. Much love to you, Suzie. Stacey Caron was kind enough to share her grandmother's rugelach recipe. Visit her at http://staceysnacksonline.com

"Happy tail" is a real malady, and yes, amputation is an option. Thanks to Dr. Nolan P. Rubin, D.V.M., for his help with my (limited) understanding of the problem.

Dr. D. P. Lyle explained to me how blood could be harvested and stored without breaking down the cell structure so that when defrosted it would seem "fresh." Doug was also kind enough to assure me that a veterinary student could, indeed, do the surgery Michelle might have performed on her mother.

Jackie Bell of Taylor & Modeen Funeral Home kindly answered my questions about the difference in the feel of embalmed and un-embalmed flesh.

Mega thanks to my agent, Paige Wheeler of Folio Literary Management, LLC, for her continued support and wise counsel.

I really appreciate the efforts of my aunt Shirley Helmly who took time to read this book and offer proofreading and suggestions.

Yes, there really are presepios on The Hill in St. Louis. The displays start around December 23 and stay up until January 2. They are lit at night, making them absolutely magical! For more information go to http://www.italystl.com/misc/m041223.htm

There's also a wonderful restaurant in St. Louis called Trattoria Marcella. When you stop by, order the lobster risotto and tell them Kiki Lowenstein sent you!

Of course, Santa's Magical Kingdom is real. It's a total treat. Find out more at http://www.santasmagicalkingdom.com/

Lanetta Holloway won her spot in this book by making a generous donation to the Guardian Angel Settlement Association (www.guardianangelsettlement.com). Thanks to my friend Olivia Kormeier for helping me connect with this worthy cause.

As for pet donkeys, Monroe really does exist. Izzy was named for a very special pup who has gone on to heaven. (I'm sure there is one with dogs and cats, otherwise it couldn't be heaven, could it?)

As for the subject matter of this book, I grew up in an abusive home. I hope that if you are experiencing abuse, you'll find the courage to talk to someone you trust. If you suspect someone is living in an abusive environment, please have the courage to reach out to them. How prevalent is this problem? According to experts, one in three women will experience domestic abuse in her life.

To all the women who read this: If he's shaming, blaming, hurting or forcing you . . . it's not love. The same goes for guys who keep you isolated. That's not about jealousy, girlfriend, that's about control. Good men don't treat women that way. No one, not one living person on God's green earth deserves to live in fear.

With all this in mind, I have donated a portion of the proceeds of this book to Lydia's House, which offers a place of healing and a voice of hope for abused women and their children.

If you are moved to make a contribution as well, please go to their website www.lydiashouse.org.

# ABOUT THE AUTHOR

**Joanna Campbell Slan** is a scrapbooker who has written seven technique books on the hobby. In fact, she loves crafts of all kinds. She is the author of twelve nonfiction books, including a college textbook, and her essays appear in five of the *Chicken Soup for the Soul* books. Joanna divides her time between Washington, DC, and Jupiter Island, Florida. Visit Joanna at: www.Joanna Slan.com.

We hope you have enjoyed this Large Print book. Other Thorndike, Wheeler, Kennebec, and Chivers Press Large Print books are available at your library or directly from the publishers.

For information about current and upcoming titles, please call or write, without obligation, to:

Publisher
Thorndike Press
10 Water St., Suite 310
Waterville, ME 04901
Tel. (800) 223-1244

or visit our Web site at:

http://gale.cengage.com/thorndike

OR

Chivers Large Print
published by AudioGO Ltd
St James House, The Square
Lower Bristol Road
Bath BA2 3SB
England
Tel. +44(0) 800 136919
email: info@audiogo.co.uk
www.audiogo.co.uk

All our Large Print titles are designed for easy reading, and all our books are made to last.

LP CAM
Campbell-Slan, Joanna
    Make, take, murder : a Kiki Lowenstein
scrap-n-craft mystery
A0000004728